Tanaki on the Shore

W. E. Smith

The following is a work of fiction. Names, characters, places, and incidents are either products of the author's imagination or used fictitiously. Any resemblance to actual events, locales, or persons, living or dead, is entirely coincidental.

"Tankas XII and XV" by Yokiko Asano, translated Kenneth Rexroth in *One Hundred Poems from the Japanese*, 1976 Kenneth Rexroth. Reprinted by permission, New Directions Publishing Corp

Copyright 2019 W. E. Smith
All rights reserved
ISBN: 9780998484716
ISBN: 0998484716

This book is dedicated to all those scientists, advocates, and policymakers who are working to save the Chesapeake

Tanaki on the Shore

Memory (1982)

He didn't share his reminiscences with Valerie. Nor did he tell her about the waxwings, how they came so unexpectedly that eight-year-distant spring. The medieval Dutch had believed the harmless passerines heralds of plague and disaster; now they came in great clouds, scouring the ground and trees for anything edible. Tanaki rushed to pick up the Bluebird in Pannenburg's jeep, not considering for a moment missing this invasion, a rarity in the migration world. They careened down narrow country roads searching for the flocks. When they found them swarming over a village near the coast he jammed the brakes, and he and the Bluebird jumped out with nets, cameras, and a cotton bag full of metal rings they intended to attach to as many of the birds as they could capture. The waxwings were in a state of frantic excitement, and as Tanaki and the Bluebird scampered about netting them, with a gaggle of curious Dutch villagers looking on, something curious happened. The line between Tanaki and bird blurred, and blurred some more, until he wasn't sure who was capturing whom. At one point he stopped, breathless, and found himself staring blankly into the Bluebird's face. She too was out of breath. There was a vacant savagery in her eyes that—he knew— mirrored his own state of mind. Some kind of boundary had been crossed. Who were they? What were they?

1
Tanaki (1989)

THE HONDA SLOWED as he pressed the brake pedal, carefully guiding the sedan between booths, easing it under the arching toll gate that stood like a *torii* before the Bay. He tossed four quarters into the gaping metal basket with a loud jangle, the light went to green, and the thin wooden barrier lifted on the wetlands of Maryland's Eastern Shore. Of course he knew he would be crossing the bridge—it was in the very thorough directions Guy Folker faxed from the research station a month earlier. But nothing had prepared him for the spectacle that surrounded him as he clipped up the approach ramp and climbed a floating band of concrete toward towering steel spires, where the bridge begins it descent towards Kent Island six miles away. It was near ten o'clock on an April morning, and the glittering surface of the Chesapeake reflected the pure spring light with a brilliance that was almost blinding. He stole brief glances to his right, careful to obey signs instructing STAY IN LANE or MAINTAIN SPEED, trying to get a better look down the length of the Bay toward the estuary's mouth. He wanted to stop the car and look over the railing, but more block letters warning STAY IN VEHICLE spoke to him with an authority it would not have occurred to him, at this point in his life, to question.

TANAKI ON THE SHORE

Somewhere up around the central span, four hundred feet above the Bay's waters—where giant steel cables swing like hawsers left behind by some doomed race of Titanic sailors—Tanaki began to think of Mrs. Scofield. Funny, he hadn't thought about it for years: the annual ritual, a summer vacation on the Upper Peninsula with his buddy Tom's family. But now he remembered it all clearly. The tense silence beginning an hour from the Straits, where they passed the boat repair shop. Mr. Scofield knocking himself out to maintain a patter of pleasant conversation, hoping to distract his wife from her fears. Tanaki could still see the way the sweat would bead on her forehead when the bridge came into view, hear her frantic refusals to go another inch—*please let me out, I'll walk back, you go on*—saying crazy things; it all ending with her squeezed onto the floorboards in back until solid ground was again under the wheels. Tanaki remembered also how odd it felt to have Tom's mother, who made egg salad sandwiches just the way he liked them when he visited at Tom's house, lying across his tennis shoes, hands covering a face grown red from holding her breath. He smiled reflexively (the funny story had been told at so many gatherings) about the time she convinced Mr. Scofield to shut her in the trunk for the crossing, emerging disheveled—hair mussed, dress askew—when they pulled off at the Dairy Queen on the other side.

Yes, Tanaki had always felt a kind of amused pity for Mrs. Scofield's gephyrophobia. But suddenly, as he floated high over the waters of the Chesapeake, Mrs. Scofield didn't seem so strange. After all, Tanaki thought, there was no way to prove that the bridge connected the two shores, that the two shores existed once he motored onto the bridge, or that the world encountered on the other side would be the same one that he had left behind. "People spend their lives looking for bridges . . . or fleeing them," he mused as he began his descent toward Kent Island, the Honda, a mere seventeen-hundred pounds of steel, plastic, and rubber, whirring over so many thousands of tons of infrastructure like a toy. Glancing to the north, he noted herring gulls—*larus argentatus*, he thought—wheeling aloft off the bridge's railing. Finally the span devolved onto a causeway that skimmed over the Bay's surface for the remaining half-mile to the Eastern Shore.

Ugly chain stores lined the highway on the other side of the bridge. Their stolid inertia dampened Tanaki's spirits, leaving him mute and heavy. But after a couple of miles the modern development thinned out; he passed a fishing supplies store with a blue marlin sign, and other establishments with names like *Dunes Café* and *Sea Crest Hardware*. He was now in water's realm. After following the ramp up the embankment, motoring southward into the Delmarva Peninsula, he noted flooded forest off the roadway, intercut with narrow creeks, open marsh, and spreading coves. Further on he cruised past miles of alluvial fields, some covered with a soft down of winter wheat, others bare or in stubble. Standing amid these vast spaces were lonely old farmhouses, isolated and exposed except for a few shade trees and out-buildings. In the far distance, hazy stands of forest lined the low horizon.

Folker's directions were indeed thorough. Tanaki had looked them over before setting out, noted the large star representing the Chesapeake Wetlands Research Center on the accompanying map. He hadn't referred to them since leaving Michigan, a fact not particularly remarkable, the principal highways between the Great Lakes and the Mid-Atlantic well marked and straightforward. But now, as he engaged the final phase of his journey, when he would leave the main highway and follow back roads to the research station; now, when it would have been the most natural thing in the world to reach into the glove box and remove the shiny rolled FAX paper, he declined to do so. Instead, after motoring confidently onto the low bridge crossing the ample width of the Choptank River, he bisected the commercial jetsam lining the highway as it skirted Cambridge and turned abruptly right at the Food Lion.

The fact is, he had decided against going to the research station, where Guy Folker and company were expecting his arrival that afternoon. It wasn't that he felt any aversion toward the Center's staff. He simply knew that his first encounter with the Chesapeake should be an intimate affair, something between him and Nature, so to speak. He'd been studying the Bay's ecosystems for months in preparation for this fellowship, and the estuary had taken on a personality of its own for him. He was particularly anxious to see if any tundra swans might still be in the area, though the bulk of the migrants had likely winged northward a month earlier. So he sniffed out his way to the Blackwater Wildlife Refuge, oblivious to park-service-brown signs indicating directions to the sprawling wetlands.

Turning into the preserve, he slowed the Honda to a crawl. He slipped the requisite five dollars into a metal kiosk that stood beside the drive and proceeded onto the loop road, a scar of dry earth raised out of the marshes. Cruising slowly, his arm hanging out the window—stopping at intervals to peer over the still, liquid expanses—he saw no sign of migratory waterfowl, but began to feel an unmistakable sense of peace.

After leaving the refuge he called Folker to let him know

that he was in the area but wouldn't make it to the station before five as planned. He maundered down the peninsula until he arched over a steep bridge to Hooper Island, a thin strip of land separated from the mainland by only a few feet of pulsing Bay. Near the island's southernmost tip he pulled off the road to observe two swans feeding in the shallows; stepping over an intertidal flat that sponged under his steps, he felt a breeze coming off the water. The swans weren't migratory tundras but non-indigenous mutes. They were considered a nuisance species by some folks, but he was happy to have found them anyway. Shortly an impatient man with New York plates pulled off the road. He stepped onto the flat just long enough to take a quick look at the graceful animals, then he strode back to his car with a disappointed "trash birds" and sped off to some inconceivable destination.

In the wake of the New Yorker's departure, Tanaki stood in a silence broken only by the slap of a desultory tide against the mud flat. He watched the swans, who were now drifting into a sun that rapidly declined toward the Bay's western shoreline. He wanted to call out to the birds, beckon them back, but with a twinge in the solar plexus he resigned himself to the improbability of such an inter-species communication. The sun cast a golden glow across the water, and the quiet of the place engulfed him. A novel awareness came upon him, that his feet were planted in the earth, that his eyes perceived the falling sun and rippling water, that his skin felt the moist breeze. Responding to a sudden urge, he dropped into a crouching position and listened intently. Gulls squawked in the distance; their rarefied cries seemed to whisper something.

His eyes sought out the swans. They were now well into the offing, elegant whitenesses against the frothy green of the water. As he watched them move towards the depths he reflected that they had no doubt spent their entire lives around the estuary, the Chesapeake's mute population being non-migratory. How different, he thought, than his own peripatetic existence: the life of a wandering scholar, still seeking his permanent place in the world. They seemed so much a part of the Bay, of its land and seascapes, while he would just be passing through, adding another block of understanding in his chosen field, another credential to his resumé. Yet something felt so true about being here—he felt such kinship with these two swans, indeed with everything he perceived around him—that he couldn't help but feel that right here at the Chesapeake he just might find something like home.

A stiffening in his knees forced him up; he held each leg off the ground and shook out the kinks. The quickening breeze against his chest seemed to push him along, but to where? The swans had now drifted so far out into the Bay that he could hardly make them out.

He made his way back to the arching bridge. Hooper Island seemed deserted, in spite of sea-beaten bungalows that stood in long, rectangular yards along narrow lanes that ran to the Bay, and workboats strung along docks that branched like coral reefs into the Honga River. The only sign of life was a road crew operating a backhoe at the northern end of the island. Tanaki waited in the placid afternoon light while they maneuvered the scoop out of his lane.

Darkness was already investing the quiet neighborhood of stately colonials when Tanaki eased his Honda around a late-model Jaguar parked in Folker's drive. Two girls and a boy of grade school age greeted him shyly as he emerged from the car and offered to help with his bags. After the four of them made their way clumsily to the front door, Miriam Folker introduced herself and told a hungry Tanaki that dinner would soon be ready. Guy Folker showed him to a room down a side hallway where he would stay until he found a place of his own.

After dinner the children rushed off to their entertainments, leaving the adults sipping coffee around the dining room table.

"Guy tells me you're a migration specialist," Miriam opened. "I do some painting, you know. Mainly watercolors. I especially love shorebirds. Are there any particular species you like to work with?"

"Not really," Tanaki said. "If it moves, it interests me. And just about everything, every *living* thing, anyway, moves. Due to the vagaries of research opportunities, I've seen more of birds than anything else so far." He glanced toward Guy. "But I'm definitely excited about working on some marine species while I'm here."

"You couldn't find a better place," Guy said and pulled a pipe from his jacket. "The largest estuary in the continental U. S., after all."

"With a watershed running clear up to New York and, to the west, out into West Virginia!" Tanaki's voice was suddenly alive with wonder. "And its migration-shed—well, that's even more extensive." Then, suddenly remembering Miriam, he added more calmly, "But I guess we're talking shop here. You'll have to excuse us."

"Not at all," Miriam said. "I find the Bay endlessly fascinating. But tell me more about this concept of migration-shed. I don't think I'm familiar with it."

Tanaki vigorously rubbed his hands together, warming to the subject. "Well," he began, "first imagine vast flocks of geese and swans shuttling back and forth from their summer breeding grounds, way up above the Arctic Circle. Then, consider our summer-resident songbirds, many of whom winter in deepest South America. Or Monarch butterflies, who drift here in huge swarms from Mexico every spring. As for the Bay's fish, why, some of them call the entire Atlantic home! They all migrate in and out of the Chesapeake as their seasonal cycles demand, and are thus part of its migration-shed." Tanaki looked toward Guy Folker. "You know," he said, "it's almost scary what you've tasked me to do, make sense of this gigantic web of constantly moving life."

"I hope my migration man's not saying he's got the jitters." Folker settled back into his chair.

"I didn't say I'm not up for it," Tanaki countered gamely. "But there are so many ways you can go wrong, with so much data in constant flux." He glanced at Miriam, found friendly reassurance in her eyes, and then turned again to Guy. "I've got to admit," he confided, "sometimes I envy those lab researchers. It would be so much easier if we could just put the entire estuary in a test tube, control the inputs and the outputs, all the variables . . ."

"If pigs had wings . . ." Folker remarked slyly.

"I'd probably be studying them!" Tanaki quipped, followed by a burst of nervous laughter that brought a mere smile to Miriam's lips and failed utterly to unlock Folker's bemused expression. "But seriously," Tanaki took up again after an awkward silence, "I've come to believe that it's really just the integrity of your system that counts. That's where the order comes in. Out there it's pure, you know, chaos. I don't mean that in a bad way, in particular."

Folker was occupied stuffing his pipe. "It may seem odd,"

Miriam suddenly came in, "but that rather reminds me of painting."

There was a pause, and then Tanaki remarked, "Really, I would have never thought of it like that."

"But it's true, isn't it?" she said. "And isn't it that challenge—bringing meaning to the chaos of experience—that keeps our tasks endlessly interesting?"

"Well, I suppose I do enjoy it."

"Good," Folker said and drew deeply on his pipe. "I like a man who rises to a struggle. Faint hearts never won fair maidens, as they say. But listen, why don't we step out to the porch? I'm sure Miriam, speaking of fair maidens, would like to show you her watercolors."

The three spent the rest of the evening on a screened porch, reviewing Miriam's artistic efforts (mostly gulls and beached sailboats) before slipping into a discussion of the local real estate market, the ever-changing weather patterns of the Shore, and odd scraps from the news of the day. With his steady gaze and relaxed demeanor Folker came across as professorial, settled into a wicker armchair, puffing leisurely on his pipe. Miriam was thoughtful and quite lovely. But Tanaki felt an odd disquiet in their presence, as if some unseen force, operating on the household, threatened to bring him as well within its grip. He was actually relieved when they excused themselves to put the children to bed; it gave him a pretext to turn in himself. Once retired to his quiet room, he lay enjoying a view of pines and stars before fading into a fitful sleep.

2
The Bluebird

"WHO'S THERE?"

The voice was faint but direct.

"David Tanaki," he replied. Tanaki stood on the porch of a three-story Victorian fronted by two great magnolias, forcing his voice through a door encrusted with dark green paint scored with myriad vertical fissures. The door creaked slowly and the musty odor of a house kept by the elderly wafted onto the porch; it filled his nostrils, encroached even into his hair, his eyes, his shoes. Straining to see into the dimness, he perceived a shadowy figure drifting backward into the hallway without any discernible movement of limbs, the way he imagined a ghost might move. When his eyes finally adjusted he made out a woman, probably pushing ninety, standing beside an antique cabinet the doors of which were alive with swirling fish and other marine motifs. The outline of a staircase now emerged from the left side of the foyer, yet still there was something about the woman's appearance—perhaps it was the faded cotton print dress, or the way her hair seemed to float above her head—that compounded the wraith-life quality he had sensed in her movements.

"You've come about the room?" she inquired, her drawly southern voice rising in a wan glissando.

"Yes. . . I'm beginning a fellowship at the research station down in Benton," Tanaki began, but he suddenly truncated his remarks, sensing that the details of his life held little interest for his prospective landlady. In fact, she was already moving toward the foot of the staircase, drawing a large key ring from the pocket of her house dress with a shaky hand. She took hold of the banister, placed a foot on the first step, and climbed without a word until reaching a capacious landing on the second floor. Here she turned and presented the keys to Tanaki. She weakly gestured to one side as she did so.

"This is the apartment," she said hoarsely, "examine it carefully."

Tanaki stepped aside to let her pass; she descended the staircase with the same gliding fatigue with which she had ascended it. He looked around the landing. Like the foyer, it was furnished with several objects of apparent antiquity—a dark, ornate sideboard, a rudely carved cigar store Indian, and a weathered sailor's trunk. After taking in these objects with a sort of halting familiarity, he placed the key in the lock and stepped over the apartment's threshold. His footsteps echoed on the hardwood floor. The apartment consisted of a living room of ample dimensions with two windows facing the magnolias out front, a galley kitchen with an adjoining breakfast nook, and a bedroom overlooking a shaded back yard.

After slowly walking through each of the rooms, Tanaki stood in the center of the living room and tried to assess what sort of feeling the place gave him. His career had involved many a change of residence over the past twelve years, and he had determined that his first impression was normally the best indicator of whether a place would work out or not. This had something to do, he suspected, with the same faculty some researchers believed helped birds on their first migrations know when they've reached the right place. Possessed of an innate impression of how a habitat should feel, look, and smell (the nature of the terrain and the flora, the quality of the sunlight, the levels of humidity—or so the theory went) they simply orient themselves to the proper compass direction and stop flying when they reach a site that corresponds to their inner Shangri-las. As he stood quietly in the vacant apartment, Tanaki now attempted to follow the same principle. The only trick was to relax enough to let his instincts take over.

He didn't know what to make of the landlady. She, like the artifacts in the hallway, seemed to belong to an earlier century. But that fact didn't come to the fore as he stood in the empty room making his decision. He was instead struck by a certain austerity about the apartment which he found distinctly agreeable. He even considered leaving the rooms largely unfurnished, to accentuate the worn hardwood floors and the blankness of the oyster-shell white walls. After all, he figured, the view out the windows would provide plenty of color in the waxy greenness of the magnolias' leaves. Making up his mind all at once, he moved briskly to the door and descended the stairs to tell the old crone that he was ready to sign the lease.

As he passed through the dilapidated gate onto Talbot Street he was aware of a raw, misty drizzle in his face. This, along with the sense of antiquity surrounding his new digs, reminded him of the Netherlands, where he had spent a couple of years doing doctoral research. Then, at an eighteenth-century church with a rose window above the entrance, it came piercing into his mind in sudden, repeating waves. Another place, another new beginning: the night, eight years before, when he had met the Bluebird.

It was a café in a coastal town where folks rode right out onto the beach in their automobiles. He had been in Europe only a few weeks; she was a Belgian who had studied at the Sorbonne and in Spain and Heidelberg. She told him later that she had known right away that he was a *navigationist*, meaning that his abiding interest was in getting to the bottom of the Italian naturalist Perdecci's astonishing work . . .

Tanaki arrived first with Pannenburg, his academic sponsor and natural mentor. Pannenburg ran a research station at the tip of one of the headlands that jut into the North Sea—a windswept place, among dunes and dune grasses, ideal for spotting the migrating flocks that collect there in epic numbers before crossing the Channel *en masse*. A bear of a man, with battleship-gray hair falling over a bluff forehead, Pannenburg enjoyed a reputation for sound science and creative thinking that reached all the way to the States. For some reason, incomprehensible to his protégé, he had taken Tanaki under his wing from the start; the two were already working together as if they had been collaborating for years.

The café lay right off the beach, and from where Tanaki sat sipping beers with Pannenburg, he watched iridescent glintings of moonlight illuminating the surf in the distance. Suddenly Pannenburg pushed back his chair and arose with a great clatter; Tanaki turned to see an angular young man and the Bluebird coming toward the table with Dietrich Moeller, one of the reigning demigods of the migration field. Moeller was in charge of a European-wide banding project that had been initiated with great fanfare in the fifties. Impeccably tailored, his thin dark hair combed back from a receding hairline, he had been a friend of Pannenburg's since they had both studied under the illustrious Perdecci years before.

Moeller introduced the Bluebird as his assistant. The connection of the young biologist Heinz Euler wasn't spelled out, and Tanaki didn't ask.

Pannenburg opened the conversation by praising Tanaki effusively.

"Yes, I have high hopes for this fellow," he had said. "He's a man to watch."

"Really. . ." an embarrassed Tanaki protested.

"You hear that Ani," Moeller teased with a sly wink, "I hope you're watching him. That is, unless you'd rather watch Heinz here."

"Maybe I'll watch them both," she countered deftly. "Or focus on my own career, if you don't mind."

"And why not?" Pannenburg put in. "She's much nicer to watch than Heinz or David, after all. And besides, isn't her talent second to none?"

"Of course," Moeller replied. "That's precisely why I hired her. In fact, she's the most capable student I've ever had." Seemingly disconcerted by this open praise of his assistant, Moeller added more quietly, looking into his own lap, "She knows I'm only teasing."

"Nothing wrong with a little levity, that's what I always say," Pannenburg bellowed. "Now, as for Heinz, well . . ."

"If you're going to start picking on me . . ." Euler began.

"Now, now," Pannenburg cajoled. "In fact, I was just predicting—it was just the other day—that your ascent into the scientific firmament will be nothing short of meteoric. Ask Dietrich, he was there. But first, why don't you see if you can't get that waitress's attention, get some food over here, more beer . . ."

THE BLUEBIRD

After a discussion of academic appointments (*Moeller: Really, Gunther, can you believe they're giving the Heidelberg post to Fanon? Remember how we all used to call him Fussypants?*) the conversation turned to the research that then consumed the waking lives of everyone at the table. Those were heady days in migration studies, and conversations between migration biologists could flame into passions normally reserved for questions of political moment, or affairs of the heart. They were all working in the wake of Perdecci, scrambling to make sense of his paradigm-shattering experiments of the sixties, and it seemed that new worlds were always on the verge of opening up—though they were never as clearly perceptible as the researchers might have wished.

Tanaki watched Pannenburg and Moeller, two shaggy-maned old lions, heatedly argue the possibility that birds use the earth's magnetic field to orient themselves, interjecting no more than an occasional clarifying question, reluctant to enter the fray. But he noted that Euler and the Bluebird—after warming to the exchange—freely traded views with their older colleagues, taking part in the banter, the thrust and parry, with evident relish . . .

During the course of the evening, Tanaki grew increasingly interested in Moeller's young assistant, though at first he hadn't found her remarkable. She was of medium height, her tawny hair long and straight. If there was anything that distinguished her appearance, it was the intelligence of her expression. But it was her style of argument, more than anything, that drew Tanaki irresistibly toward her. Instead of taking on a point directly, she would strike obliquely with a remark that, while not seeming to contradict either Pannenburg or Moeller, invariably subverted their entire train of thought in some insidious way. In fact, he conjectured, the older guys probably thought that she was agreeing with them most of the time. But on one occasion she stopped the discussion short by responding to Pannenburg's glowing description of a new songbird trap with: "Perhaps we should examine to what extent this wonderful device elucidates the neurotic projections of its inventors," before breaking into laughter as she quashed her cigarette butt.

Ashtrays filled and beer bottles emptied, and Tanaki experienced the unsettling but inescapable feeling that he had assumed the role of spectator, the Bluebird performing some kind of high-wire routine for his personal benefit. He couldn't begin to guess why. Still, when he awoke the next morning in his spartan room back at Pannenburg's research station, all he could remember was watching her through a haze of smoke as she laughed at one of Moeller's witticisms, or affected a pensive air, as though she were taking Euler's remarks seriously...

The hoarse blast of a car's horn—just as he was about to wander into an intersection against the light—wrenched Tanaki from his reminiscences. He shook off the old chain of memories with an effort and, pulling himself back to the present, noticed a hollow feeling in the pit of his stomach. Whether its cause was hunger spiritual or biological he wasn't sure, but seeing a luncheonette across the way, situated between a laundromat and an insurance agency, he remembered that he hadn't eaten all day. He entered and took a seat at the counter, ordered a cup of coffee and a sandwich and looked through a newspaper left by an earlier customer. On A-4 he lit upon the following item:

THE BLUEBIRD

> An unidentified woman was found dead yesterday morning in the lion pavilion at National Zoo. Her severely mauled body was encountered by two zoo employees who feed the powerful beasts every morning.
>
> The victim's motivation for entering the pavilion isn't yet clear, and police haven't ruled out the possibility that she was forced into the enclosure against her will. The coroner's office placed the time of death at shortly after midnight.
>
> According to Joseph Scalotti, who manages the pavilion, it is likely that the large carnivores attacked the woman out of fear, or in defense of their territory, since the cats are well fed on a diet of ground horse meat. Nonetheless it appears that portions of the victim's left arm are missing.
>
> The lion pavilion, constructed in 1979, is not enclosed by bars. A moat twenty feet wide and fifteen feet deep prevents the dangerous predators from escaping. However, the structure cannot, zoo officials concede, prevent a determined visitor from entering the animals' habitat.
>
> Officials are attempting to determine the woman's identity. According to police, a key found on the body has been traced to an apartment building in Nashville.

Tanaki's sandwich came and he dug in without ceremony. While he finished his coffee, he congratulated himself on having found a place to stay so quickly, the first he'd looked at, in fact. But the apartment was perfectly suitable, and he resisted any temptation to question whether he had acted too rashly.

"Sometimes," he said to himself, "you just get lucky."

Rising from the counter, his hunger satiated and a sense of purpose taking hold, he decided to go directly to the research station and get settled in. The season was advancing, and much of his work could only be done during specific phases of the annual cycle. Great blue herons, majestic messengers from a world of dream, were already congregating in their noisy rookeries; osprey, elegant dive bombers only just arrived from points south, would soon begin their elaborate breeding rituals; and if luck were with him, it wouldn't be too late to catch the herring runs . . . millions of the silvered beauties thrashing up the Bay's tributaries after having found their way home from watery way-stations up and down the Atlantic Seaboard. And so it went with myriad other animal species, as well plants, like the aquatic vegetation that was aborning again in the shoals and the marshes. Each new season, each new week, in fact, brought significant changes to the Chesapeake's ecosystems. The cycle repeated itself year after year, a cosmic carousel ride, and an enthralled Tanaki could only smile with the thought that he had season tickets to this year's show.

He stood at the rail of the four-car ferry as it puttered its way across the broad river, taking in the breeze coming off the water. A distaff group of mallards floated near the dock at Benton. The research station was situated on a narrow point of land that extended like a pseudopod into the Bay south of town. Tanaki cruised down the main drag, past the guest inns, restaurants, and gift shops, and pulled into the station's parking lot to the sound of gravel crunching under the Honda's tires.

The receptionist looked up when he entered the lobby. She wore her bronzed hair clipped short in a stylish French cut. "You must be Dr. Tanaki."

"It's so damned hard to be anonymous," Tanaki thought, figuring his Asian features had once again given him away. "David," he said and held out his hand.

"David, then." She smiled and placed a sinuous hand in his. "I'm Cynthia. We've been looking forward to your arrival."

He followed her down a dark corridor to a large and open room surrounded by windows. It offered spectacular views of the Bay on three sides. Around its periphery were laboratories demarcated by partial walls. Each of these, Cynthia informed him, was occupied by one of the Center's scientists.

The two made the rounds and Tanaki tried to fix all the names in his memory. But only one of his new colleagues made a particular impression on him. He was an invertebrate biologist by the name of Mark DeForrest, a stocky man of medium height with a dark beard, glasses, and a knowing gleam in his eye.

Cynthia showed Tanaki large common laboratories with specialized equipment not available in the scientists' individual labs, also holding pens with sluices emptying into the Bay, and a big scale model of the estuary. Then she escorted him to Folker's office, which was located in a wing of its own. Tanaki thanked the director for his hospitality and let him know that he would be moving out within the week.

His orientation out of the way, Tanaki settled into his lab and began to inventory equipment and supplies. He spent much of the afternoon going back and forth to Cynthia for things he needed. At one juncture Mark DeForrest's face appeared over the partition of his cubicle.

"Don't be afraid to ask for it," DeForrest said with that glimmer in his eye. He took a furtive glance over each shoulder before adding in a lowered voice, "Believe me, this place is loaded." With that he disappeared across the room.

Tanaki stayed until late, determined to get his lab in order as soon as possible. He was motivated by a feeling, mysterious yet distinct, that the Bay was rapidly receding into some inaccessible distance, that there was no time to lose.

3
Reynolds

"IT WILL BE DARK around eight."

Reynolds sunk the pole into the thick mud, leaning in as the boat brushed against the willowy grasses that lined the narrow watercourse. He and Tanaki had floated away from the research station at first light and it was now approaching four in the afternoon. Tanaki had eagerly wanted to explore the tidal creeks that meander through the marshes south of Benton. It was a pleasant spring day, sunny and clear. When they weren't taking water samples and pulling up bouquets of aquatic plants, he and Reynolds poled and paddled far into a labyrinthine network of interconnecting waterways.

It wasn't long after they first entered the marshes that Reynolds had begun to entertain doubts about Tanaki. He'd been working at the station for twelve years and had come to expect a fair degree of levelheadedness on the part of the fellows. But he couldn't quite figure this new guy. Since it was the first time Tanaki had been on the water, Reynolds could understand his innocence regarding the difficulty of navigating out of that maze of uncharted creeks. But the scientist's unconcern in the face of his repeated efforts to recommend simple precautions left him thoroughly nonplussed. Gleefully examining marsh grasses, lovingly massaging bottom muck in his hands, Tanaki appeared oblivious to the passage of time. Hence Reynolds' reminder about the hour of sunset. In fact, it hadn't been the first. He had initially offered this parcel of information around noon, when his thoughts first turned toward getting out of the marshes by nightfall.

"It'll be getting dark around eight this evening," he had said, assuming a word to the wise . . .

And then again, around one—"Like I said, it gets dark around eight this time of year."

At two he tried a variation on the theme, as his earlier remarks had failed to elicit even the slightest reaction from the biologist:

"You know, we'd better leave enough time to make our way out of here before nightfall."

This last drew nothing more than unintelligible mumblings from Tanaki, who was deeply intent on a vial filled with cloudy marsh water.

Reynolds had lived around the Bay for the better part of his sixty-odd years. Descended from a long line of slaves, sharecroppers, and watermen, with a bit of planter and a slice of Nanticoke Indian to boot, he'd worked on farms as a boy and took to the water after returning from the Big War. On their way to the marshes Tanaki had asked how he came to work at the research station.

"It just kept getting harder and harder to make a living on the water," Reynolds explained. "No more clams, no more oysters. All those long faces at the dock at the end of the day. Least ways here there's a regular paycheck."

He was well liked at the Center; his avuncular manner especially appealed to the younger staff. Steady and efficient in his work, neither hurrying nor slacking, he seemed almost a part of the Bay, with its quiet marshes, perennial fish runs, and regular tides. He had a lot of patience; but like an old song said, that's a lot to lose. He could deal with spending the night shivering in the marshes, if it came to that. But Shirley would be worried as hell, and how would he face his waterman friends if the Coast Guard had to come in after him? Though he hated to dampen Tanaki's enthusiasm—having romanced the estuary for a lifetime, he could well understand the newcomer's excitement on his first date—he figured it was time to speak plainly.

"Listen chief, if we don't start heading back soon, we'll never get out of here before dark."

"Dark?" Tanaki hardly shifted his attention from the clump of eelgrass he was examining.

"Normally there wouldn't be any difficulty, but the way you wanted to get in here, I'm not sure about the way out. We're probably going to have to work it by trial and error."

"Trial and error . . ." Tanaki mouthed dreamily.

Reynolds settled back into the boat with a deep exhalation. He observed Tanaki closely, searching for some clue about this character he would have to be dealing with. Early to mid-thirties, he figured. Clear skin. Neither thin nor fat, with Japanese features. A shock of dark hair falling over a broad forehead. Blue nylon windbreaker and white golf shirt. He marveled at the guy's concentration. For all the scores of scientists Reynolds had worked with over the years, he had never seen anyone so enraptured with the objects of his study. In spite of his irritation at the difficulty of communicating with the newcomer, he experienced a sympathetic satisfaction that the young man had found something to which he could devote himself with such a whole heart. Focusing on the dripping vegetation Tanaki held in his hands, Reynolds was suddenly overwhelmed by a deep and inexplicable sense of connection to the new researcher.

And then something peculiar happened. The bright glare of the sunlight coming off the marshes penetrated deep into Reynolds' mind. His vision went hazy, and he began to hear phantom sounds: the unmistakable riveting of a machine gun, punctuated by terrific, earth-thumping explosions.

The next he knew Tanaki was shaking him by the shoulders. "Excuse me, Mr. Reynolds! Are you okay?"

Reynolds began to come out of it. He looked dazedly at Tanaki.

"Are you all right?" Tanaki asked again. "Do you have any medical conditions that I ought to know about?"

Reynolds shook his head vigorously as he forcefully pulled himself back to consciousness. "No, I'm okay." He rubbed a hand across his face to clear his vision.

"Sure you're all right?"

"Nothing to sweat about," he said. "I'm fine." He pulled himself off the boat's bottom and reached for the seat. "Don't you worry about it."

Tanaki helped him onto the bench. "Maybe you've gotten too much sun." He lightly brushed dirt from Reynolds' jacket. "You better see a doctor, get that checked out."

"I suppose so," Reynolds responded abstractedly and reached into the back pocket of his trousers for a handkerchief.

"I guess we had better be getting back," Tanaki fretted.

"That's what I've been saying all afternoon." Reynolds wiped his forehead with the handkerchief while he checked his watch. "But it'll be a close thing if we can get out of here before dark."

Tanaki squinted over the wide expanses of the marshes. "It's around this mound up ahead." He spoke assuredly as he took up the pole.

Good guess, Reynolds thought. But feeling out of sorts after his fainting spell, what he said was, "Whatever you say . . ."

The sun was still riding a few degrees over the Bay's western shore, however, when with a whoop from Tanaki the two men spotted the station's motorboat anchored at the edge of the marshes. Reynolds figured Tanaki had surreptitiously employed some subtle system for marking the route, though he couldn't imagine why the guy would want to mystify the thing. He didn't figure him for the wise-acre type. Still, as the two men fastened the motorboat's lines to the station dock, the sky growing dark over the Bay, Reynolds couldn't resist—an ironic smile cornered on his mouth—letting out with, "That was a cute little trick you pulled back there."

Tanaki looked at Reynolds with pure puzzlement on his face. Slyly smiling, Reynolds gave Tanaki a light slug on the side of the shoulder before ambling across the Center's lot and climbing into his pickup.

4
Valerie

HE MANAGED a heroic job of putting up a good front, but Tanaki often experienced the odd sensation that he didn't know exactly what he was doing. It was as if, underlying his day-to-day comings and goings, there was some inner migration always taking place. To where, or even from where, he would have been hard-pressed to define; and he was equally at a loss to determine whether this migration was (like that of a cabbage moth) one uninterrupted journey from birth to death in a straight line, never returning to the point of departure, or whether it constituted a chain of "return" migrations—an endless loop, like that of songbirds and waterfowl. He only knew that for the moment he was bearing west, back over the magisterial span of the Bay Bridge, back toward the realm of solid ground: of commerce, of law, and of industry.

More specifically he was on his way to Baltimore, where he had agreed to represent the Center at a conference on environmental problems facing the Chesapeake estuary. To his objections that he had only been on the Shore for three weeks, Folker replied that he knew more than enough to put on a dog and pony show for the policy wonks who would make up most of the conference's attendance. Of course it was to be expected that the new guy would get stuck with more of the unpleasant chores no one wanted to interrupt their research for. Public relations was part of the job, Folker explained. "Sure, in an ideal world, we'd all love to be doing nothing but pure science. But the unfortunate fact is, we've got to keep up our visibility. That's what keeps the moolah flowing out of Annapolis!"

Tanaki was already beginning to hate Folker's glib way of dismissing such an obvious inconvenience.

"You know how it is," Folker continued as he stepped around his desk and placed a fatherly arm on Tanaki's shoulder. "We've got to get out there and show the public that we're doing something useful. It's all about spin, my man. Spin! We may not like it, but I'm afraid that's the way the world operates these days."

Tanaki mulled over Folker's comments as he approached Baltimore, dodging tractor-trailer trucks and trying to maintain a decent speed. Aside from his annoyance at Folker's whole PR take on things, one particular remark struck him in an unexpected way, hinting at a truth about himself he had no doubt been growing into but hadn't yet taken stock of. When Folker said, "we'd all love to be doing nothing but pure science," Tanaki had sensed a nagging desire to qualify the statement, though he didn't then voice his feelings. He would not even have known how to limn them at that moment. He had fallen deeply in love with science once upon a time and, as is always the case with love affairs, he hadn't stopped to consider where his infatuation was leading him. And though he still mightily loved his research—was sure he always would, in fact—he was beginning to sense that he may have failed to attend to other strata of his being, other aspects of his nature that continued their own migrations, unheeding of his conscious complicity.

One thing was certain, he did regret leaving the Shore,

if only for a day. His work was commencing as nicely as he might have hoped. He was starting to get a feel for the Bay: its marshes and tributaries, its fish, water grasses, muskrats, and birds. Moreover, he didn't relish coming into the city's ambit. The intensity of Baltimore's traffic had already started to rattle the inner calm that had come over him his first day on the Shore. It was some consolation at least, as he approached the shining new aquarium on Pratt Street, to see the broad harbor nudging its way into the metropolis. He knew that this placid space of water was part of the same estuarial web, by way of the Patapsco River, that filled the broad panes of his lab's windows with its radiance, its shifting planes of light.

While listening to the moderator introduce him, he looked over the sleekly modern room—a conference facility on one of the aquarium's upper floors—full of lawyers, nature non-profit staff and journalists. Then, as he shuffled through the index cards on which he had jotted some talking points, he realized with a sudden sense of panic that he hadn't yet decided how he was going to begin. Out floor-to-ceiling windows the harbor glistened in the morning sun. His eyes were pulled toward the water and he took in the view. With that image in mind, amid scattered applause, he stepped to the podium.

He began to speak, almost without conscious direction, of the primeval Bay's tremendous fecundity. He invoked English explorers who wrote of skies darkened by waterfowl, and fish so dense they could be caught in prodigious numbers merely by dipping nets over a boat's gunwales. He exalted over the millions of acres of wetlands along the Bay's vast shoreline, which together constitute an ecosystem many times more productive than even the most fertile farmland. The Bay's shallow profile, which favors a profusion of bottom vegetation upon which complex communities of aquatic life depend, brought him to rhapsodic heights. Then he dialed it back and professorially detailed the Bay's ever-changing salinity portrait, which allows those species—like the blue crab—which tolerate such variable conditions to thrive and reproduce in fantastic numbers. "As a result of these serendipitous circumstances," he summed up, gesturing toward the harbor, "this estuary has, throughout the millennia, acted as an irresistible magnet for migrating fish and waterfowl. As you may know, it's North America's most productive fishery after the Atlantic and Pacific oceans."

Tanaki coughed and then, with another glance toward the harbor, he shifted gears. He began soberly to describe the gradual but relentless degradation of the Bay environment that had taken place in modern times. He lamented the scores of species, once extravagantly plentiful, whose numbers were rapidly dwindling. In a voice tinged with sadness, he touched on the case of the American shad, whose bountiful spawning runs were once desperately awaited by hungry colonists at the end of lean winters; they were now rarely found in the Bay system, their spawning grounds blocked by the giant power dam that proudly bestrides the Susquehanna River. He lauded the fabled canvasback duck, once a favorite of Tidewater sportsmen but now seldom encountered in the estuary, thanks to the decimation of the bottom grasses upon which it feeds. He meticulously detailed the problem of over-enrichment from fertilizer run-off, and he explained its role in the algae blooms that smothered life beneath the water's surface. This led to a primer on sewage disposal, and other pressures that a burgeoning human population was placing on the ecosystem. Finally, with a sense of deepening tragedy, he explained the vital role once played by oysters in filtering the estuary's waters—a species whose numbers had now fallen to a minuscule fraction of their nineteenth-century levels.

Much of the audience strained to follow Tanaki's discursive presentation, strewn, as it was, with biological concepts and terminology. But Tanaki held their interest, and even surprised himself—he had never considered himself much of a rhetorician—with the intensifying ardor with which he delivered his remarks. Taking a final look down on the harbor, he closed with reference to a document Folker had provided him, the report of a commission that Maryland's governor had convened to evaluate the health of the Bay.

"Listen to this." He flourished the report over his head before opening it and beginning to read:

"Item—alarming decline of striped bass stocks;

"Item—Black duck populations down from 300,000 to 30,000;

"Item—Redhead ducks completely abandoning the Bay, due to the loss of submersed vegetation;

"Item—Millions of fish dead from effluent in the James River;

"Item—Wholesale clearing of forests needed by bald eagles for nesting;

"Item—Politically directed management of oysters at the behest of harvesters."

Tanaki peered intently at the audience. "And get this," he concluded, slapping the pages of the report with the back of his hand, "repeated warnings of numerous scientists and commissions of inquiry *ignored* by the Virginia and Maryland legislatures!"

His face was flushed as he stammered out these last remarks, and he once again raised the report over his head. He fell silent then, still holding the booklet aloft, frozen into some sort of living tableau. The audience sat in mute embarrassment at what they considered, no doubt, an affected attempt at a dramatic close. But it wasn't an act. Tanaki's evocation of the destruction wrought upon the Chesapeake over the last century had left him in a state of profound shock, as if he himself had incurred all of the violations and assaults he had just described.

After what seemed like forever a woman stood up in the center of the room. "Dr. Tanaki," she coaxed, nudging him from his stupor, "I want to thank you for that wonderful presentation." Tanaki shook his head groggily and peered out over the room. The woman continued. "Could you tell us," she said, "what you now consider to be the most serious threat to the Bay's ecological health?"

Tanaki spoke uncertainly as he tried to focus on the indistinct figure—her blonde hair delicately braided around her temples—wearing a light green suit. "There are so many threats," he began. "Over-enrichment from fertilizer run-off . . . the filling of wetlands . . . inorganic pollutants . . . irresponsible harvesting . . . recreational boating. Excuse me if I'm rambling. I feel a bit strange."

He firmly pressed his left temple and squinted his eyes tightly.

"You're doing just fine," the woman said with an encouraging smile. The moderator began to rise.

"On a more general level," Tanaki resumed weakly now, but with more focus, "I've seen the situation in the Bay characterized as *death-by-a-thousand-cuts*. An ecosystem is like a living entity, it can only take so much abuse. You can kill it with one massive blow, or with a series of small but unrelenting ones."

A representative from an industry association rose to speak.

"Mr. Tanaki, can you tell us how long you've been at the Center?"

Sensing a trap, Tanaki hemmed and hawed. Coming to his side, the moderator bailed him out. "I'm afraid that's all the time we have for questions. We've got a very busy agenda for the afternoon. Lunch is to your left as you leave the room."

The woman in the green suit approached Tanaki as the conferees filtered out of the hall. She held a cup of water before her. "Here," she said, "this should help. Are you all right?" Tanaki took a small sip before answering her. "I'm a little better, thanks." The woman introduced herself as Valerie Stanton. Her name tag revealed an association with the University of Maryland's law school. As they walked together toward the luncheon, they talked about the Bay. Though brief, their conversation was long enough for Tanaki to appreciate a searching mind and a keen regard for the natural environment. Before splitting up to take their respective seats, he had accepted her invitation to meet for dinner when the conference ended.

Following the yellow Miata with the Chesapeake Bay tag toward Little Italy, Tanaki wondered what Valerie's take might be. Was she only interested in his ideas on ecology, or was something else going on? He did find her attractive. She seemed sincere and good-hearted. And she dimly reminded him of someone, though he couldn't quite put his finger on it. Someone distant, from long ago . . .

He parked behind her on a street lined with trim row houses with formstone facades and marble stoops. A humid breeze engulfed them from the harbor as they walked to a corner restaurant with the modest but pleasant aura of an Italian-American working-class home of the fifties.

"That was a pretty lame way to end a talk." Tanaki slowly rocked his head in amused disbelief.

"I wouldn't worry about it," Valerie said. "A little drama can leave a lasting impression. Ask any trial lawyer."

Tanaki looked at her doubtfully. "I'll have to take your word on that. It's not the kind of thing I normally do. I was more or less corralled into this one."

"But you're good at it," she said while a waiter poured wine between them. "You should do more advocacy work."

Tanaki watched the silky red liquid flow into the glasses. "I don't know about that. Perhaps I should leave that to you lawyers. Or was it law professor?"

"Both, actually. I teach environmental law at the university. But I also do some pro bono work on the side."

"Pro bono? Isn't that where you help some character who's short of cash get out of jail?"

"Criminal law isn't my area," she said, "but I will take on a case when the legal defense project is overloaded. Most of my outside work is environment related. These last couple of years I've been serving on a commission looking at land use along the coast. I'm also working on a project with the Chesapeake Bay Fund, drafting regulations for fertilizer run-off."

Tanaki found her interest in fertilizer run-off strangely beguiling but didn't say as much. Instead he said, "You seem to have gotten yourself pretty heavily involved."

"Nature advocacy is a big part of my life." She looked away and added, "maybe too big, I don't know."

"Don't you enjoy legal work?"

She grew thoughtful. "It's really more about protecting things I care about."

Tanaki gazed toward the table and nodded noncommittally. As he remained wordless, almost awkward, Valerie continued.

"I grew up outside the city," she said, "in what used to be the far fringes of suburbia. The subdivisions had just begun to be cut, ever so sparsely, into the surrounding forests and farms. It wasn't the kind of breathtaking wilderness one goes to the national parks to find, but the balance between nature and man-made was still solidly in nature's favor, if you know what I mean. In its own quiet way, that upbringing embedded in me a profound sense of connection to the untrammeled earth. I have such fond memories of exploring the fields and forests in tow of my older brothers, or the stables where I rode horses. Or all the old farms, like the one where we bought our little lab puppy. Looking back, I think I can say that no matter how much madness was going on in my world—you would see it on the television screen every evening—I was always aware of the earth and sky, the fields and forests. I sensed it all around me, with a calming force that I still feel to this day."

"It sounds like you had a pretty happy childhood," Tanaki noted wistfully.

"I suppose it was," she reflected. "In my younger years, anyway. Once I got into my teens everything wasn't so rosy. I was angry about Vietnam and Nixon, racism, sexism—and also about environmental degradation, of course. I affected a counterculture stance, which instigated endless, heated conflicts with my mother. At school, it seemed like our teachers had just given up on us. Then my father started running around, which led to my parents' divorce. I have to admit, I was a little rudderless there for a while . . ."

"I suppose they were strange times for a lot of people."

"Thank goodness for my friends," Valerie said, a smile suddenly forming on her lips. "We'd skip school and go to this abandoned quarry, and when it was warm we'd go skinny dipping in one of the pools that had formed. We'd build bonfires and stay late into the night, drink cheap wine and smoke stuff I'd be disbarred for today. I recognize now that some of it was a little reckless; but still, there was something unspeakably beautiful about it all."

She must have sensed Tanaki imagining—perhaps even exaggerating—her more reckless behaviors, because she moved abruptly past her adolescent years. "When I was in law school at Charlottesville," she said, "I did a lot of hiking in the Shenandoahs. Have you ever been down there?"

"Not yet," he said, "but I'd love to explore the Appalachian flora system sometime."

"You really should," she said. "There are such beautiful waterfalls on the mountainslopes. And the sunsets are amazing, all those hazy blue ranges overlapping one another like palimpsests. We'd always end our hikes at this place called Spittler's Knoll. The view from that ridgeline is absolutely unbelievable."

"We?"

"Oh—" she said with surprise, as if she was not aware of having brought another party into her narrative. "That would be Ron . . . this man I was involved with in those days."

Tanaki just squinted at her; his very silence seemed to beg an explanation.

Valerie fumbled delicately with her napkin. "We were together for a few years," she said. "I went through a lot of changes for that guy, but he just wasn't ready to make any kind of meaningful commitment . . ."

Her eyes had grown moist. "Excuse me." She reached into her purse for tissues. "Allergies," she lied.

"They're really kicking in right now," Tanaki said helpfully. "The trees are still pollinating, and the grasses are already starting to come on line. I believe the hickory and sweet vernals are especially active this week."

She nodded appreciatively as she daubed at her eyes.

Their dinners came then and they chatted about the conference, their opinions of the other presenters, and about the Bay. Over spumoni ice cream Valerie attempted to extract a *curriculum vitae* from her companion. But along with his native sense of privacy, Tanaki was still feeling shaken by his contretemps at the conference, and he was even more reticent than usual.

"Science, that's me in a nutshell," he said, only vaguely aware of the unflattering metaphor. "I live for my work. That's pretty much the way it's been since grad school."

"Now, come on," Valerie coaxed. "I'll bet there's been more to it than that."

Tanaki blushed slightly and polished off his wine. "I'm not so sure." He cast his eyes away, and Valerie let him off the hook.

They stood on the curb to say goodnight. Valerie gave him a warm hug and said that she'd like to get together again, both of which instigated vaguely pleasurable feelings in Tanaki. Driving back to the Shore, he kept seeing her pale blue eyes.

When he got to his apartment, he switched on the black and white TV that sat on a shaky table, the only piece of furniture in his living room besides a stuffed chair he had bought at a secondhand shop in town. His attention was immediately riveted by horrific images of a bloodied and prostrate black swan. A female anchor voiced-over the story:

The National Zoo is in the news again today as yet another encounter between man and animal leaves zoo officials, police and concerned citizens reeling. An Australian black swan, one of the zoo's prized possessions, was found dead this morning in the waterfowl pavilion. It appears that the nineteen-pound bird, which had lived at the zoo for over six years, was deliberately killed by a blow to the head with a large stone found nearby. Police are holding a fifteen-year-old male in the incident. The adolescent turned himself in this evening at the third precinct headquarters, feeling remorse over the slaying in which he claims to have participated with two other youths. According to sources, the teenager gave no reason for killing the bird other than, to quote the youth, "we just felt like it." Since they are juveniles, the names of all three suspects are being withheld. It remains unclear whether the incident is related to the fatal mauling of a Tennessee woman by the zoo's lions last month.

"Damn!" Tanaki whispered. He was stunned. He had always considered the Australian black—its glossy nocturnal elegance, the startling scarlet beak—to be one of the most gorgeous creatures on the planet. Observing them at close range in Tasmania, he had never tired of their sleek beauty. He desperately wanted more information, but when the broadcast resumed after a commercial, the announcer moved on to a story about a neighborhood clinic closing.

Tanaki went to bed in a dark mood and was soon engulfed in dream. Standing at the edge of a beautiful pool, surrounded by rushes and flowers, he watched a black swan glide over the surface. The Edenic environment, designed with a perfect balance of nature and artifice, pleased him immensely. He turned at the sound of a loud noise but, seeing nothing, turned again to the pool. The swan had disappeared. Instead Valerie, clad in a clutching black bathing suit, now cut through the water. She beckoned him to jump in. He walked onto a delicately arching footbridge but encountered—Mrs. Scofield, fearfully pleading with him to go no further. He looked over the pond, seeking Valerie, but saw only a bloody streak running through the water. The scene shifted. He stood beside the highway, and a crisp breeze blew through his hair. There was a car on the shoulder with its trunk open. Mrs. Scofield lolled inside, licking her lips in an incredibly suggestive way. He took a step, another, and found himself in . . . Valerie's waiting arms!

5
Folker

BY THE TIME the azaleas on Talbot Street arrayed themselves in all their crimson glory, and while the green of the marshes burgeoned forth with an amazing profligacy, Tanaki was finding his stride. He had made several trips into the Bay with Reynolds: exploring swamps, oyster reefs, shoals, and creeks; taking water samples or yanking up great dripping hanks of submersed aquatic vegetation; sighting birds and trapping fish; checking crab pots, and peeking into ospreys' nests. Eager to jump-start his research, he spent most evenings at the lab evaluating samples and writing up results. He was methodically coming to grips with reducing the web of migration in and out of—and within—the Bay to some kind of intelligible schema.

He had started where he had to start, getting a feel for the various habitats, observing the animals when possible. As the season advanced he would concentrate on particular species as they underwent critical phases of their life cycles. Summer-resident birds would be nesting and breeding, raising the year's young, and then undergoing their moults before a slew of bodily changes prepared them for their fall migrations. Meanwhile a score or more fish species would migrate into the estuary, some to spawn in the relative safety of the Bay and its tributaries, others to feast on the eruption of plant and animal life—much of it on the planktonic level—that characterizes the estuary's warmer months. And a host of migratory dramas would occur entirely within the ambit of the Bay's home waters: like that of the Chesapeake blue crab whose mated females, having been romanced for the first and only time in their lives, would spend the summer clawing the shoals towards the saltier waters of their Virginia Capes spawning grounds (passing, along the way, the prior year's young migrating up-Bay where, after growing to maturity, they would repeat the cycle in their turn).

Not long after the Baltimore conference, Tanaki experienced what was to be the first of several puzzling encounters with Guy Folker. It was established protocol for the Center's researchers to clear their outings around the Bay with the director. Not only was Folker responsible for producing a coordinated research effort, aside from logistical hurdles, there were serious safety issues to be considered. The Bay's waters, after all, were not always benign. In fact, Tanaki's enthusiasm would have gotten him into trouble on more than one occasion, had it not been for Reynolds' seasoned prudence.

But Tanaki was unaware of any storm warnings on a bright Friday morning when he stopped by Folker's office to let him know that he intended to cruise down-Bay toward Smith Island. He was eager to take a close look at the salt grass meadows that extended for thousands of acres like aquatic prairies in the lower reaches of the estuary.

Folker's face clouded with consternation. "Listen, Dave," he said, "I'm sorry, but that portion of the Bay is off-limits for the time being. Why don't you head north instead? There are some real nice underwater beds up around Elk Neck."

"But Guy," Tanaki responded quizzically, "you know that's a completely different habitat from down in the lower Bay. The salinity portraits aren't even close."

"Sorry, Dave. Them's the rules. What can I say?"

What could he say? Tanaki thought. He could say something that made sense, for one thing. "Is the weather predicted to turn bad?" Tanaki hardly managed to mask his irritation.

"Could be, you never know. Anyhow, I've really got to get back to all this paperwork." Folker displayed the scattered papers on his desk with an outstretched hand.

"Fine," Tanaki replied. He gritted his teeth as he turned to go.

"Oh, and Dave," Folker called out from within his office.

Tanaki wheeled a couple of steps and leaned into the doorway, grasped the door jamb with one hand. "Yes?"

"I've got another dog and pony show I need someone for—some nice little ladies who happen to be among our most active supporters . . ."

"But—" Tanaki began to protest, thinking of the intensifying schedule of research on his plate. But while he hesitated, Folker added with unruffled bonhomie, "Sorry, old man. You were such a hit at the last meeting, I'm afraid you've made yourself indispensable. Yeah, those folks in Baltimore ate up that shtick of yours like a Belgian waffle piled high with whipped cream. I heard all about your dramatic close. That was pure inspiration! I wish I'd been there to see it. I had no idea we were hiring such a great front man."

Tanaki didn't respond. But as he walked down the narrow hallway toward his lab he grumbled to himself, an occasional word emerging into audibility, had there been anyone there to hear it.

"... arbitrary ..."
"... stupid ..."
"... bullshit! ..."
Unfortunately he had to content himself with this private venting of frustration, for it would have been unlike him to blow up at work. It's true that his parents had been given every encouragement, while growing up, to master an American cultural idiom that had eluded his immigrant grandparents. But some traditions die harder than others, and Tanaki père never ceased to remind his son of the old Japanese proverb: *the nail that sticks up gets hammered down*. In fact, the phrase now floated into his mind involuntarily, like some importunate harpy.

"I'd like to hammer something all right," he thought to himself as he entered the open area surrounded by his colleagues' labs. Crossing the sunlit room toward his cubicle, he ran into DeForrest, whom he had failed to notice in his self-absorption.

"Whoa, Nelly," DeForrest joked. "Where's the fire?"

DeForrest's mirth was like a splash of cold water on Tanaki and called him back from his preoccupations.

"Sorry, Mark." Tanaki flung out one arm in exasperation. "Herr Folker has just disrupted my entire work schedule for the week."

"Well," DeForrest said, "join the club."

"It's happened to you?"

"To me? It's happened to everybody." DeForrest took Tanaki by the elbow and guided him to an empty corner where he resumed more quietly. "The problem, you see, is that the guy's clueless. Doesn't know a thing about what we're doing here. He sits in his gold-plated office surrounded by his precious paperwork, making pronouncements about how we've got to keep the bucks coming out of Annapolis and prove we're useful, and all that bunk. Annapolis, sure he's interested in Annapolis! He's some kind of political appointment, after all. Tell me," he said, "had you ever heard of the guy before you came here?"

"I was a little concerned about that," Tanaki said. "But frankly, I really needed the job."

"Well no one else has either. That should tell you something right there. No reputation in the field whatsoever. Why he's here is anybody's guess! Probably somebody's brother-in-law, or a major campaign donor. All this obstructionism, it's unprecedented in my experience. And I've been around a few years, if you know what I mean. Anyhow, none of us really get it, but I'm starting to think there's something fishy about the whole thing. No pun intended, natch."

Tanaki spotted Cynthia coming toward them from the front office. He raised his eyebrows in his best exaggerated manner and DeForrest fell silent. After she passed, DeForrest again grasped Tanaki by the elbow.

"Tell me," he said, "what kind of story did he give you? Weather? Turbulence? Too many ocean freighters out there?"

"He didn't give me any explanation at all."

DeForrest caressed his beard in long, slow strokes.

"Now, that's unusual," he said. "Maybe he's finally lost his nut for good."

6
The Yamaguchis

THE NEXT DAY, as Tanaki prepared for another long evening at the lab, he felt a sense of depletion. His dust-up with Folker had dented his morale, precipitating a bottoming-out already brewing on account of his herculean work schedule. After staring mindlessly at the Bay for half an hour from the chair in his lab he decided to head home. He had hardly been in his apartment since the move and figured a quiet evening would do him good.

There was a warm southerly breeze coming off the water when he left the station. He stopped by the neighborhood market to pick up some spaghetti and bottled sauce. Sitting on an orange crate in the dining nook, he gazed at the magnolias out front and forked the slippery noodles off of one of the two dinner plates he owned.

It was quiet on the street except for the songs of birds. It felt good to look around and realize that he had made two good decisions: to take the apartment, and to furnish it sparingly. It was like a vacuum, a vacuum that sucked up all the striving that had lately marked his existence.

After putting his plate in the sink he made himself

comfortable in his easy chair. He turned over the cover of a scientific journal that had lain unopened by the door since it arrived a week earlier. He smiled when he noticed an article by Dietrich Moeller in the contents; it somehow confirmed the validity of his decision to knock off early. Its title: *Competing philosophical angles on current migrational evolutionary paradigms.*

"Sounds like he's at it again," Tanaki thought. Moeller had a reputation for taking hard science beyond its normal boundaries; Tanaki had personally witnessed his famously speculative flights over beers and coffee in cafés along the North Sea coast. In the middle of the following passage, which Tanaki couldn't help but hear in Moeller's refined German accent: *If it is true that in the evolutionary game there are only winners and losers, with no exiguous pay-offs*—Tanaki was interrupted by a crisp rapping at the door.

Expecting his ancient landlady, he blanched at finding two young women, Japanese in appearance, standing on the landing. The one who introduced herself as Setsuko Yamaguchi was elegant, thin, and radiated confidence. Her softly rounded companion, whom she introduced as her sister, Nariko, shrunk upon herself and smiled with a pained shyness.

Tanaki, confounded, stared blankly at the two females.

"We just came by to say hello," the one named Setsuko said in accented but assured English.

Tanaki mustered a weak smile, standing there holding his journal at his side. He was struggling to wrench his mind from scholarly delight to the protocols of social interaction.

"We live up on the third floor," Setsuko continued. "Mrs. Stafford said that you were new in town. And well, we just thought you might like to come to dinner sometime."

"That's certainly nice of you," Tanaki said with a careful formality, thinking of his pressing work schedule, his need for quiet rest . . .

"How about tomorrow evening?" she went on. "It is Saturday, after all." She took a long glance down at Tanaki's journal. "You know, all work and no play can make Jack a pretty dull boy."

"That might be possible," Tanaki offered hesitantly, wondering vaguely if he had just been called dull.

"Great!" she said. "See you at six. Ciao!"

Tanaki groped for a rejoinder while Setsuko Yamaguchi wheeled gaily toward the staircase. The one named Nariko, embarrassed by her sister's audaciousness, bowed awkwardly and turned to follow. Tanaki stiffly returned the gesture and closed the door. He stood dumbfounded for a moment, wondering what had just happened. "Odd," he thought, "just when I'm trying to have a quiet evening."

He made his way back to his easy chair but couldn't concentrate on Moeller's article. Something about those two women was nagging at him. Something to do with . . . their Japanese-ness. For one thing, it was a strange coincidence, and coincidences always made him nervous. And then there was the possibility that they would look to him as some kind of local protector, just because they shared a common ethnic ancestry. That made him even more nervous. It was hard for him to believe that it was simply a matter of good fortune that two attractive and friendly women happened to be living upstairs. His speculations on the matter led nowhere, however, and after a few minutes he settled back in his chair and again lost himself in Moeller's evolutionary ruminations.

As it happened, when Tanaki awoke the next morning, after

a night of heavy and luxuriant sleep, he found himself looking positively forward to the proposed get-together. Lying in bed, staring at the ceiling, he couldn't deny that there had been something missing in his life—something having to do with being with people. Not to work with them, but to feel their presences, hear their voices, smell their scents. And now, with both a quiet evening and a good night's sleep under his belt, he was more alive to the fact that the Yamaguchi sisters were of an age to make good companions, seemingly intelligent, not unattractive, and FEMALE. As for coincidences and the imponderabilities of fate, he would not, for the moment, ponder them. He spent most of his day at the lab, ran a few errands, and then made his way past the cigar store Indian and up the creaking stairs of Mrs. Stafford's shambling Victorian to the third floor.

He carried a bottle of wine he had picked up at the corner market.

Setsuko answered the door with a welcoming smile and thanked him for the wine with a quick bow. "Please come in," she said in her refined inflections. "Nari's in the kitchen. Make yourself comfortable while we finish dinner." She disappeared around a partition toward what Tanaki presumed was the kitchen.

He removed his shoes and placed them on a small shelf beside several ridiculously small pair that must have belonged to the sisters. He looked around the living room. It was furnished in spare Japanese style, with paper fans and classic prints on the walls. It was unclear how the effect had been achieved, but there was a warm, reddish glow about the place, as if the room had absorbed the colors of a thousand sunsets. Perhaps it had something to do with the highly polished floor, the wood of which was of a reddish cast. Then again, the orange light of the dying day may have been responsible.

Tatami mats surrounded a low table in the center of the room. Tanaki sat on one of them and soon lost himself in a print that depicted a white crane flying over a snow-draped forest. He was still immersed in speculations about the bird's life-cycle when Setsuko and Nariko emerged from the kitchen through a cloud of steam.

"If you'll excuse us, we just have to do a brief service before dinner," Setsuko said.

He had no idea what she was referring to but didn't ask for an explanation.

The women briskly moved to a table before a window facing the Choptank River through which Tanaki saw fragments of nacred water beyond the trees in the neighboring yards. The room was growing dark and Nariko lit some candles. She and Setsuko knelt before the table, apparently an altar of some kind. It supported a magnificent color photograph of a blue marlin and an ornately carved frame bearing the portrait of an elderly man with an open face and kind eyes. A sprig of loblolly pine lay across the front of the table. There were also flowers, and a sake cup which Nariko filled from a decanter she had carried in from the kitchen.

The women knelt silently for a few minutes, eyes closed, and then began to intone some kind of chant in delicate and high-pitched voices. Tanaki remained seated on his mat, examining the photos on the altar, looking out the window toward the river, or observing Setsuko and Nariko. He couldn't understand a word of their chanting, never having learned Japanese, and the whole thing seemed odd and made him feel queasy and uncomfortable. This was clearly some kind of spiritual practice, and Tanaki had steered clear of such exercises ever since his parents released him from the bondage of attending Sunday School when he was in the ninth grade. But the sisters' keeningly soulful vocalizations, which seemed to well from some hidden reserve not strictly appertaining to them, affected him nonetheless—along with the reddish glow in the candlelit room, the pungent aromas of seared seafood coming from the kitchen, and the gleaming shards of river out the window. He began to feel something novel, a sort of expansiveness he had never encountered at Trinity Episcopal Church in Saginaw. When he tried to objectify the experience he could only identify a kind of pulsing, a pulsing that seemed to link him with the sisters, the sunset, the river, the marlin in the photograph, and the old man with kind eyes whom he was sure he had never seen before.

When after five minutes the sisters fell into silent meditation Tanaki noticed something unusual. It was as though the sound of their voices was still in the room. Perhaps not the sound, *per se*, nor even a reverberation or an echo. But he sensed some quality that hadn't been there when he came in, what seemed an almost tangible substance that occupied every molecule of air. For some reason he connected it with the reddish glow. It made him feel a little off-center, but curious to explore the phenomenon further. When Setsuko sprang to her feet and began to rearrange the ritual paraphernalia, he felt almost cheated.

"Ready to eat?" she asked matter-of-factly. She and Nariko slipped back into the kitchen. Before Tanaki could respond, they were returning with two sizable platters loaded with seafood delicacies that he soon learned were cooked to perfection.

"Mmmm—where'd you get this seafood?" he asked by way of compliment.

"We've got a very special source," Setsuko hinted solemnly. She shot a conspiratorial glance at Nariko. Nariko reddened and pressed her lips tightly, suppressing an urge to laugh.

Tanaki decided to go along with their little female game. He wasn't new to these kinds of flirtations, though he hadn't expected it to start so soon. "So this seafood source of yours, it's some kind of secret?" he asked slyly.

"Oh, no, it's not a secret." Setsuko gazed soulfully toward the river, her chopsticks suspended before her. Tanaki, now thoroughly nonplussed, quit chewing the mouthful of squid he was working on and stared dumbly at her.

Setsuko glanced again toward the Choptank, and a thin smile formed on her lips. "If you really must know," she then said calmly, "our special source is . . . the sea!" At that she erupted into a gay laughter that Nariko also joined in her quiet way, leaving Tanaki blushing at the thought of having been so amusing to his hostesses.

Nariko began shyly. "I think we . . . joke . . . too much."

On hearing Nariko speak, Tanaki realized why Setsuko did most of the talking. Her younger sister's English was halting and unsteady. Nariko continued uncertainly. "You see," she said, "we have . . . a . . . seafood business."

"Ahhh," Tanaki said. He pincered a piece of whitish flesh in his chopsticks. "Looks like a variety of sea bream, if I had to guess." He intently examined the dangling morsel.

"You certainly know your fish," Setsuko said.

"Well, I am a biologist," he rejoined.

"A *biologist*," Setsuko purred. She and Nariko exchanged another one of their knowing looks, sustaining the cryptic theme they seemed to find so amusing.

"But bream isn't found in the Chesapeake, is it?" Tanaki asked seriously. He scrutinized another piece, anxious to break up a species of conspiracy that he didn't understand, one that was beginning to make him vaguely nervous.

"Oh, no," Setsuko said, "we take it offshore."

"Special . . . delicacy," Nariko added as she chewed a mouthful of the delectable animal.

"It's considered good luck, especially for us fisherwomen," Setsuko explained. "That is, if you go in for that kind of thing. Omens, signs, astrological forecasts . . ."

"People say it's—" Nariko struggled for her English words.

"Auspicious," Setsuko offered. Expertly mixing sauces in a small bowl, she hiked her head toward the kitchen. "That print over there by the kitchen," she went on, "that's the god *Ebiso*. He's supposed to be the patron of us fisherwomen. If you look closely, you can see there's a sea bream under his left arm."

Tanaki looked past Nariko's head to the portrait of the god. It depicted a stoutly built figure with flaring eyes and a topknot, his flowing kimono swirling about him like a whirlwind. His impressive form rose amidst the kind of stylized waves Tanaki remembered seeing in those Hokusai prints that everyone had on their walls at college. Beyond Ebiso, a red *torii* rose from the sea. In the distance, snow-capped mountains pierced the sky. The god strode through the waves wearing an expression of wild glee, his step an exuberant dance . . .

Tanaki turned his attention again to his dinner. "So all of this came from your seafood business?" he asked.

"Well," Setsuko said, "it's actually father's business."

"Good old *Chichi*," Nariko added, her tone tinged with

homesickness.

"But we're in charge of the Chesapeake operation," Setsuko picked up gallantly. "We have twenty ships. We started with just two."

"My sister is . . . good . . . businesswoman," Nariko added.

"It sounds that way." Tanaki sipped his sake with warm relish.

"All us Japanese are completely gaga over fish, of course," Setsuko took up again. "But this was my idea, the Chesapeake operation. It's funny. Though I'd never been here before, from the earliest age I felt a bizarre attraction to the Bay. Especially those old Colonial times. The English settlers, Jamestown, Pocahontas, the whole enchilada. I read about it in the encyclopedia, and did countless school projects on the subject. When I got involved with father's business, after university, I begged and pleaded—observing the best filial devotion, of course—until he agreed to set up an operation here. I ran the numbers, naturally, and convinced him that it just made good business sense to cut out the middlemen."

After collecting the dinner plates, the women excused themselves and disappeared into the kitchen again. They soon returned with a Japanese tea service. While they were setting out the cups, Tanaki heard their chanting voices—from their pre-dinner ritual—echoing back from some unknown region within his own consciousness. The sensation was so real, and it increased in force to such a point that he was finally compelled to ignore the discretion he had been taught was appropriate where other folks' spiritual practices are concerned.

"If you don't mind my asking, what religion was that?" he asked forthrightly. "You know, with the chanting, the photographs on the altar, the sake, and the flowers?"

THE YAMAGUCHIS

Setsuko took a long, luxurious sip of tea and then said, as if it explained everything, "Oh that, it's just one of the new religions."

"New religions?"

"You know," she said, "part of the rush hour of the gods." She dumped a small spoonful of sugar into her tea and stirred it.

"Rush hour of the gods?" Tanaki said. "I don't believe I'm familiar with that phrase. I was brought up in an Episcopalian . . ."

Setsuko trained a steady, inquisitorial gaze on him. "Wait a minute," she said. "Are you telling me you're that clueless about Japan? Your own ancestral culture?"

Tanaki was taken aback both by her blunt tone and the persistence of her gaze. He wasn't really sure what he felt as he replied, "I guess my family was pretty Americanized."

"Hm, I see." Setsuko spoke as if she didn't quite believe him. But as she topped off Tanaki's tea, she carefully explained. "After the war," she began, "there was an awful lot of confusion in Japan, and plenty of downright soul-searching. After all, the home islands were in ruins. Our cities were burned out, cluttered with rubble, the streets filled with paupers and grotesquely maimed soldiers—the few who had survived, anyway. And then there was the big one—Hiroshima, Nagasaki—apocalyptic devastation. Yes, humanity had finally broken into the atom, and we Japanese got to be the lucky guinea pigs for its less-benign uses. Guaranteed to bring on a major case of existential angst for any society. For sure. As for our ancient codes of honor, and all that malarkey, it was clear that the almighty emperor and the crazy samurai types hadn't been able to keep us from getting ourselves bombed silly. Well, human nature being what it is, people turned to the supernatural, and a bunch of new religions got started. There were so many back in the fifties, one clever wag dubbed it the *rush hour of the gods*."

Nariko nodded in agreement as Setsuko spoke. When she finished and fell silent, Nariko added, in quiet tones, "It's mainly about *kami*."

"*Kami*?" Tanaki asked.

"*Kami* means something like *spirit*," Setsuko explained. "It's a Shinto term."

"Oh, Shinto," Tanaki said bravely, "I have heard of that one. It's some kind of nature worship, isn't it?"

"*Kami* is in mountains, trees . . . rivers," Nariko recited wistfully.

"But also, supposedly, in ancestors and buddhas," Setsuko added.

"Ahhh, so this is some form of Buddhism." Tanaki hoped to bring the conversation around to something that he had a familiar, universally recognized category for.

Setsuko disappointed his expectations with a sort of careless nonchalance, seeming more interested in the sweet bean cake she nibbled than the fine points of religious categories. "Not really," she said between bites. "But Buddhist doctrines do play a certain role . . ."

After a moment of silence, Nariko looked up from her tea and spoke. "It's called—" She turned to Setsuko, her face flushed in helpless exasperation, and quickly pronounced a Japanese phrase.

Setsuko thought for a moment before translating. "It means something like . . . *pure action*," she said. "This guy named Ato Matsunawa started it . . ."

THE YAMAGUCHIS

"Hold the phone," Tanaki said. "Some guy just up and started a religion? Just like that?" Tanaki had developed the opinion over his thirty-four years that religions, by definition, could only be founded by mystery-cloaked figures from the depths of ancient history; that they required centuries of elaboration by solemn bureaucracies . . .

Setsuko laughed at Tanaki's incredulous expression—and at his naiveté about the world in which he lived. But settling down into her tatami, with a ring of laughter still in her voice, she patiently explained it all:

"It was like this," she said. "Ato-san, Pure Action's founder, was born in some nowheresville fishing village . . ." She glanced toward the ceiling, thinking. "It was, oh, way the bejeezis up north somewhere. On the island of Hokkaido, I think. Anyway, in 1945, when Ato-san was just a teenager, his father was killed in the brutal, pyschopathic fighting at Okinawa. Well, Ato was the oldest boy, and according to the hoary old customs of those days, the support of the now fatherless family rested entirely in the hands of number-one son. As you can imagine, young Ato felt overwhelmed by these new responsibilities, and this was on top of a growing existential distress—as he wrote in his autobiography—occasioned by the insanity of an entire world at war. It seems that Ato-san felt that everything around him, not just his personal life, was sort of, like, out of whack. So, being one of these religious types—you know, probably a fantasy-prone personality—he decided to pray to the *kami* for relief. According to sect legend, in fact, Ato prayed and fasted non-stop for days on end, until he felt directed, in some inward way, to take a job with one of the big fishing companies. Well, he followed up on that vague, sort of supernatural, inner prompting, and a few months later, in a sudden fit of inspiration, he invented a new and more efficient method for netting shrimp! It was a huge advance over then-existing techniques, and he made a real killing in the process. In more ways than one, I guess you could say."

She smiled, and Tanaki tipped his cup in acknowledgment of her quip.

Setsuko took up a tray of cookies then and held it before Tanaki; he chose several and placed them on his plate. She settled back onto her tatami and, after an elegant sip at her tea, extended her palm-down hand before her. "So, now," she took up again, "Ato-san is rolling in dough—lettuce, greenbacks—thanks to this shrimp-harvesting contraption he had invented. But instead of doing the usual thing—you know, crowding out competitors, living the high life, geishas, caviar—he used his profits to start a religion based on respect for the *kami*. And there must have been real hunger on the islands for the kind of spiritual goods he was retailing, because before long he had thousands of converts." Setsuko gestured to Nariko. "Our dear old papa-san was one of the first among them. It so happens that Chichi had just started his own seafood business. He hadn't even met Mom yet. And, call it coincidence, but after joining Ato-san's sect, his bottom line went through the roof! Now he's forever proclaiming how we owe everything to the *kami*, just like old Ato-san, and how we have to appreciate everything they've done for us . . ."

Tanaki took a moment to process it all. Then he asked, "Could the Bay be considered a *kami*?"

"The Bay is a huge *kami*," Nariko asserted unhesitatingly.

"Some people call it the shrimp religion," Setsuko remarked casually, as she chomped into an orange-flavored cookie.

"At least it's not the . . . golf religion," Nariko stammered.

"Golf religion?" Tanaki asked over the sisters' laughter. He felt mystified. And certain that he was being sucked into something. Something not necessarily unpleasant.

Just something.

7
Birdwatchers

THE HOTEL was a Georgian structure of whitewashed board surrounded by spreading elms. Tanaki was here to dispatch Folker's latest interruption of his research—a talk before the Chesapeake Avian Support League, the "nice little ladies" the director had referred to.

Helen Conway was waiting in the lobby when he arrived. Short and of medium build, with graying brown hair only partly drawn behind her head, she moved with a fluidity that belied Folker's description. And though she impressed Tanaki as being smartly dressed, there was about her clothing a Bohemian sentimentality, an almost gypsy wildness, that betrayed her identification with the flighted world. Silken scarf. Floral blouse under a loose-fitting, tailored jacket. Translucent, bluish eyeglasses that rose to points at the sides.

Her speech was softly articulate.

"Most of our members are long-time residents of the Shore," she explained as they rounded a corner towards the meeting room, "though we're getting quite a number of retirees these days. Escaping those dreadful cities across the Bay, I suppose."

Tanaki grunted earnestly.

"Our members are quite active in the conservation scene,"

she explained. "Most belong to several organizations. You know, Audubon, Sierra, Greenpeace . . ."

Tanaki nodded politely. He took care not to betray his bemusement at the idea of some quaint little ladies in a provincial backwater spearheading the fight against Despoilers of the Earth. He couldn't imagine that Helen, judging from her demeanor, was brewing up a cauldron of eco-activism on the Shore. More likely, he figured, he'd be addressing what could only be described as a bird-watching club, a coterie of aging gals who occasionally tiptoed to the edge of a marsh to thrill at the sight of a red-winged blackbird, a diversion from their normal round of coffee klatches and church bazaars.

None of that is to say that Tanaki felt any aversion toward people who simply liked birds. He was quite fond of them himself. And the subject matter was a cakewalk. Judging from Folker's scanty remarks, the club was expecting some kind of primer on migration. Tanaki figured they were appreciative to have an expert—a real scientist!—spend some time with them. In fact, he was starting to feel like a damned nice guy.

When he and Helen arrived at the Wicomico Room a crowd of ladies were already in their seats, chatting together or quietly waiting. As he looked them over, observing the collection of shiny or dumpy handbags, the funny hats, a couple with small bits of netting, he felt a certain pity, a pity tinged with tenderness. And he noted the ways in which each of them, like Helen, had been transformed through her fascination with our avian cousins. There was a plump little wren, a lanky, almost aristocratic egret, a boisterous mockingbird, a sleek swallow, a silently observing owl . . .

After Helen introduced him to the group he stepped to the front of the room and causally leaned an elbow on the podium. Having successfully scraped through the Baltimore assignment, he hadn't bothered to reflect on what he might say to the ladies until he was on his way to the hotel. He certainly wasn't about to waste his precious research time putting together a formal talk. Nor had he looked at the information packet Folker had provided him the day before. After all, if the closest thing to a religion he possessed was biology, migration was his personal mantra; he figured he could easily throw out enough interesting tidbits to charm the roll-up stockings off his eager auditors.

"You know," he began, "we once reserved the term *migration* for those spectacular, thousand-mile journeys, like you've all no doubt seen on National Geographic TV specials."

"Never watch TV," the wren piped up. "If you want my opinion, it's a complete waste of time."

"Half of it's sordid," added the egret.

"The other half is infantile," a bunting put in.

Tanaki glanced toward Helen Conway in the front row; her expression was fixed in a benign smile. He chuckled pleasantly. He didn't want to lose his momentum.

"Good point," he said. "But as I was saying, now we migration guys look at all sorts of movement—actually any movement, no matter how small, and by any form of life—as a *migration*."

The ladies, one and all, stared blankly ahead. Not a single gasp of epiphany. Tanaki forced an edge of excitement into his voice.

"Take the amoeba," he enthused, pinching together his thumb and index finger. "Imagine this microscopic organism, painstakingly displacing its minuscule body by the extension of its pseudopods, looking for a more promising solute." He glanced out the window, saw the leaves of the bigs elms shifting mildly in the breeze. He gestured in their direction. "Or a spore from a tree, floating on the wind, waiting to drop on a fresh patch of soil. Well, it's all now considered part of our world of migration studies!"

"We knew that," cried the mockingbird. Her raspy voice sliced through the room like a stainless steel scalpel, and a ripple of nodding hats advised Tanaki that her opinion was general.

"It certainly looks like you've been doing some reading," Tanaki replied, while he thought to himself, *there's always one wiseacre in the crowd.*

Deciding that he had better up the ante, he slyly wagged his finger toward the ladies. "But have you ever considered the idea," he said, "that we humans migrate? And I'm not referring to those major episodes of transhumance"—he figured this fifty-cent term would throw the know-it-alls off the scent—"that fill the pages of history texts, but any human movement, even your simple trip down to the corner grocery store."

"Of course!" the grackle squawked from a back corner of the room.

A little flustered now, Tanaki gave up all pretense to linearity and began to riff in the general key of animal migration. Somewhere in the mélange of words there was something about whales moving between Antarctic feeding grounds and warm water birthing territories; about the flight of the diminutive blackpoll warbler over a thousand miles of open ocean; about the movements of beehives, the swarming of locusts, and the free flights of such "aerial plankton" as aphids.

It was the owl who finally interrupted him, stating calmly but firmly, "Now you're starting to sound like a National

Geographic TV special!" Her remark instigated a round of laughter that put a decisive kibosh on Tanaki's disjointed monologue.

Inspired by her cohort, the swallow said, "But what does all of this have to do with conservation? After all, we're a *conservation* group."

"Conservation?"

"Yes," piped the bunting, "we were hoping you would discuss Operation Recovery. Don't you know that our group is an authorized participant in the Atlantic Flyway banding project?"

"You work with Operation Recovery?" Tanaki asked incredulously. Operation Recovery, a volunteer effort to document songbird migrations, was an invaluable resource which Tanaki and other scientists used regularly. The ladies nodded their affirmation in unison and Tanaki looked to Helen. She must have sensed the helplessness in his expression.

"Perhaps Director Folker didn't forward our information along," she offered helpfully.

The information packet! Tanaki thought to himself and then lied, "I must have missed it."

He took a few steps away from the podium, face toward the floor. He searched within, solidly embarrassed and needing some way to emerge from the hole into which he had dug himself with these women. "The data you're helping compile is incredibly important to understanding songbird migrations—and, more critically, the effects of habitat loss on their populations," he finally blurted out, more to himself than to his auditors. He raised his eyes and gazed thoughtfully out the window for a long moment. A host of chickadees played through the elms and through the crepe myrtles that graced the hotel's grounds. He watched them, smiled involuntarily at their joyous antics, and then turned back toward the ladies. One or two of them smiled, and Tanaki suddenly felt collegial and chatty. "You know," he said, "I got a call from a friend of mine, a fellow researcher out in central Ohio, the other day. She's been studying obstacles songbirds face in their migratory journeys. If you can believe it, she had just counted some thousand starling cadavers around the base of a radio tower out there. And they had all collided with it in a single night!"

"Oh my"—the swallow.

"Poor dears," added the egret.

There was silence for a moment.

"But doesn't that just show how high the stakes are?" the blackbird finally announced with deep authority.

"Yes," Tanaki replied. "Exactly . . ."

"After all," a warbler chimed in, "migration's no pleasure cruise. These animals need to escape lethal cold, find food, or seek out suitable habitats for rearing their young. For them, migration is a matter of life or death. The very viability of their species depends upon it!"

"I couldn't have said it better," Tanaki responded with surprise. "In fact, you've just stated a fundamental premise in my field of study: that no migrant would undergo all of these risks and rigors if an easier avenue to survival existed."

The ladies shook their heads in unison, smiling politely now.

"There is one thing I think migrating animals have going for them, though" Tanaki continued, back into his professorial mode. "And that's their tendency toward gregariousness. Even species that generally prefer to spend their days in complete solitude will come together when it's time to migrate, due to the hazards of the journey, the exigencies of the mating process . . . and no doubt for other reasons we don't yet fully understand." The ladies' expressions had begun to turn listless again. "But you probably know all of that," Tanaki conceded, wishing anew that he had taken a close look at Folker's packet.

To his relief, Helen stood up, took him by the arm, and warmly thanked him for his lecture. Then she led him into an adjoining room where refreshments were laid out on draped tables. The women of the club surrounded him as he sipped a glass of punch. They peppered him with questions on every detail of his research, quizzing him on air currents, incubation rates, salinity gradients, freshwater flows, and the growth rates of aquatic vegetation. He was a little diffident at first, feeling the fool for having so completely misjudged his audience. But as he dutifully fielded their queries, he warmed to the exchange, until he felt downright happy that he had come. And he began to feel that they liked him, too. They hovered about him as he satisfied their scientific curiosity in extensive detail, and by the time he was preparing to leave, while they all nibbled cookies and chatted together, he began to suspect that the ladies viewed him as if *he* were a bird—some displaced nestling who simply needed understanding and a little nurturing. He couldn't explain it, but as he drove back to the research station, he experienced the odd but unmistakable sensation that he had been taken into a new flock.

8
Ocean City

CYNTHIA buzzed Tanaki to let him know that Valerie Stanton was on the line.

The call came as a surprise. Caught up in a rapidly evolving season of research, Tanaki hadn't had much chance to think about Valerie since the Baltimore meeting. It's true that every now and then, while floating through some marshy creek with Reynolds, a pleasant recollection of their dinner in Little Italy crossed his mind. But if he had thought about calling her once or twice, the occasion never seemed propitious. He picked up the phone while looking over the Bay's waters, blue under the intense June sun.

"Is this David?"

At the sound of Valerie's voice, Tanaki felt abashed at not having called her. Though that wasn't supposed to be the man's role these days, it may have been plain rude not to venture the gesture. Valerie's tone was free of reproach, but he a hard time getting started.

"Valerie . . . yeah . . . Hi . . ."

"Listen, I'm going out to Ocean City this Saturday," she began in a voice full of sunshine, seemingly oblivious to his difficulties. "There are some shoreline issues I'm dealing with on the Commission, and I need to get out there and see a few things with my own eyes."

"That's the best way to do it, I always say."

"Of course, for recreational purposes I would much prefer Rehobeth. It's so much quieter. But it's an excuse to get out of town, and it looks like the weather will be splendid. So, anyway, I thought you might like to drive out with me. I'll be coming right past Cambridge, and I can easily stop by for you."

She made it all seem utterly casual, not hinting at anything intimate—while at the same time not ruling it out. He reflected that he had been meaning to get down to the coast anyway, to the great islands of shifting sand that constitute the Eastern Seaboard's vanguard against the relentless pounding of the Atlantic surf. He also remembered Valerie's attractive figure and soft blue eyes, so with a comment about scientific interest that didn't rule out other kinds of interest, he gave her directions and told her that he would be ready Saturday morning.

He recognized the yellow Miata when it pulled up to the curb, and grabbing his overnight bag, bounded down the steps with only a passing glance at the cigar store Indian. Valerie drove like an ace and seemed benignly oblivious to the speed limits. Her eyes were hidden behind large tortoise shell shades. Strokes of white along her neck betrayed an earlier application of suntan lotion. The top was down, and her golden hair flew in the wind.

They arrived at the coast in a little over an hour. It was apparent that Valerie knew Ocean City well. She negotiated the throbbing traffic that clotted the main thoroughfare without flinching, then maneuvered onto a side street where she found a coveted parking space near the beach. As for the great barrier island, there wasn't much of it to be seen, most of it having long since been covered with hotels, restaurants, honky-tonks, boutiques, and a broad swath of asphalt that carried a never-ending flow of raving automobiles up and down its length.

Tanaki and Valerie crossed the boardwalk and made their way across the hot sand of the wide beach. Valerie looked around with an arm-spreading gesture that betokened animal health and said, "Don't you love the sun?"

Tanaki meanwhile was adjusting to the brightness, shaking himself out of a reverie that had overtaken him on the bridge across the Isle of Wight Bay, a placid body of water that separates the barrier island from the mainland. Looking over its waters, he had drifted into a series of speculations about levels of salinity, tides, and water temperatures. Now, as he and Valerie walked down the beach toward the surf, the distinctive rhythm of which was already playing on his consciousness, he became aware of the holiday horde that covered the sand with their blankets and umbrellas. He had spent the previous summer in the far north, observing tundra swans in their breeding grounds, and most of the fall and winter in a small Michigan town waiting to hear about the Chesapeake grant. The presence of so many people all in one place downright startled him.

They spent the day sunbathing, making heroic forays into the freezing Mid-Atlantic surf, and listening to pop tunes on Valerie's boom box. At intervals she perused a report she had brought along, one having to do with the coastal land-use issues she was studying for her commission. Tanaki, for his part, wasn't interested in reading. When they weren't in the water, he lay on his side gazing incredulously at the sea of shining bodies spread under the baking sun; or sat facing the ocean, watching the swimmers, rafters, and body-surfers.

TANAKI ON THE SHORE

Valerie closed the report on itself and sat up. "Wow," she said, "it's amazing to think that a hundred years ago there wasn't anything along this shoreline but a few simple cottages." She peered northward, where towering condo buildings rose one after another, like some gargantuan army marching upon the Atlantic.

"No kidding?" Tanaki replied, following her gaze.

"The thing is," she said, "there was no viable way to even get out here until they ran a railroad across the Eastern Shore in the early part of the century. After that, the vacationers from Washington and Baltimore could ferry across the Bay, and then catch the train the rest of the way."

A gaggle of children careened by the blanket, spraying sand across Tanaki's legs. He brushed it off with emphatic swats. Valerie set the report down, adjusted her hair band, and gazed out over the ocean.

"It seems this was just a quaint seaside town as late as the nineteen-forties. A few hotels and fishing camps. Then—in '52—they put up the Bay Bridge. That opened up the Shore to automobile traffic . . ."

And the swarms came, Tanaki announced deeply, like the narrator of some cheap sci-fi flick. He glanced around at the beach-going crowd.

Valerie laughed. "See that huge barge out there?" She pointed to a fuzzy dark bar suspended in the hazy offing.

Tanaki squinted through the glare that blazed off the sand and sea.

"It's part of this Sisyphean effort to prevent erosion of the shoreline."

"I can imagine," Tanaki replied. "A barrier island has to be one of the most fragile ecosystems on the planet."

Valerie turned suddenly toward him. "That's right," she said. "I guess we're getting into your area of expertise now, aren't we, Dr. Tanaki?"

"No, no" he protested. "Please go on. I'd like to hear your take on it."

Valerie blushed under Tanaki's approval. "Well, in addition to its fragility, this barrier island happens to be smack dab in the middle of the Atlantic storm zone."

"Of course!" he replied.

"In fact, a major hurricane made landfall here in 1933. Slashed right through. That's where the inlet is now, down south of town."

"Just wait until a *really* big one comes," Tanaki said.

"That's exactly what the meteorologists are saying. They say that when the big one hits, this whole place could be history."

A gull squawked loudly.

"So," Tanaki said, "I suppose that barge is doing some kind of dredging work."

"Yeah. They pump sand onto the beach through these huge plastic tubes. You should see them. They look like the tentacles of some weird sea monster, lying across the beach, the other end disappearing into the surf."

Attack of the sea tubes, Tanaki jested in his movie voice, just to make her laugh again. He wanted to see her eyes sparkle, and to see her throw her head back, her shining golden hair bouncing and bobbing. When he resumed, he spoke more seriously. "Do they really think they can take on Mother Nature with a couple of barges and some plastic tubes?"

"Good question. It seems like every other year a big storm erases an entire season's worth of restoration work."

"I can imagine."

"But the town keeps pouring money into erosion control," Valerie said. "This place is big business, after all." She looked north toward all the swanky condo towers. "Its entire economy depends on the beach."

The two new friends fell suddenly silent, struck by the extent to which man will go to secure his pleasures, undaunted by the ephemerality of the structures upon which they are built.

Then after a moment, as she had throughout the afternoon, Valerie pulled down the straps of her suit and enlisted Tanaki's aid in covering her back with suntan lotion. When, in spite of these ministrations, her shoulders began to turn an unhealthy shade of pink, they gathered up their blanket and headed toward the boardwalk. After browsing in a few shops they returned to the car. There they decided to get a room, speaking only of a place to shower and change. They bathed and dressed—she in a slinky number that really showed off her figure—and walked to a breezy dining spot on the sound. As they began to sip their beers she said, a little sheepishly, "The last time we dined, I believe I told you about my student years. I may have even touched on my big, famous heartbreak."

"Oh yes," Tanaki replied with a sly gleam in his eyes, "I took extensive notes . . ."

She looked at him wryly.

"As a biologist," he went on, running a finger around the rim of his beer mug, "I'd be remiss if I didn't fully document all new life forms."

"So the women you date," Valerie countered with a fetching smile, "they're just so many interesting specimens?"

He'd taken enough tests to know that the answer to this

question was *none of the above*. "Scratch the bit about the notes," he said. "But I do remember those hazy Shenandoah ridges, the fireflies on summer lawns . . ."

She was pleased that he had passed the test, and also that he remembered. It showed in her blush. But she didn't want to talk about her life again. Tonight she was determined to find out who lurked behind the thick glasses, a shock of dark hair falling across his forehead; a man who, she'd learned on the beach, could watch hovering gulls for twenty minutes as if nothing else in the universe existed.

"You seem to really love observing animals," she said.

"I suppose I do." He spoke almost as if he had just realized it himself.

"That's all connected with your work, I imagine."

"Well . . . yes," he started thoughtfully, feeling his way along. "But I guess it goes back beyond that, probably to the fishing trips I used to take with my father, up on the Upper Peninsula."

"I hear it's very beautiful up there!"

"Yes, in a rugged sort of way."

"So you'd go fishing with your Dad?"

"When he first started to take me, actually, I was too small for fly fishing. Just five or six. But he would let me carry the tackle box as we explored up and down the streams, looking for a good spot. I'd sit and watch him cast his line into that frothing whitewater for hours."

Tanaki directed his eyes obliquely across the table, as though observing something unseen to Valerie. When he turned his gaze back to her, there was a distant look in his eyes.

"Dad knew everything about trout," he picked up again. "He'd tell me stuff as he fished. About their habits, what they'd do, where they'd turn up. To me it was like a game. I would try to figure out what the fish were thinking. So we could win the game, I guess!"

He looked away again. "You know how kids are."

They fell into a moment of quiet beer sipping. Tanaki inhaled and took in his surroundings. The deck on which he sat with Valerie hung out over the sound. There was a rich magenta wash across the water, and a cooling breeze washed over them in continuous waves. Valerie looked beautifully flushed with the sun and exercise she had taken during the day. Tanaki unthinkingly allowed his gaze to rest languidly across her body.

Valerie spoke to break the spell. She wasn't ready for this kind of observation—not, at least, until she was certain she wasn't just another *specimen*. She thought back to Tanaki's Baltimore lecture. "I know so little about migration," she said. "Just what I've seen on those National Geographic specials . . ."

"Funny you mention that," Tanaki said with a small laugh, thinking of Helen Conway's birdwatchers.

"Why?"

"Oh, nothing," he said. "It's just more complicated than most people think"

"But I enjoy complexity," she said gamely.

"I don't suppose you've ever heard of Aldo Perdecci," Tanaki queried doubtfully.

"Aldo. . . ?"

"Perdecci. It was reading about his work, when I was at Cornell, that got me hooked on migration studies."

"Hooked? That sounds pretty serious." She took a long draught of her beer.

"I guess it is," he said. "It's rather hard to explain . . ."

"But it started with this Aldo—"

"Perdecci. Yes. You see, before him, everybody thought that migration was painfully simple. The classic idea was that animals operate on raw instinct, mechanically driven by hormones. Utterly without thought processes of any kind . . ."

"Kind of like dating," Valerie effortlessly quipped.

Tanaki laughed. "You know," he said, "that could make for an interesting thesis . . ."

"I suppose it could," Valerie replied, and she smiled. "But for now," she added, swallowing her mirth along with a sip of beer, "I want to hear about your scientific hero. Perdecci, the name was?"

Tanaki was delighted with Valerie's sense of humor, a playful persona she seemed to have put on with the slinky dress and dangly, glittering earrings. He was also glad that she was interested in his work. He wondered hopefully whether she might find migration research as fascinating as he did . . .

"Before Perdecci," he took up after a brief, foamy sip, "it was thought that, after orienting themselves to an instinct-driven compass direction, cued by light levels and such, birds fly unthinkingly—on auto-pilot, so to speak—until they reach their final destinations. The idea was that they have no idea where they are from moment to moment."

"I'd bring up dating again," Valerie purred, "but I don't want to sidetrack you . . ."

But it was too late; Tanaki was already getting sidetracked, and beginning to wonder about Valerie's instincts. But she had said she wanted to hear about his life's obsession, and so he proceeded right into the heart of the matter . . .

"In 1964," he began, "Perdecci conducted an experiment that swept the carpet from under all previous migration theory. It was quite simple in design, really. First, he captured some Swedish starlings in the Netherlands. Now, at the time, these birds were in the midst of their autumnal migration toward Brittany, which is southwest of there. After loading the starlings into a van—in covered cages—Perdecci then transported them to Switzerland, where he released them. Well, if the birds were simply following an instinct-driven, pre-programmed direction, they should have continued to fly on a southwesterly course, through southern France and ultimately into Spain. But instead they winged north-by-west, and arrived right where they belonged—in their normal Breton wintering grounds."

"So, somehow, they knew . . ."

"Yes! They apparently were able to determine precisely where they were on the earth's surface at any given moment. And this was done without visual clues; remember, they were transported to Switzerland in black-out cages. They also clearly understood their relationship to their desired destination. It was as if these birds have a built-in geo-positioning system, including a complete inner map of the planet. Long before we humans invented one, of course! On top of that, they appear to have possessed the data-crunching ability to calculate, and then recalculate, the vectors needed to bring them to their customary winter home."

"That's really awesome," Valerie said with genuine enthusiasm. "And quite beautiful to ponder."

"I guess it is," Tanaki said. "But you can imagine how it shook up the migration community. Everyone suddenly went into a frenzy of new protocols, testing birds' sensitivity to wind currents, the ionization of the atmosphere or magnetic isotherms. They blindfolded birds, put frosted contact lenses on them, or strapped magnets onto their heads. Sometimes they even mutilated them—removed pineal glands, severed optic nerves, or destroyed the inner ear—all so they could figure out how on earth these birds were committing these amazing feats of navigation."

Valerie recoiled upon herself. "Those poor creatures needed a lawyer," she said as a waitress approached with their dinners: sole for her, flounder for him.

Tanaki leaned back in his chair. "Fortunately," he said, "most of us modern researchers have abandoned those methods. I'm happy to say that nowadays, by and large, we prefer to observe the animals in their normal condition and state of health."

Valerie commented approvingly; Tanaki straightened himself and picked up his silverware. But casting nothing more than a bare glance at his food, he took up again with surprising focus, emphatically punching his fork into the air. "There was something about Perdecci's data that I just couldn't walk away from. The idea that these birds, with their proverbial 'bird brains,' could figure out—whether based on magnetic fields, celestial soundings, or the ever-changing ionization of the atmosphere—their precise position, and then calculate a vector to their destination, well, that simply amazed me!"

After taking a moment to cut up his flounder, and testing a few bites, he resumed more casually . . .

"In a way," he said, "I guess it was like those trout. I couldn't understand why these animals were behaving the way they did. That bothered me, that not being able to understand. It was like these animals possessed some . . . wisdom . . . that I didn't. Now it was more than a boy's game. The stakes seemed higher. Life or death, almost. It's hard to explain . . ."

"Sounds terribly serious," Valerie said through a mouthful of sole.

They ate quietly for a moment. Finally Valerie looked up at Tanaki.

"So what did you ultimately do about this conundrum?" she asked. "This mystery, with which you could not abide?"

Tanaki sat back. He thought for a moment and tried to recall. He wasn't used to explaining himself to others, or even to himself. But as he dredged up the long-ago years of his college days, a rough picture began to emerge. "In short," he finally said, "I buried myself in migration studies. I suppose I figured that if I learned everything there was to know about the topic, the answers *had* to reveal themselves. Consequently, I spent most evenings of my junior and senior years in the library, investigating everything from whales to aphids, or sitting up late in my dorm, calculating the energy requirements of long-distance migrants. You know, metabolism of stored fats, that kind of thing . . ."

After a respectful silence, Valerie said, "I hope I'm not treading on too private ground here. But what you just described sounds like a pretty one-dimensional—not to mention, lonely—existence."

Tanaki put down his fork with an air of revelation. "Now that you mention it, I suppose it was. But I don't know that I suffered any lasting damage. Looking back on my student days, it seems that I was like an insect that spends part of its life cycle in a cocoon, preparing for its next metamorphosis."

Valerie leaned back in her chair, where she could take in her companion in his totality. "And when that metamorphosis came," she asked, "what sort of creature—strange and beautiful, I'm sure—emerged?"

"Just what you're seeing here," he replied. "More strange than beautiful, I'm afraid."

She laughed kindly while he organized his thoughts.

"Since graduation I've had some papers published," he said after a moment. "There have been a couple of temporary teaching posts, and a few research grants along the way. The typical aspiration for someone in my shoes, of course, would be a tenured teaching position." He looked off, as if making some inner calculation. "And I've put in some applications. But I've never pushed that track very hard. The only real constant since my college days has been migration research. That seems to be the thing that's driving me."

Valerie grew thoughtful, gazing at the stars that had begun to emerge out of a darkening sky. "I can see how you could get hooked on migration studies," she said. "It's sounds truly fascinating. All the creatures of the earth, constantly on the move, each trying to find its own happiness. So much like us, when you think about it."

"I guess you're right," Tanaki said. He looked down with a vaguely uncomfortable expression, and an awkward silence ensued.

Valerie's feminine intuition was on overdrive, and she sensed something unsaid, something that hovered about their conversation like a phantom. She thought she knew what it had to do with, and though she knew it was a buzzkill to speak of past lovers with a new date, she also sensed that she would never really know David Tanaki were she not to breach the topic. Needing connection more than buzz, she spoke.

"Yes", she said with a brief hesitation, "I can really understand your passion for nature over the years. But I also sense something missing from the story, some crucial element . . ."

He looked at her quizzically.

"*Cherchez la femme* is how the French put it, I believe."

"A woman?" he began, exhausting his familiarity with the language of the Gauls.

"Yes, mixed up in all of this, somewhere. I sense it. How are my instincts?"

To his display of reticence, she responded, "Now don't go getting shy on me. After all, I've shown you the heart on my sleeve . . ."

It was true, and Tanaki, though discomfited, perceived a kind of strength in Valerie's forthrightness. He took up his napkin and stared at it a moment, as if searching for something. Then he spoke flatly, with little emotion. "There was one woman who was, I guess you could say, mixed up in all this. We worked together when I was in Europe."

"Of course," Valerie replied with just the slightest air of triumph. "And will said woman remain nameless?" She made her voice playful now.

He looked up with a muted smile. "No need for that," he said. "Her name is Anna." He hesitated a moment, before adding, "but I used to call her Bluebird."

"That's cute," Valerie said, and Tanaki was too self-absorbed to note his companion's forced gaiety. "And she didn't mind?"

"Aside from when I first got to know her, I don't believe I ever called her anything else."

"An allusion to the bluebird of happiness, I imagine?" she coaxed.

"I don't know about that," Tanaki countered, looking away. Then he rallied, wanting to dispel a *blue* note left by his remark. "It started with a sort of game we used to play. She might say, *you're acting like a beluga whale during mating season.*

Then I would say something like, *I can't help it, I feel like a blackpoll warbler in late November.* That kind of thing. Maybe you had to be there—or be a biologist."

The waitress came to clear the table. Amid the clatter, Tanaki succumbed to other memories of the Bluebird: how they would meet in quiet Belgian towns, spend the night on a Zeeland beach wrapped in his old sleeping bag.

He didn't share these reminiscences with Valerie. Nor did he tell her about the waxwings, how they came so unexpectedly that eight-year-distant spring:

The medieval Dutch had believed the harmless passerines heralds of plague and disaster; now they came in great clouds, scouring the ground and trees for anything edible. Tanaki rushed to pick up the Bluebird in Pannenburg's jeep, not considering for a moment missing this invasion, a rarity in the migration world. They careened down narrow country roads searching for the flocks. When they found them swarming over a village near the coast he jammed the brakes, and he and the Bluebird jumped out with nets, cameras, and a cotton bag full of metal rings they intended to attach to as many of the birds as they could capture. The waxwings were in a state of frantic excitement, and as Tanaki and the Bluebird scampered about netting them, with a gaggle of curious Dutch villagers looking on, something curious happened. The line between Tanaki and bird blurred, and blurred some more, until he wasn't sure who was capturing whom. At one point he stopped, breathless, and found himself staring blankly into the Bluebird's face. She too was out of breath. There was a vacant savagery in her eyes that—he knew— mirrored his own state of mind. Some kind of boundary had been crossed. Who were they? What were they?

Of course Tanaki didn't tell Valerie how, that night, he and the Bluebird loved one another with a rapture unlike anything either of them had ever experienced. Tender and hungry at once, with a fluttering of wings . . .

As the waitress wrapped up her duties, Tanaki looked at Valerie again with that peculiar sadness in his eyes. She smiled reassuringly, knowing that he had been far away, and also where his thoughts had wandered. Night had fallen, and spots of light bounced on the sound. Valerie, inwardly questioning why she hadn't stuck with migration studies, steered the conversation back around to science.

"So, about the great mystery," she said, "how these fragile creatures find their way across their trackless destinies—that question you hoped to resolve by exploring the depths of migration—have the answers yet revealed themselves?"

"I'm afraid not," Tanaki replied. "Not yet, anyway." He squinted painfully at her.

"I suppose you're still collecting your data," she said helpfully.

"Yes. But the scary part is, it's starting to feel like there may be no end of data to collect. You see, the data keeps changing. And growing. Or perhaps it is I, or my need for data, that keeps changing . . ."

Both of them were quite beery now, and it was natural to put their arms around one another as they walked toward the motel. When Valerie leaned her head against Tanaki's shoulder he felt a thrill at the brush of her hair against his face. Once in the room they came together without any real deliberation. It had been a long dry spell for him, and he liked how she was patient, letting him take the time he needed to try and get it right.

They lay facing one another in the wee hours.

"There's this diminutive little bird in Africa," Tanaki began out of the blue. "And it ekes out its difficult existence in some of the most barren desert regions of the continent . . ."

Valerie ran her fingers lazily through his hair. He continued excitedly.

"But when the brief rainy season comes, all of a sudden, the desert bursts forth with all kinds of new life!"

"How nice," she said, and they shifted onto their backs and gazed together toward the ceiling.

"What I find so cool about it all," Tanaki began again after a moment, "is that these little birds — these black-faced sparrows, to be precise—they have enough sense to mate within moments of the arrival of the first showers. That way, when their chicks hatch, the parents can nurture them on all the fruits and insects that will soon be springing up everywhere."

"That's almost romantic," she said drowsily. She shifted onto her side and nuzzled into him. They lay quietly, breathing softly together, until they both dropped off to sleep.

Tanaki opened his eyes. It wasn't yet dawn, but he felt wide awake. He was surprised—almost shocked—to see Valerie lying there, breathing heavily. An image of the previous evening came to mind: their confessional conversation, the beery slide back to the hotel, all the rest. Valerie grunted slightly and laughed in her dream. Strands of gauzy hair lay across her scrunched-up face. The way she lay on her side, all of her womanly curves showed themselves to great advantage. Tanaki smiled at the thought that just a few hours earlier she had pantingly cried out his name and pulled him impossibly close. She was a good-looking woman, and intelligent as well. He thought of the Bluebird, the way they used to sleep like spoons in the wee hours of the morning, cupping themselves into one another. He even considered whether he oughtn't to sidle over and wrap himself protectively around Valerie. But somehow it didn't seem right; he just didn't know her that well.

He looked around the room and began to feel restless. And a little awkward. Why was he here? he asked himself. He had no clear answer, other than beer and hormones. He looked at the clock. Sunrise was near. He decided to walk down to the surf. There was a chance the dolphins would be running, and that magnificent sight always inspired him, steadied his mind. Valerie, from the looks of her, wouldn't be waking up any time soon. Moving quietly, he pulled on his pants. Slipping into the flip-flops he had left by the door the evening before, he thought of the Yamaguchis, removing his shoes when he visited at their apartment. That small ritual had already imprinted itself upon his consciousness . . .

The air was moist and cool as he strode over the sand toward the water. After walking up and down the beach a bit he stood peering out past the breaker line. No dolphins. When the sun began to rise, he sat cross-legged, a few feet from the surf's high water mark. He tried to put the previous night into perspective but concluded only that he wasn't sure what to make of it. He pictured Valerie sleeping soundly in the motel room. She was nice, and he really appreciated her love of nature. As for their sentimental operations, they had been undeniably sweet. Then why this sense of apprehension? Could it be, he thought, the fear that he had backed himself into some kind of corner? The kind spelled E-X-P-E-C-T-A-T-I-O-N-S? For Tanaki felt at heart that he was fated to remain—for how long, who could tell!—as free and unfettered as the objects of his research.

Staring over the water, he forcefully put it all out of his

mind. The extensive nautical vista beckoned him toward a feeling of expansion, while the rush and swoosh of the waves anchored him in the cool sand. He recalled some lines of verse, the few that had made any real impression on him in his obligatory college lit class:

> *Once, far over the breakers,*
> *I caught a glimpse*
> *Of a white bird*
> *And fell in love*
> *With this dream which obsesses me.*
>
> *Swifter than hail*
> *Lighter than a feather*
> *A vague sorrow*
> *Crossed my mind.*

A sudden inner clamor. For some reason, he closed his eyes and began to try to meditate like he had seen the Yamaguchi sisters doing. The plunging breakers gradually pulled him away from his unfocused feelings, until he was soon aware of nothing but the sound of the surf and his own breathing. He sat this way for some time, for the first time in his life thinking nothing at all. Then, without warning, he dropped into a deep and soundless void. An indeterminate amount of time went by. When he opened his eyes, the sky was lightening over the horizon. He felt emptied and light. Gulls wheeled overhead, and sandpipers ran along the surf-line. There was someone fishing up the shore; an early-rising, middle-aged couple strolled in the sand. Out past the breaker line, a troupe of dolphins gaily leapt through the surf.

After watching the dolphins awhile he got up and walked over the beach. He crossed the boardwalk into town and then made the four or five blocks that separate the ocean from the sound. Everything was quiet. He walked along the Isle of Wight Bay until he came to the inlet, where he stood and watched the vigorous green seawater surge and thrash through great stone seawalls. When he got back to the beach the sun was well over the horizon.

There were a few surfers floating in the offing waiting for something worth the trouble. He went down to the water's edge and started toward the hotel, figuring he would check in with Valerie. But as he walked along the surf-line he noticed, with a small shock, that along the trash-strewn beach stretching ahead of him, gulls and terns indiscriminately pecked at plastic bags, cellophane hot dog wrappers, and styrofoam cups. He knew that if they were to swallow such junk they could be irremediably injured.

He tried to shoo the birds away, but they scattered further up the beach and continued their scavenging. He felt sickened. He began to pick up trash, waving his arms and shushing loudly to scare off the birds. When his hands were full he looked about for a receptacle, but the nearest trash cans were up at the boardwalk—a solid, tedious trek across loose sand. Nonetheless, as he watched a black-backed gull snatch at a waterlogged plastic bag sloshing in the foam, he resolved to clean up the mess there and then. He trudged up to the trash can, deposited his handful of wrappers and cups and then returned to ocean's edge to continue picking up refuse, all the while vainly trying to frighten away the stubborn birds.

He didn't notice the sun moving overhead, or the growing crowds that had begun to cover the beach, until their blankets made it difficult for him to continue his task. He had likewise failed to consider Valerie. She had woken around ten, and after patiently waiting for more than an hour was now making her way down the beach to look for him.

When she sighted him a few blocks up the beach from the hotel, out near the surf, she wasn't sure what to think. He was in the process of lifting the blanket of an apparent stranger to look underneath for garbage. When she approached him he looked at her dazedly, as if he had been on a long journey in the wilderness and hers was the first human face he had seen in months. He grasped a large wad of trash in his left hand. Particles of sand and salt formed a crusty film across his jaw. She followed along as he walked toward a trash receptacle on the boardwalk.

"This stuff can kill these birds!" he said. "I can't believe someone doesn't do something about it."

"They're supposed to clean the beach every night."

"*Supposed* isn't going to help these gulls!"

"It must have been an accidental spill."

He was turning toward the water. She watched him walk away. "Don't you want some breakfast?"

He made a vague gesture and walked on. She stood on the beach and watched. His thoroughness was frightening. He went to each blanket, politely explained the problem, and asked the sunbathers in question if they wouldn't mind if he serviced the area. The sun rose higher, bore relentlessly down on the burning sand. Valerie returned to the room, where she changed into her suit and applied some sunscreen. She breakfasted alone and spent the rest of day on the beach, taking occasional dips and reading her report.

As the dinner hour approached, shadows from buildings along the boardwalk began their slow invasion of the beach; successive groups of bathers retired from the waning light, until Tanaki was able to work unimpededly. He knew that he had been taken for a nut case more than once, but he didn't let that bother him. His species had trashed up the beach, he figured, and if no one else was going to take responsibility for cleaning up the mess, that wouldn't deter him from setting things right. It wasn't until the last oblique rays skimmed the gleaming surf that Valerie persuaded him, not without some difficulty, that he had done everything humanly possible. They loaded the car in an awkward silence. Finally he apologized for not having been much of a companion during the day.

"I hope you don't think I'm losing it," he said.

"No, not *losing* it," she replied.

After a tense silence, she added, "I do appreciate you caring about the birds."

He didn't ask any more questions, and they hardly spoke on the drive back to Cambridge. Tanaki wondered about the events of the day. Clearly something unusual had taken hold of him. He was reminded of his experience at the Baltimore conference when, at the end of his lecture, his mind locked up. He was a little worried about himself, and he wondered what Valerie was thinking. Her face betrayed scant emotion as she listened to the popular love songs that followed one another on the radio, oscillating between hope and despair like some migrating bird whose homing mechanisms had gone pitifully awry. When they pulled up under the big magnolias, she reached over the console and gave him a decidedly perfunctory hug. He said that he would call, pulled his bag from the back, and pushed shut the low and insubstantial sports car's door.

9
Reynolds

REYNOLDS POSSESSED a knowledge of the Bay that Tanaki, in spite of his prodigious scientific investigations, would never share. He was descended from a long line of oyster tongers and crab catchers; his ancestors had lived around the estuary for a score of generations; he had imbibed a sense of the life in its waters with his mother's milk. While Tanaki could minutely describe the endocrinal functions going on inside some mollusk, he turned to Reynolds when he wanted to know the best place to find oyster spat or how to bait a crab pot. In fact, Reynolds' knowledge of the marine resources of the Chesapeake was nothing short of encyclopedic. He was reflexively aware of when certain fish species would be running, and where to locate them.

"They're a tasty fish, them drum, but you have to know how to fix them," he explained one evening as he and Tanaki motored into the station's dock. "They have this tough bone at the back, and you have to pull that bone straight forward. A lot of people say they're too bony—but that's just because they don't know how to debone them properly. The trick is to start it out right. You have to get ahold of that piece near the tail, then it'll lift right out . . ."

As time went by, Tanaki also came to appreciate the older

man's advanced understanding of the human animal. Though Reynolds was a passed master at steering clear of the Center's politics, his habits of observation, long practiced on the water, and the propensity of the Center's staff to confide in him, left him unaware of little that went on at the station. One bright day a frustrated Tanaki approached him on the docks. "He's done it again!"

"No trip down to Tangiers, I suppose."

Tanaki didn't respond as he made a turn on the dock; he looked out on the Bay as if seeking an answer from its silent surging. "Has it always been like this?"

"Oh no," Reynolds said. "Only since Guy came on board—just before you got here. Before that the day-to-day made more sense, at least most of the time. Now every scientist on staff's been fouled up one way or another. And there doesn't seem to be much rhyme or reason to it."

"He claims he's following Coast Guard guidelines," Tanaki said.

Reynolds took a deep breath of Bay air before revealing his skepticism. "That's the *official* explanation. Let me tell you something I've learned over the years. Usually the purpose of the official explanation is to hide the facts, not to let folks know what's going on."

"But why would he want to mess with our research?"

"I don't have a clue," Reynolds said with a sigh as he unwrapped one of the motorboat's lines from a cleat on the dock. "But if you ask me, something's definitely not cool about the whole thing."

Over the course of several trips in and around the Bay the two men developed a simple division of labor. The scientist would succumb to a pitch of investigative intensity, while

REYNOLDS

Reynolds took care of logistical matters and helped Tanaki find what he was looking for. One thing Reynolds never worried about, though, was getting back to the Center. Since that first outing together Reynolds had watched Tanaki carefully, alert to any sign of the notation system he had adduced could be the only means by which the scientist had been able to find his way out of those uncharted marshes. But he had observed nothing but a sort of distracted nonchalance as, on one occasion after another, Tanaki seemed to know each and every turn. By summer, in fact, Tanaki had so impressed Reynolds with his uncanny sense of direction that the native son, laying aside his earlier suspicions, had surrendered to a nearly unquestioning faith in the path-finding abilities of the newcomer . . .

They would often stop for meals or, as the approaching solstice brought a stronger sun, for cold drinks at a dockside market. At every stop Reynolds was hailed by old acquaintances, retired watermen with time to linger and chat with the proprietor or their buddies, waiting to see who or what might happen along.

Mid-morning. Tanaki stands on the shaded porch of Frankie's Bayside Market, waiting for Reynolds, who's gone around back to wash up. Buzz Richardson, a stout man of seventy-odd years with spotty white stubble covering his fleshy face, wisps of fine hair lying across a blotchy scalp, stands beside him. Richardson leans on a cane for support.

"So how is everything?" Buzz asked. He gazed out toward the dock.

"It's going pretty well, I guess," Tanaki said. He popped the tab of his soda and then held it away, waiting for the momentary eruption of foam to subside. "What about you?"

"Oh, fair to middling. And what about Johnny?" He turned

and glanced back toward the market. "How does he seem to be doing these days?"

Tanaki wondered why Richardson, if he was interested in Reynolds' well-being, didn't just ask Reynolds himself. "Seems fine to me," he replied.

"Everything normal, then?" Richardson persisted. "I mean, he's in good health and all?"

Something clicked, and Tanaki suddenly sensed what Buzz must be driving at. "Since you mention it," he said, scuffing his feet on the dock, "something funny did happen a few weeks ago." Tanaki recounted Reynolds' difficulties that first day they had gone out in the marshes together, when Reynolds briefly lost consciousness and collapsed into the bottom of the skiff.

"So it was, sort of like, some kind of spell?"

"Something like that," Tanaki said. "I figured he'd probably just gotten too much sun."

"Sun, naw," Buzz said. "I've worked beside the man in the height of the summer's strength for more hours than I can tell, pulling oysters in. No, I think it's something about that old war injury of his."

"Really?" Tanaki said. "I heard he was in the war—someone back at the Center mentioned it—but they didn't say anything about any injuries."

"Well, he had one, sure enough. And I never saw him falter for many a year. But then, a little before he retired, he started to have these sort of spells. Just every now and then, mind you. Like he wasn't all there, you might say. All I could figure was that it must have been that old war injury coming back on him somehow, just like this stupid leg of mine. I told him he should get it checked out, but he just wouldn't go to a doctor.

I even called over to Shirley, but she couldn't get him to the doc either. I guess the man just don't like doctors."

Reynolds was approaching. "Smells like a thunderstorm," Buzz announced ostentatiously. "Ya'll better be careful out there."

The day was sultry; otherwise there was no sign of the storm Buzz had prophesied in the baby blue sky full of fluffy cumuli. Dragonflies darted through the air and skimmers leapt over the oil-dark surface of a brackish marsh near the mouth of the Wicomico River. Tanaki was sorting through a hunk of vegetation he had just pulled up. He could see Reynolds out the corner of his eye, standing in the aft of the skiff, surveying the marsh with a fathomless expression on his face.

It was oddly difficult for Tanaki to concentrate, for he couldn't get Buzz Richardson's remarks out of his mind. He had grown truly fond of Reynolds, and it dragged on him that the stalwart old salt might be oppressed by some disorder that could be treated if only Reynolds could be convinced to seek medical help. He hated to bring up the fainting spell, concerned that it might embarrass the older man. So after careful deliberation, he decided on an oblique approach.

"I've heard that you were in the war." Tanaki tried to sound as though he were making casual conversation, but his voice set the quiet of the marsh vibrating with a strange, melancholy music.

"*The* war," Reynolds replied, turning his head slightly to acknowledge the remark.

"Do you mind my asking about it?"

Reynolds sighed as he shifted and sank onto the bench that ran across the back of the skiff. It was as if the mere mention of the twentieth century's great and terrible bloodletting had exhausted his forces. "Not really," he said, pulling a handkerchief from his pocket to wipe his brow. "It seems so long ago. Some ways, at least. In other ways, it seems like it all just happened yesterday..."

Tanaki replied with an earnest grunt. He lay the water grasses he had been examining across the skiff's gunwales and stared at Reynolds, who sat carefully mopping his face with the handkerchief. When the older man looked up he seemed uncertain as to whether he wished to say more, but Tanaki's stare, squinty-eyed into the sun, bore into him with an intensity against which he possessed few defenses. Everything seemed to have gone deadly quiet; it was if the very marshes were calling out the story; as if the green and watery earth required some expiatory telling of griefs too long hidden, of murderous enmities which had scarred its plains and forests, cleaved its frothy, fertile seas with bombs and torpedoes.

"If you're really interested," Reynolds finally managed to get out, I suppose I could tell you something about it. Who knows, it might do you some little good to hear it..."

Tanaki nodded solemnly, and Reynolds folded his handkerchief and replaced it in his pocket, took a moment to collect himself.

"It started with this friend of mine," he began after a moment, peering into the bottom of the skiff, his voice level. "His name was Henry, but we always used to call him Boots." Tanaki smiled at the whimsical moniker, which occasioned nothing more than a faint light in Reynolds eyes. "Now, me and Boots," Reynolds continued, "we had quit school about that time, and we were both working at this cannery up in Cambridge. And let me tell you, life was just plain scary back then for us folks who are more gifted, you might say, in the pigmentation department. They were still lynching people out here on the Eastern Shore. Can you imagine?"

Tanaki involuntarily winced at mention of the barbarism that marred too much of his nation's history. But Reynolds took no particular notice and, after glancing athwart at the surrounding marshes, he carried on in his steady way . . .

"We were at the cannery one day, me and Boots," Reynolds went on, "and Boots comes up to me with this Negro newspaper he had picked up in Baltimore. (Boots, you see, he was over across the Bay most Saturday nights, sporting around. That's how he was, Boots. Fun-loving, I guess you'd call it.)" Now Reynolds did smile, if only faintly, an expression that to Tanaki's mind was tinged with an unmistakable sadness. "Anyway," Reynolds continued, reaching again for his handkerchief, "that newspaper's got this big old advertisement, full page, and it says that we black folk ought to enlist in the United States armed forces. And the slogan—you know, they always got to have a slogan—it was *Double* Victory. 'Double Victory, the ad said, 'End Fascism Abroad, and Racism at Home.' 'Well,' I said to Boots, 'that sounds like a lot of victory.' And he looked at me with that gleam he'd get in his eyes, and he just said, 'Let's sign up.'"

"Okay, I'm thinking, I never planned on being a soldier. I was just a farm boy, and a fishing boy, and now I'm working at the local cannery. It wasn't much of a job, but I had my gal—me and Shirley were already steady—and we were planning on getting hitched up. There were plenty of things that weren't cool on the Shore, sure, but I was doing my damnedest to ignore them. You couldn't cross Race Street—funny name, isn't it—without getting jumped by a bunch of thugs, for one thing. And the cannery foreman was always on our backs, just because our ancestors were Africans. So anyway, I say to Boots, 'What, fight a white man's war?' 'Well, what would you rather do,' he shoots back, 'hang around here for the rest of your life, slaving at jobs whites won't do, for half the pay?' 'Listen,' I told him, 'you really think anything's gonna change? I mean, Double Victory, it all sounds good, but . . .' Well," Reynolds continued with a small laugh, "that's when Boots got that look he'd get when a parcel of that crazy Boots wisdom was about to come at you. And he says to me, 'The way I see it, anything's got to be better than yes-sirrin' that nasty cannery foreman day-in, day-out, seven to six, Monday to Saturday.' I got to tell you," Reynolds went on," he almost had me with that one. But there was one little detail I figured maybe Boots hadn't thought too hard about. 'That all sounds fine,' I said, 'but have you thought about the fact that we could get ourselves killed over there?' And what does he say to me, that same wild-wisdom look in his eyes? 'Yeah, he says, 'but having that nice warm rifle in our hands might just make us feel like something better than second-class citizens for a change.'

"I told Boots he was crazy, and we got back to work. But that night I couldn't sleep for thinking about what he had said. And, as I lay there, I had to admit that I was sick of the life I was living. The more I thought about it, in fact, I couldn't see how I was going to spend the rest of my life that same way. I started to think on Shirley. How was I going to look her in the eye every evening, I'm thinking, after I done spent the day kissing some man's behind, just because his skin's a different shade than mine?

"The more I dwelled on it," Reynolds said, "the more troubled I felt. Sleep was out of the question. So I decided to get up and see if there wasn't something on the radio. I went out in the main room and turned it on, real quiet, so as not to wake up the rest of the folks. Put my ear right up to the speaker. And it so happened they were talking about this book Hitler wrote—you know the one, *Mein Kampf*—where he laid out this grand plan to put us blacks—along with everybody else he didn't like—back into slavery. And let me tell you, I can't imagine anything that could have made a bigger impression on me at that moment in my life. It was almost like some higher power was talking to me! I mean, how much of a clue did I need? If I couldn't fight the stupidity on the Eastern Shore, it seemed like, here was my chance to take it on someplace else. So a couple days later, there's Boots and me, Baltimore's Pennsylvania Station, bound for Fort McClellan, Alabama."

Reynolds stood up and poled the skiff away from a hummock it had knocked up against. He spent a moment looking over the marsh before he settled again onto the bench.

"Of course," he picked up again with laughter in his voice, "us being in uniform didn't suddenly change everything. I guess that shouldn't have been any surprise. We were in *colored* units. (Always loved that term. Like white folks don't have any color?) Except, naturally, the officers were all white. If we went off base, even in uniform, we couldn't so much as buy a soda at the local market. That's how ridiculous it was. Us black soldiers were being treated so bad down there, in fact, the army almost had a mutiny on its hands. I wasn't seeing any Double Victory, if you know what I mean. Not even a single victory. It may seem crazy, but I was downright glad when they rushed us out to our staging bases on the West Coast."

The two men sat in silence, the midday southern sun pressing on their faces. They both knew the story had to continue. Finally Tanaki spoke, close to a whisper.

"You were heading into the combat zone?"

Reynolds looked into the bottom of the skiff, ran his hand across his head, seemed almost to twitch once or twice.

"Sure you don't mind talking about it?" Tanaki offered, sensing Reynolds' difficulties.

"No, it's okay." Reynolds raised his face, stared out over the marshes toward the Bay, and began to speak in halting phrases. "My unit was in the Pacific. It was just after Guadalcanal, and we were taking back all those tropical islands, one by one. But those Japanese"—his voice caught slightly at the word, and he glanced oddly at Tanaki—"were dug in like you wouldn't believe. And I've got to tell you, it was a hard-fought thing clearing those goddamn bunkers . . ."

He stopped as though he might end the story there. He even took hold of the pole and made to stand up. But then he settled back into the bench. He dug the pole into the bottom of the marsh and began to push the skiff along with tentative strokes.

"Make a long story short," he said as the skiff began to drift along, "after an unfriendly encounter with a mortar shell, I was evac'd to Hawaii. I sat out the rest of the war in a military hospital, getting my insides put back together again." Now Reynolds got up for real and began to push more determinedly. He peered straight ahead, his face expressionless. "What say we get some lunch?"

Tanaki assented, took up a paddle and joined Reynolds in moving the skiff along. After a moment, he broke their silence. "Whatever happened to that double victory they talked about in the newspaper advertisement?" he asked. He turned around to face Reynolds, squinted into the sun.

"Well," Reynolds said, "we certainly beat the pants off

them fascists. But I guess you know that."

"Yeah, I do. But what about that other part of the slogan, the part about ending racism?"

Reynolds slackened his poling. He grew thoughtful and let the skiff coast for a moment, and then he laughed a little. "Thing's didn't change overnight, that's for sure. You might say that the Eastern Shore was still the Eastern Shore. For that matter, America was still America. Maybe the change was more in me than in the folks around me. You see, when I came back after four months in that hospital, I was a different man. Grown up in a whole new way. I figured Boots and me put ourselves on the line for the Double Victory. I wasn't about to let some ignorant racist mess it up for us. Me and Shirley had got ourselves hitched by then, and little Louis was on the way. And man, when I thought about my boy growing up in the same messed up world I did, well, I just couldn't figure it."

"I don't suppose you went back to work at the cannery."

"Noooo." There was palpable satisfaction in Reynolds' voice. "After all those months in that hospital bed I didn't want to be cooped up anymore. And I wasn't too crazy about seeing old Mr. Foreman again, you want to know the truth. No, that's when I started to work on the water. And you know what? People seemed to get on easier with each other out here. Seems like there was more respect. Maybe being on the Bay made everybody a little more human, I don't know. All us watermen were struggling to make a living, black or white. Dealing with the same struggles, day by day. And out on that water"—here Reynolds gestured toward the wide waters of the Bay—"you never know when you're gonna need somebody's help. When that day comes, let me tell you, you're not gonna be looking at what color that rescue boat is. When you think about it, I guess you could say we were all in the same boat; well, maybe different boats, but we'd be out there working the same oyster bed, side by side."

Reynolds interrupted his story to disentangle his pole from some stubborn bottom grasses.

"Sure," he said after he had gotten the skiff going again, "there was still plenty of that old racism on the Shore. I had to deal with it all the time. Still have to, on occasion. But you see, I had that new attitude. Maybe Boots was right about having that gun in my hands. I just quit accepting it. I got into a brawl or two, that's for sure. But it was worth it. And you know what, eventually, little by little, things began to change. Other blacks were just as sick of the old routine as I was. Plenty of whites, too. We had a real time of it back in the sixties. I remember when H. Rap came out to Cambridge. I was in a few of those struggles myself. Yeah, I've definitely inhaled my share of tear gas . . ."

Reynolds poled steadily now. A contented smile formed on his lips, and he drew in the thick air of the marsh in deep, easy breaths.

"Whatever became of Boots?" Tanaki asked suddenly. "Is he still around?"

"Boots?" Reynolds started, his body stiffened, and the skiff glided aimlessly as he let the pole go slack. He gazed into the turgid marsh water long enough to say, "Same mortar round," and then, "only he didn't make it." He lifted his head and resumed directing the little craft. Tanaki didn't turn around, but still he registered Reynolds' momentary distance, felt the skiff drifting; in some way he even sensed the single tear that now rolled down Reynolds' cheek. Then, as Reynolds regained his form, working his strong arms into the pole, Tanaki worked his paddle and he soon felt the skiff skimming along again at a good pace.

As they boarded the motorboat for lunch, Reynolds put an arm around Tanaki's shoulders. "I got to tell you," he said, "this war business ain't no picnic. But I'd still say that there are a *few* things worth fighting for. Just make sure you choose your battles carefully. All right?"

Tanaki couldn't imagine why he might need such advice, but Reynolds' embrace felt so fatherly he couldn't argue. "Sure," he said. "I'll do that."

10
The Eel

NO ONE COULD SAY precisely when Tanaki's fascination with the eel began; though it must have been sometime after the ospreys nested, for he had been much too busy with the flashing raptors to think about anything else; but not much later than the epic bluefish runs, for he would soon be caught up with a brilliant horde of Monarch butterflies.

The American eel—*anguilla rostrata*—is the only truly *catadromous* fish in the estuary, spending its adult life in the Bay and its tributaries, returning to open ocean only to spawn (the exact opposite approach, this, to that taken by the Bay's other resident fish species, which use the sheltering estuary to spawn and grow to maturity before venturing into the bounteous deeps of open ocean to pursue their adult dreams.) Though the most numerous species in the watershed, present in every river and stream, *anguilla* is virtually unknown to most human denizens of the Bay region. With its murky-yellow to mud-brown skin, and its propensity to burrow into bottom muck during the day—emerging to feed only under the cover of darkness—it happily remains a non-entity to millions of suburbanites who occupy the Bay's watershed in bedroom communities surrounding Washington and Baltimore.

Its breeding rites, which Tanaki thought heroic, might be

considered ghoulish by those with less appreciation for nature's mysteries. An a*nguilla* spawns only once in a lifetime, its dramatic ritual of regeneration marking the end of its existence. Biologists still don't know how an eel decides when its hour has come, and the age of spawning seems to vary wildly: on this score, as on others, the eel has kept its reasons to itself. But each year on a dark November night, the moon in first quarter, countless *anguilla* move stealthily downstream, riding the wake of an autumn storm, aided by the prevailing currents in an inexorable procession toward the trackless sea.

Biologists for many years were at a loss to describe the trajectory of the spawning *anguilla* once they reach the Atlantic. It was clear that they mate somewhere in the great deep, as the larval phase of the creature—which look like small, glassy willow leaves—had been identified as early as the nineteenth century floating in the Mediterranean's Strait of Messina. But the location of the spawning rites remained as much an enigma to early twentieth-century biologists as it had to the ancients: who subscribed to the theory, for want of a better idea, that the eels spontaneously generated from river slime.

In 1920 the Dutch government commissioned the otherwise obscure biologist Johannes Schmidt to explore the matter. For years Schmidt's trawlers scoured the Atlantic, from Newfoundland to the Orkneys, from the Straits of Gibraltar to the Antilles, dragging nets of a mesh fine enough to entrap the diminutive larvae. The searching vessels finally converged on the seaweed-mantled Sargasso Sea, where growing numbers of ever-smaller larvae in their nets made it clear that the provenance of the elusive animal had finally been discovered. Further investigation determined that after reaching the surface from deep spawning grounds, the larvae float effortlessly, unhurriedly, on the clockwise currents that wash both shores of the Atlantic, until arriving at the mouth of a suitable estuary. Having by now matured into small eels known as elvers, they swim up-current to the stream or tributary where they will nourish themselves and grow, living unobtrusively until they feel an inescapable urge to again return to the sea.

In spite of the progress that had been made, by the time Tanaki began his career, in clarifying *anguilla rostrata's* life history, there remained one great mystery concerning the animal. Though it was clear that all Atlantic eels travel to the Sargasso Sea to spawn, researchers remained frustrated in their attempts to locate an adult *anguilla* in open ocean. This left a gaping lacuna in our understanding of the animal's epic migrations. One thing was certain, however: the eels swim to their spawning grounds at very great depths. This was the only way to explain their having avoided turning up in fishermen's nets over so many centuries.

It was equally clear that spawning eels never return to their home streams, but leave their lifeless carcasses under the Sargasso Sea. This was evidenced by the physiological changes undergone prior to migration—a process by which, for all practical purposes, a freshwater fish becomes a deep-sea breeding machine. The eel's eyes bulge to twice their normal size, enabling it to see through the murky waters of the great depths through which it must travel; the air bladder toughens; even the shape of the skull alters to withstand the tremendous pressures experienced in the abyss. Muddy brown skin metamorphoses into shifting bronzed planes of pinks, greens, and purples (perhaps so that the animals, Tanaki liked to muse, can be encouraged in their awesome journey by the iridescent glintings of their fellow spawners all around). The eel's normal coating of slime thickens as a prophylactic against the salty waters it will traverse, and the animal eats enormously, laying on great deposits of stored fat.

As the hour of departure nears the eel's digestive tract begins to atrophy, for once the spawning migration is underway, the animal will not eat again. From this moment forward, all of its biological processes are geared to one thing and one thing alone—so imperative is the eel's procreative urge, kept in abeyance for a lifetime, that the animal will now sacrifice everything to its eventual fulfillment. Tanaki personally verified the metabolic equations, satisfying himself that by the time the spawning eel reaches the Sargasso Sea, it will be utterly emaciated, bones and tissues disintegrating, with no remaining energy reserves. Once there, in a final spasm of excitement, surrounded by an international convocation of millions of its own kind both male and female, it will release its precious cargo of milt or spawn, adding to the misty stew from which the next generation of *anguilla* will arise. Its destiny achieved, it will sink quietly to the bottom and die.

Needless to say, a biologist who could locate an adult eel in open ocean would register a coup that, if not equaling Perdecci's, would surely be considered in the same class. Of course Tanaki had his own reasons—beyond professional glory, that is—for his fascination with the eel. Its unobtrusive behavior through the years of its freshwater existence, thriving under our noses with hardly a soul aware of its existence; its spot-on intuition in sensing its hour of departure; its tremendous bravery, setting out on its final mission through *mare incognita*; and its last burst of ecstasy under a vegetation-shrouded sea: these all appealed greatly to our hero. Yet it must be conceded that, as Tanaki's thoughts became increasingly fixed on the object of following a migrating spawner beyond the continental shelf, he couldn't help but entertain the odd fantasy about the astonished acclaim which would accrue to his credit should he pull it off.

The morning the telemetry system arrived, Tanaki rushed to the Center's shipping room to find Reynolds standing over an open cardboard box. The older man was staring with admiration at some shiny-new devices he had just liberated from their plastic wrappings.

"This is some beautiful gear you got here," Reynolds said.

"Ever seen anything like it?" Tanaki lifted a receiver out of the box.

"You kidding?" Reynolds stiffened into military attention and raised his billed hand in a mock salute. "You're looking at Radio-Specialist-First-Class-John-D-Reynolds-United-States-Ar—mee-Sir!"

Tanaki handed Reynolds the receiver. "I didn't know you'd worked with radios."

"You never asked." Reynolds ran his fingers along the receiver's smooth steel casement. "Granted, the devices we had in WWII were dinosaurs compared to these babies. Yeah, look at this stuff. It's gorgeous!"

"I just hope it's gorgeous enough to do the job."

Reynolds turned to Tanaki. "And what would that be?"

"Tracking an *anguilla rostrata* in open ocean."

"Hmm." Reynolds stepped back from the equipment and thoughtfully scratched his jawline. "That could be a problem."

"Really? Why is that?"

"The first difficulty is going to be losing your signal. From what I've heard, them eels swim mighty deep once they clear the continental shelf. A radio signal will attenuate pretty bad in salt water."

"Sure, but we'll be using *acoustic* telemetry. It uses sound waves, not radio waves. I've been in touch with some old colleagues of mine, and they've been having pretty good luck with it."

"At these kinds of depths?" Reynolds raised an eyebrow.

"Okay," Tanaki conceded, "I know I may be pushing the envelope, but I think there's at least an even chance that it will get the job done." He almost added "Faint hearts never won fair maidens," but remembering Folker's schmarmy use of the phrase at their first meeting, thought the better of it.

"I guess it's worth a try," Reynolds said. "But there's another thing to consider. Do you really think some skinny ol' eel can carry all this weight?" He lifted the receiver on the palm of his hand, balanced it there, let it fall of its own mass and then lifted it again.

"I don't know," Tanaki said. "My research tells me it will take a lot to stop one of these guys once it decides to embark on its spawning migration."

Reynolds gently nudged Tanaki with his elbow. "Sounds a lot like us humans, doesn't it?"

"Maybe even worse," Tanaki said with a laugh. "They're incredibly tenacious. I recently came across an article about this New York plumber. It seems the guy got a call for a clogged drain in some thirteenth-floor Manhattan apartment . . ."

"I see where this is heading. . ."

"Exactly. When he comes out to the place, and takes the pipes apart, what does he find? Yep, an *anguilla rostrata*, lodged in the drainpipe. Thirteen stories up!"

"Amazing," Reynolds purred. He turned the receiver this

way and that, examining it from every angle.

"The engineering folks have come a long way with this gear in the last few years," Tanaki said. "The transmitters I worked with over in Europe—only a few years back—they didn't have anywhere near this kind of range. I remember following a herd of swans all over the French countryside one summer afternoon. Damn, what a riot!" Tanaki's face lit up, and a smile formed involuntarily on his lips. "This friend was with me, and she was sighting the swans with a pair of binoculars, while I drove. We were on these winding country roads. Of course the birds didn't have to follow the damned roads! If you let them get too far ahead, they were gone for good."

"That's the way it goes sometimes . . ." Reynolds spoke absently, still absorbed in his examination of the electronics.

"With some of the satellites that are starting to come on board," Tanaki said, "we'll soon be able to follow the animals anywhere. Right from the comfort of our own labs!"

"You don't say," Reynolds said, finally turning his attention from the receiver to Tanaki.

"It will definitely be more efficient," Tanaki said. Then he added wistfully, "probably take some of the fun out of it, though."

Reynolds carefully laid the receiver back in its box. "I guess you had a right bit of fun with that *friend* of yours over there."

"I suppose we did." Tanaki looked flustered. He removed his glasses, pulled out his shirt tail, and began to wipe the lenses.

Reynolds placed a hand on his shoulder. "Listen, Dave," he said bravely, "don't you worry about all this. I'm going to take a good look at this gear and test it out thoroughly. Really run it through its paces."

THE EEL

Tanaki stiffened involuntarily. "Are you sure you know what you're doing?"

Reynolds pulled back in mock amazement. "Know what I'm doing? Know what I'm doing! Davy, just leave this to me. We'll get that eel, you can bet on it."

And Reynolds set out at once to make good on his assertion. He spent every minute for the next two weeks, when he wasn't out on the water, going over the technical manuals that had come with the gear. He showed up one morning with some tattered books, bound in army green, that he had used in the service. He was determined not merely to master the devices, but to improve them.

"Dave," he said one morning, "I'm gonna have to rebuild these hydrophones."

Not wanting to hurt his friend's feelings, Tanaki masked his apprehension. But when he found him in the shop that evening, standing over the costly devices with a soldering iron, his widened eyes betrayed his fears.

"Quit your worrying, Dave," Reynolds said, "when I'm finished with these units, that eel can swim to Timbuktu and we'll find it."

And so a strange troika came into being: Tanaki, whose Japanese ancestors once crossed the Pacific in search of prosperity undreamed of by their cautious village neighbors; Reynolds, whose more remote predecessors migrated involuntarily across the Atlantic in the cramped and stinking hold of a slaver; and *anguilla rostrata*, oblivious to the commotion its ancient and inevitable migratory cycle had stirred up in a couple of human minds. Reynolds would have until autumn to work his electronic wizardry, when he and Tanaki would attempt to capture one of the spawners prior to its journey toward open ocean. They would affix the transmitter and then follow in the Center's ocean-going cruiser, hoping finally to retrieve the defunct specimen over the Sargasso Sea, conveniently delivered to the surface by a pressure-sensitive flotation device.

11
Obon

TANAKI'S ACQUAINTANCE with the Yamaguchis had advanced considerably by the time the tidewater summer inflicted its oppressive sultriness upon Cambridge. On the sporadic occasions when he left the Center at a reasonable hour, they would have him to dinner. Afterwards the three would take advantage of the cooler air of evening to walk through the elm-lined streets of their neighborhood, or sit on the porch talking until all hours of the night. From the porch there was a clear view to the river, and when there was a moon, they quietly marveled at its silvered gleamings.

The sisters virtually adopted him. They spoiled him unabashedly, explaining that in him they had found the brother they had always wanted. And Tanaki sensed at times, if it wasn't his vanity running away with him, another element: a competition for his attentions that wasn't strictly sororal. Though worlds apart in character and personality, the Yamaguchi sisters seemed to belong inextricably together, like different facets of the same gemstone. Tanaki often wondered if it would be possible for a man to fall in love with only one of them. One day, he figured, they might have to resort to polygamy.

One thing that intrigued, perplexed, and even exasperated him, was a sense of unshakable calm about the sisters, an inner satisfaction of sorts. He wasn't sure to what to attribute it: their being women, their close sibling relationship, or something in their family upbringing or culture. Maybe it involved their being heirs to a substantial fortune, a luxury that Tanaki was sure he would never have to contend with.

Perhaps, he sometimes mused, it had to do with their peculiar religion, as this seemed to permeate their lives in a subtle, yet unmistakable, fashion. Gleaning information from late night conversations, Tanaki discovered that there was a good deal more to the so-called "shrimp religion" than Setsuko's first skeletal description had indicated. Its founder Ato-san was, by any measure, an exceptional character. After the death of his father in the Second World War, he had not only prayed to the *kami* but, loin-cloth clad, fasted for weeks on a windy headland in the dead of winter, citing the need for what he called a "sincere act of rectification," both for himself and for his violence-intoxicated nation. He became punctilious in the observance of the traditional rites, never failing to honor the *kami* at the appointed times. He applied himself to his work in the fishing fleet with an uncanny vigor, giving everything he had for no reason other than a desire to serve others. And when his own business prospered, he lived frugally, donating the concern's profits to the rebuilding of temples. As his religious movement gathered strength in the fifties, he earned notoriety by campaigning for a national day of atonement for the savagery perpetrated under the country's militarist leaders before and during the recent war.

Ato's doctrine was normally translated by the Yamaguchis as "pure action." He preached that the chief impediment to living well consisted of fear of the future. Ato typically referred to this sad syndrome as *what-might-happen* thinking, such as working to achieve economic security, for fear of *what-might-happen* if one were to follow one's inner springs of passion; or, on the national level, adopting a bellicose stance in foreign affairs for fear of *what-might-happen* if a conciliatory policy were to be pursued. For Ato, the only activity worthy of one's energies was that which was purely spontaneous, growing out of one's inmost nature; albeit, inspired through regular communion with the *kami* and a sure knowledge of one's connection to all beings. As to work, he maintained that it should be undertaken not out of fear of penury, but as a joyous sharing of one's best gifts, just as nature, buddhas, and the ancestors bestow their priceless boons without expecting recompense. *What-might-happen* thinking, Ato counseled, can only lead to emotional and spiritual *blockage*. If not checked in time, he warned, personal and collective disaster will inevitably follow in its train.

One evening, while the three friends sat on the front porch gazing toward the Choptank, the sisters recounted to Tanaki how, in the sixties, Ato had again plunged into the political arena. This time he spearheaded a prolonged fight to protect the natural environment—imbued as it was, for him and his followers, with the spirit of *kami*.

"It really threw old papa-san for a loop, let me tell you," Setsuko remarked. "Whaling was a major profit center for the firm back then, and it wasn't easy for the old man to divest himself of that lucrative line of business."

"But surely the right thing to do," Tanaki said soberly.

"What choice did Chichi have," Setsuko replied, "with his revered Ato-san conducting hunger strikes left and right, wasting away to nothing? I mean, I could see Ato's point, but one can carry a *sincere act of rectification* too far, if you want my opinion. And all of Ato-san's efforts, dramatic as they were, still failed to put an end to whaling, though they did contribute to his premature death."

"Don't forget the . . . dolphins," Nariko put in.

"Oh yeah," Setsuko rejoined, "that cost dear old dad a few more millions, retooling our fleets to keep dolphins out of the nets. But like you say, David-san, it was the right thing to do. Even if it put us at a competitive disadvantage against outfits that didn't give a flying fish for biodiversity . . ."

The three sat in silence for a moment, listening to the crickets in the lawns and the spring peepers in the nearby marshes. Then Nariko, waving a hand softly across the nightscape, taking in the lawns and trees but also the shining river, spoke again.

"It's all *kami*," she said. "All of it."

It was a warm Saturday night. Tanaki had spent most of the day at the refuge, but he had made a point of getting back before dark. Setsuko had said that she and Nariko had some special plans for him that evening. The idea of polygamy didn't cross his mind.

Not much, anyway.

He had no sooner stepped into his apartment than there was a knock at the door. It was Nariko. "Sorry to bother you . . . too soon," she began. "It's almost time . . . to start."

"No problem, Nari," Tanaki said. "By the way, it's *so* soon, not *too* soon. And what is it we're going to start, anyway?"

"I can't . . . explain now. Setsuko said don't waste . . . time. You know . . . my sister. She gets a little . . . anal. Is that the right word?"

Tanaki chuckled at Nariko's growing familiarity with the subtleties of character description in English. He went to the bathroom and splashed cold water on his face. After brushing his teeth and changing into fresh clothes he headed downstairs.

When he stepped onto the porch he was greeted by a vision of the Yamaguchi sisters in traditional Japanese kimonos. Setsuko had been more painstaking in her approach, right down to the traditional makeup, whereas Nariko's costume left the impression of, not a studied *deshabille*, but a hurried effort at meeting the requirements of the occasion. At first the delicate refinement of the shimmering silk garments seemed glaringly out of place on Talbot Street. But as the three friends stepped off the porch and walked toward the river, the sisters radiated a transcendent beauty that suffused their surroundings, and found an echo in every feature of the townscape.

The sisters led Tanaki toward the small harbor where Church Creek debouches into the Choptank River, a minor embayment that was the locus of the Cambridge community in colonial times. Their destination was the Chesapeake headquarters of Yamaguchi Enterprises, a large, hangar-like structure of corrugated metal extending over the harbor. After walking alongside the building on a boardwalk, they entered the small front office. Tanaki's first impression was of a powerful odor of fish. He followed the sisters through the office and through a door on its back wall. This brought them into a cavernous space that was half-terrestrial, half-marine. The floor, composed of the same planking used on the outdoor piers and walkways, did not extend over the entire area of the enclosure but terminated at steel railings, where the waters of the harbor were exposed. Here, Yamaguchi ships could enter and unload their catch.

Nariko, with apparent pride, pointed out a placard hanging over the office door. It bore the company credo which, she informed Tanaki, was chanted *en masse* by Yamaguchi employees before beginning each day's work. Without ceremony, she straightened her shoulders and began to recite the credo out loud. Tanaki joined in with playful solemnity:

> *We are grateful to the people of the world.*
> *We will not forget that our fleet exists for the sake of*
>   *our customers.*
> *Sharing good times and bad, we will cooperate,*
> *And not forget to encourage one another.*
> *Setting aside the past, and worries for tomorrow,*
> *We will find our joy in the task set before us today.*
> *Remembering that all beings are precious,*
> *We resolve to be good stewards of the earth.*
> *We will not fail to show our gratitude,*
> *To the ancestors and the kami,*
> *For all we have and will receive.*

Nariko squeezed Tanaki's arm in delighted recognition of their moment of camaraderie. Then she drew his attention, down one of the building's long walls, to a shrine of rich, dark wood. It housed a larger-than-life image that Tanaki easily recognized from the print in the Yamaguchi's living room as the god, and patron saint of fishing folk, Ebisu.

He followed Nariko and Setsuko to a corner where a large number of paper lanterns had been stockpiled. There he watched them place them in shallow baskets of fine workmanship. It was only after he helped carry the lanterns onto the landing, and the three friends sat relaxing on the thick planking, that Setsuko offered an explanation of what was going on.

"You don't know about *O-bon*?" she asked incredulously.

"I think my mother told me something about it once."

"Once! Is that all?" Setsuko asked.

Tanaki turned up his palms and looked at her blankly. She exchanged a pitying glance with Nariko.

"It looks like some kind of party," Tanaki finally offered.

"Not exactly," Setsuko said, "but you're not entirely wrong. Are you sure you've never honored your ancestors? Ever?"

"I can certainly say that I respect them. I don't know much about them, actually."

"These lanterns are called *toro*." Setsuko picked up one of the delicate boxes. "See the candle inside." Tanaki glanced briefly toward the apparatus. Setsuko thrust the lantern into his face. "Now little brother, pay attention!"

Tanaki exaggeratedly scratched his head in jest and Nariko softly giggled. Setsuko set the *toro* on the landing and addressed Tanaki more earnestly. "A few days ago Nariko and I placed some special offerings on our household shrine. Flowers, sake, rice dumplings. Nari, am I forgetting anything?"

Nariko shook her head.

"Those offerings were a way of showing our respect, and our appreciation, to our ancestors. All those people, even those lost in the mists of history who, through their tireless struggles against hardships beyond anything we puny modern people can conceive of, made our comfy little lives of today possible."

A shrill chorus of frogs and insects swelled beyond the harbor.

"Then, night before last," she went on, "we lit a *makaebi*

fire. The light of the fire helped the old ones—at least that's the idea—to find their way back across the great divide. Those flames, and the offerings at the shrine, were our way of welcoming them back. For a little visit, you might say. You know, to hang out for a couple of days."

"What are we doing now?" Tanaki peered into the gathering dusk and wondered in spite of himself if they—the ancestors—were out there somewhere, watching, listening.

"Tonight," Setsuko said, "we're sending them home, back to the other side." Her kimono rustled as she began to stir. "The purpose of these lanterns is to light their paths, help them find their way back through the void."

The three friends crouched on the landing. A humid breeze washed over them. It softly ruffled the paper of the *toro* as the sisters arranged them in neat rows. After they were in order, Nariko knelt at the edge of the pier and Setsuko grasped one of the lanterns. She removed a box of wooden matches from the folds of her kimono, lit the small candle inside, and handed it to her sister. Bending toward the water, Nariko floated the glowing box on the surface and gave it a gentle push away from the landing. The *toro* floated towards the river's channel, echoed by fireflies that hovered in the air. Setsuko lit another and passed it to Nariko, who sent it on its way after the first, and so on, until an ethereal parade of luminous points extended far into the Choptank.

Darkness had fallen.

"You know," Setsuko said as the last of the lanterns made its way into the river, "it's interesting. Since *O-bon* welcomes ancestors back to their home towns, I'm really not sure I can say whose ancestors we've been venerating."

"You mean . . ." Nariko began.

"I mean that it's just possible we've been entertaining the ancestors of Cambridge for the past two days, and not our own."

Nariko was thoughtful for a moment before responding, almost to herself, "Does it really matter?"

12
Ancestors

THOUGHTS OF THE O-BON ceremony lingered in Tanaki's mind for days. The three friends had danced at a local nightspot afterwards, the closest feasible substitute for the jubilant street parties that mark the close of the ceremony in Japan. But it was the quiet moments watching the *toro* drift into the river that penetrated Tanaki with an odd longing, a longing he identified with a desire, now intensified in remembrance, to dive in and follow the lanterns on toward the Bay. He had never thought much about ancestors before, his or anyone else's. "How ironic," Setsuko had said, forcing her voice over the loud music at the Happy Clam Bar and Grill. "You, a migration specialist, never studied the migrations of your very own ancestors. I'll bet your grandparents caused quite a stir when they left their little village for America." Tanaki countered that his parents had made no attempt to pass on what they knew of their antecedents. "My folks didn't even like discussing their own experiences in life, much less those of their ancestors," Tanaki explained. "I guess I've always thought that that was normal."

But can a human being really live without a past beyond his own personal history? And if so, how? Tanaki had never pondered the question, absorbed, as he had been throughout his life, in his investigations of nature. But his simple participation in the *O-bon* ceremony awakened a dormant region of his being. He became preoccupied with the idea of the past. And he no longer found it possible, as he walked through the streets of his river-washed town, to think only of an assortment of services that answered to the practical needs of David Tanaki: the dry cleaners, the diner, the bank, the post office, the drug store. Now every street, every old house, every quiet yard was haunted by the spirits of those who had walked those streets, inhabited the houses, and sat quietly of a summer evening in yards full of birdsong and the scents of flowers. He pondered over Setsuko's last remarks on the landing of Yamaguchi Enterprises—about honoring the ancestors of Cambridge—and on a quiet Saturday morning walked to the town's library, a squat brick building near the courthouse. He addressed himself to the precise, matronly ladies who ran the place, and one of them directed him to a quirky assemblage of colonial history with a title that appealed to the biologist in him: *Albion's Spawn in the Great Shellfish Bay*.

His interest in any but the broadest strokes of history had been so perfunctory, a couple of required undergraduate courses he looked upon as rude interruptions of his migration studies, that his encounter with Professor Huntley's tome had an effect upon his imagination similar to that which might have attended a voyage to some distant planet. There were the first European explorations, so poorly documented that it's uncertain whether the Italian explorer Giovanni da Verrazanno actually spotted the Virginia capes in 1524. The brief, fruitless attempt by Spanish Jesuits to settle the banks of the James River prior to the arrival of the English in 1607. There was the "starving time" at Jamestown, when the living dug up graves to devour the dead; when John Radcliffe, sent to the much-abused Indians for food, instead had the flesh scraped from his bones with seashells; when a crazed colonist ran through the marketplace crying that there was no God, only to fall victim to the indigenous inhabitants while hunting in the forest that day. There was the amazing Opechancanough (rumored to have been the young brave educated by remnants of the failed Jesuit mission) who, after years of cagey sparring with the better-armed colonists, master-minded the bloody but futile massacre of 1622. There was even a pitched naval battle involving all of three sailing vessels on the waters of the Bay, a battle which settled once and for all Lord Calvert's claim to jurisdiction over Kent Island.

Tanaki was entranced by all of the improbable characters who made up the Chesapeake's early history. But nothing intrigued him more than the story of Margaret and Mary Brent, daughters of a fishing captain, who migrated to the estuary in the early years of the Maryland colony. Reading about how they established their own household, eschewing the protection of their brother Giles, Tanaki couldn't escape an odd feeling that he knew them. He inwardly cheered when Margaret Brent displayed a genius for legal matters, representing herself in the myriad land disputes inevitable in an era of poorly defined property rights. He even experienced a prideful satisfaction when she began to represent her neighbors as well, profiting so much from the parcels they gave her in payment that she became one of the colony's largest landholders. When she came to the attention of the Maryland governor, however, Tanaki felt an odd unease—a premonition of trouble. Still she became one of Leonard Calvert's closest advisors and the executor of his will.

ANCESTORS

It seemed to Tanaki that Margaret Brent's hardiness of character was never displayed more clearly than on the occasion of Ingels' rebellion, a short-lived spin-off of the English Revolution. He paused carefully over Huntley's words:

After the governor's supporters managed to drive Ingels and his Roundheads from St. Mary's City, a new crisis arose when the governor found himself unable to pay the soldiers. When these mutinied, threatening to take the city on their own account, Margaret Brent stepped into the breach. After chastising the mutineers for their greed and disloyalty, she promised to use her influence to see that they be paid—but then threatened to take her cane to anyone still lingering on the parade grounds after five minutes!

Tanaki would have preferred that the story end there, at the zenith of Margaret Brent's star. He would liked to have seen her retire happily on her estates, enjoying the prestige that was clearly her due, having rendered such services both to her neighbors and to the colony. But when the governor—and her protector—died, she ran into trouble. It was correct in both law and conscience to liquidate the governor's properties to pay off his debts. But the governor's brother (and the colony's Lord Proprietor, comfortably ensconced in England) didn't take the loss to the Calvert family estates gently. In a letter by the first ship bound for North America, he relieved Margaret Brent of her official duties and, in the bargain, he impugned her probity.

For some reason, Tanaki felt personally stung by this long-past injustice. He stood up from where he sat at the library and made a couple of turns around the table. He didn't really want to know more, but the chapter was near its end. He sat down and picked up his reading where he had left off:

TANAKI ON THE SHORE

The Lord Proprietor closed his letter with a slighting reference to Margaret Brent's parentage. "This mortification," Calvert inveighed, "might well be brought upon us by the spawn of a fishmonger."

"Fishmonger!" Tanaki blurted and broke into laughter, a laughter stifled by an ominous glance from the reference librarian. "Of course, Setsuko and Nariko!" he thought to himself. "I knew those Brent sisters reminded me of someone." Finishing the chapter in Huntley's book, his feelings were somewhat assuaged by the episode's conclusion, which described how Margaret and Mary sold off their Maryland properties and moved to Pennsylvania, where they enjoyed a bountiful retirement. While walking home, burdened with tomes on everything from the Underground Railroad to the development of Maryland's colonial tobacco trade, Tanaki again thought of the Yamaguchis. "I wonder if they could ever run into problems with the authorities?" he asked himself. But, as the crowns of Mrs. Stafford's magnolias came into view, hastening his pace, he just as quickly dismissed the thought.

13
Haskel

BY MID-SUMMER a new pattern had developed in Folker's incessant meddling. He increasingly cloistered himself in his office, refusing calls or visitors. All interaction with staff was funneled through Cynthia, who made the rounds distributing memos and communiqués.

Sitting in his cubicle one afternoon with a freshly denied boat request in hand, Tanaki knew he needed a change of scene. He thought of Bob Haskel, a biologist he met at a professional meeting he had recently attended at Folker's behest. Haskel had invited him to visit the Muddy Creek Wildlife Management Area to look into some intriguing research he was conducting with a network of committed scientists.

Haskel and his colleagues were working to address the displacement of waterfowl from their wetland habitats. Whether in the Central Valley of California, across the pothole country of the Northern Plains, or around the Chesapeake itself, everything from filling for agriculture and development to fouling by pollutants had instigated profound disturbances in the life-cycles of creatures Tanaki considered among the most noble on earth.

He arrived at Muddy Creek in little over an hour. To the sound of gravel crunching under his tires he pulled off the paved road onto a dirt drive that wound through the ubiquitous loblolly pines, rolling up the windows to close out a cloud of dust that rose from the wheels. At the end of the drive he entered a clearing. A redwood-clad house sat in the middle of a broad lawn. A considerable number of snow geese—upwards of two hundred, Tanaki figured—milled around in groups of ten or twenty.

He was parking the car to one side when Bob Haskel emerged from the house and strode energetically across the front porch and onto the lawn. As he crossed the yard, excited geese surrounded him in a tight peloton, shadowing his every step. Soon the entire gaggle, Haskel included, were at the car. Tanaki couldn't help laughing as Haskel reached over his honking charges to shake his hand.

"We'd better go inside," Haskel said, "or we'll have no peace."

As they headed for the porch, sidestepping blotches of geese guano that nearly covered the lawn, Haskel told Tanaki to go in through the front door and wait for him in the kitchen. "I'll meet you inside," he clipped in rapid staccato before bolting around the side of the house, the geese setting off after him. Tanaki walked down a hallway to the rear of the house and entered the kitchen just in time to see Haskel squeeze through the back door, a flurry of white forms fluttering and flapping behind him. Haskel briskly snapped the door shut and then calmly walked across the rough tile floor toward Tanaki. Winded, he invited Tanaki to sit at the kitchen table, a pine plank affair on delicate iron legs.

"Okay," he said once they were seated. He was still catching his breath, but his face bore a welcoming smile. "Where were we?"

HASKEL

Tanaki stared at him for a long moment, unable to dislodge the image of him edging through the door surrounded by an hysterical mob of crazed waterfowl. He was a man of fifty-some years, with short-cropped, reddish hair and a build that, while slight, was admirably taut. His gold-rimmed glasses had slid down his nose.

The geese hopped about wildly outside the kitchen, fluttering to the windows and flapping their wings outrageously, trying to get Haskel's attention. Beyond them Tanaki made out a small aircraft parked in an long open space behind the house.

"This must get distracting," he remarked.

"Just an over-heated mimetic instinct," Haskel said. He looked toward the windows along the kitchen's back wall. "It's funny," he continued, "I feel like they know I'm their last, best chance." He silently watched the geese for a moment, with evident tenderness, before turning back to Tanaki. "I can't complain. It's really just a testament to how effective my research procedures have turned out to be."

"That may be," Tanaki said. "And maybe I shouldn't say this. I mean, I don't know you very well. But it appears that these geese have made you a prisoner in your own house. I don't suspect that was envisioned in your research procedures."

"No, it wasn't," Haskel said. "But you can't blame the geese. After all, they probably think I'm their mother. And truth be told, I've got a soft spot right here for those silly birds."

Haskel patted his chest.

"I'm surprised to see them here this time of year," Tanaki remarked after a moment. "Shouldn't they be up north, at their breeding areas?"

"That's true. They should be. But, obviously, they aren't. You see, this was one of the first groups I trained to follow my plane."

Tanaki leaned forward, straining to hear over all the honking and flapping going on outside. Haskel raised his voice.

"They were HATCHED up in CANADA," Haskel yelled. "But when the CANADIAN GOVERNMENT got wind that they were being used for experiments in the STATES, a big bureaucratic FUSS ensued and they REFUSED to let me bring them back into the COUNTRY. So they're REFUGEES, at least for the time being. The fact is, I'm all they've GOT until we can sort this mess OUT."

"Good God," Tanaki said, "what do they expect, passports?"

Haskel gestured that he couldn't hear him. "We'd better relocate," he hollered.

He got up from the table and showed Tanaki to the family room. There were several photos, Haskel at various stages of his life with a woman and a couple of handsome children. Tanaki bent down to examine one.

"The wife and kids," Haskel offered.

"Cute little ones," Tanaki said.

"That's an old photo." Haskel picked up the framed image, looked at it tenderly. "The kids are in college now."

"What about your wife? What does she do?"

"That's a long story," Haskel said with a small sigh. "To put it simply, you could say that she's taking a breather. Visiting friends and relatives, that sort of thing. Giving herself a break from, well, from all of this." He gestured vaguely toward the outdoors, to the frantic snow geese and all their mad cryings and flappings. His voice cracked and Tanaki felt a little alarmed. But as they got seated, Haskel gazed steadily at his bookcase. Then, turning toward Tanaki, he began to speak in carefully measured tones.

"I have to admit, it's been a bit inconvenient, and sometimes painfully lonely. But with the family gone," he went on, "I've had a lot of time to myself. Time to think deeply. I find myself sitting here nights, contemplating the way we're living on this planet. Here we are, modern *homo sapiens*, the so-called *wise* hominid. And we've evolved—if that's the word for it—to the point where we can work our will on the entire biosphere. We can take care of it, or destroy it. And look what we're doing. We're in the middle of a mass extinction, on par with the pre-Cambrian die-out. And we're causing it. Us!"

Tanaki shifted in his chair, not sure what to say. Haskel glanced toward the shimmering foliage of a red maple outside the family room window. "Sometimes I think of the earth as a Rorschach blot on which we project our psyches," he said. "And I wonder, what kind of psyche would wish for all this death and destruction, this wanton plundering of other life-forms? Each so unique, each so beautiful."

Haskel's eyes bore into Tanaki with an almost savage intensity, the kind of intensity from which his wife may have felt constrained to "take a breather." Tanaki couldn't avoid a response. "I don't know what to say, Bob," was all he managed. "I know we're facing some problems, but don't you think there's any hope?"

"Oh, there's always hope," Haskel said in a lighter vein. He even laughed a little. "And I'm sorry. I don't mean to harangue you. Preaching to the choir, I'm sure. I'm just an old man who spends too much time alone." The familiar flapping and honking noises drew his gaze to the windows, where the geese were beginning to congregate.

He began to rise from his chair. "Yes, there's hope," he repeated. "But we'll have to be very strategic from here on out. There's nothing pristine out there anymore. It pains me to say it, but the time for preserving ecosystems is past. In the future we'll be *re-creating* them—if there's anything left to re-create them with. Meanwhile we have to do what we can, even if it's only rearguard actions. That's all I'm doing with these geese. Trying to keep them safe while I train them to follow the Cessna around the refuge. My next challenge will be to find a viable breeding ground for them. Then, after a test run, I'll see if I can induce larger flocks to join in. Admittedly, a lot of this depends on untested theories on collective intelligence. Have you had the chance to look into Rupert Shelldrake's work?"

Tanaki said that he hadn't. The entire gaggle were now creating an uproar at the windows of the family room, and Haskel moved to the door and beckoned Tanaki to follow. He offered to show him around, and as his jeep carried them along the refuge road, a low-flying V cast its spreading shadow from above.

Back at the Center, Tanaki told Reynolds about Haskel's geese.

"Snowbirds, you mean."

"No, I mean snow geese."

"Wait a minute. Big white goose with black wing tips?"

"Yeah, snow geese."

"Well, we always called 'em snowbirds." Reynolds peered into the telemetry receiver in which he was making a delicate adjustment with a jeweler's screwdriver. "When I was a kid," he went on as he worked, "our folks had us convinced, you know, that those birds needed all kinds of help to keep on flying. Yeah, at the end of winter, when we'd see 'em coming across the sky, all in their magnificent formations, or just hear 'em coming in the distance, my brother and sisters and me would go running out into the yard. My grandmother'd be over on the porch, calling out to us. 'Hurry, now,' she'd holler, 'hurry!' Them geese've got a long journey to make, and they're going to need all the help they can get!' And we'd start running around like we were plum crazy, and we'd all start crying out to them geese. 'Come on, geese!' we'd yell out, 'don't stop! Come on, snowbirds, you've got to keep on flying. You've got a long journey til you can make it back home!'"

"You know," Reynolds concluded as he lay aside the screwdriver, "it wasn't until I was in the service that it occurred to me those geese didn't need any help from us to get to where they were going . . ."

He paused.

"They didn't, did they?" He stared down at Tanaki with dead seriousness.

He watched a moment longer as Tanaki tried to engineer an earnest response; and then, laughing gently, he patted him softly on the back.

14
Melanie Kersey

TANAKI'S VISIT to Haskel, while it offered a day's relief from the Center's claustrophobic atmosphere, did little to solve his wider problem. The fact remained that his research had reached a bottleneck. He simply had to investigate those sites in the lower bay, where highly saline waters support ecosystems not found elsewhere in the estuary. He particularly wanted to explore the salt grass meadows that occupy large expanses of the lower shore.

Zugenruhe, that's what the German researcher Neuman had named it. "Migratory fidgets," the tendency of caged birds to exhibit restlessness during migration season. They flutter their wings and hop about, always oriented toward the direction they would fly, were they only able to execute their urge to move.

The phenomenon had been well-studied. Researchers employed caged birds in attempts to determine the effects of photoperiodism, atmospheric pressure, and temperature on the onset of the migratory impulse. They also sought to determine whether the bird's orientation could be altered by the use of magnetic fields, or by exposing the animal to planetarium skies full of bogus celestial landmarks. Tanaki had taken part in a number of these studies himself. He always felt a certain pity for their subjects as they frantically flapped their wings with the coming of evening. He felt certain they knew they were missing a rendezvous with destiny, but utterly without the means to do anything about it.

Now he had become one of them!

Reynolds walked toward the dock at Frankie's Bayside Market, where Tanaki sat in one of the station's motorboats. He carried a soda in each hand and shook his head quizzically. As he stepped into the boat Tanaki asked what was going on.

"I was talking to some of my buddies in there, and it sounds like something's up. Some kind of demonstration or something, way down past Bristol."

"A demonstration," Tanaki said, "what's it about?"

"Hard to say," Reynolds replied. "All I could make out from the fellas inside was some hoopla about a bunch of bones." He began to hum, *dem bones, dem bones, dem dry bones* . . .

"Bones," Tanaki murmured, his scientific curiosity piqued; maybe there had been a fossil find! "Let's go down there and take a look."

Soon the faded red pickup rumbled over narrow macadam roads, with Reynolds, Tanaki, and Buzz Richardson pressed against one another on the springy seat of the hollow cab. With both windows open, the smell of chewing tobacco and fish mingled with the warm aroma exuded by trees and moist earth alongside the road. Buzz was driving Reynolds and Tanaki down the peninsula in search of the altercation that was the main topic of conversation in Frankie's Market when Reynolds stopped in for sodas.

"Wonder if it could be some old graves like they went and dug up over to St. Mary's not long ago," Buzz had said to no one in particular.

"Wasn't they looking for some of Calvert's people from back in Colonial days," a portly man in overalls, who leaned heavily against the cooler, put in.

"Lord knows, there's enough bones buried around here to keep a whole crew busy a couple a lifetimes," Buzz replied.

"Those folks sure made a fuss about digging up them graves, though, didn't they?" Frankie chimed in from behind the counter. "You'd a thought they was digging up the Virgin Mary or something."

"Seems they just wanted to know whose bones they were, way I remember it."

"Never did find out, either," the man leaning on the cooler concluded.

As Buzz chatted with Reynolds and Tanaki, he periodically stuck his head out the window to spit chaw juice on the road. His spirits were good. He had agreed to drive them down the peninsula with eagerness. He and his comrades were relics of an era when hundreds of Eastern Shore men supported their families working on the Bay's skipjacks, dredging for oysters that were once more plentiful in the Chesapeake than anywhere in the world. Now it was seldom that anyone asked him to do anything, and he was by nature a helpful sort.

"By the sounds of it, down around Marsh Bay," he offered, and then paused to spit.

"Anyways, somewhere near Sommerfield," Reynolds said. He watched the breeze play in the passing pines.

"Good hour."

Tanaki sat squashed between the two larger men watching sun glint on specks of rock in the pavement. A bird swooped down over the road, barely missing the truck's windshield. All around there was stillness, and in the afternoon heat Tanaki sensed the earth sweating. Passing cars were few and far between. The road was lined with forest broken here and there by fields—or a house with a lone child playing in the yard, a dog panting on the porch.

In the cab, conversation lagged. Lulled by the truck's movement, conscious only of the hum of the tires on the road, Tanaki didn't notice all the commotion until Buzz applied the brakes. There were several police cars edged off the road with emergency lights flashing. Four men in hard hats spoke to a couple of cops, and at a distance Tanaki saw construction equipment through a stand of pines.

Buzz pulled over. He and Reynolds swung open the doors and climbed out. Tanaki followed. The three men stepped stealthily through the pine grove, making their way toward the dull-yellow earth-moving machines that sat in a clearing a few hundred feet ahead. They heard loud voices and were able to make out several people on and around the machines by the bright colors of their clothing. When they got to the edge of the woods the scene began to make sense. The bulky rigs sat amid piles of dirt that appeared to have been excavated from several gaping holes. A vaporous dust rose from the ground into the sultry air. The Bay could be seen through the surrounding forest, not far off.

The people in the clearing wore T-shirts advertising their allegiance to the Nanticoke Indian Heritage Society. Otherwise Tanaki would have been hard-pressed to classify them as First Americans. They wore typical modern clothing, and their facial features presented a varied amalgam of their Mongoloid, Negroid, and Caucasoid ancestors. Several carried large picket signs. There were about two dozen of them, not an impressive force. But they kept up a steady stream of commentary, one voice blending into another in emphatic outbursts:

"Respect Native rights!"
"Leave the dead in peace!"
"Heritage over profits!"
"Save sacred spaces!"
"No more broken promises!"

Before Tanaki could process the confusing welter of sights and sounds, the cops began to advance into the clearing. Several of the protesters lay on the ground before the rigs. Others draped their bodies over the machines' treads. When the officers were within earshot of the protesters, a dark-haired young woman climbed onto the front end of one of the dozers and addressed them sharply.

"These are our ancestors' graves," she hollered. "How'd you like it if we were digging up your grandma's bones?"

The officers stopped and squinted up at the diminutive figure silhouetted against the blazing sun. "Why don't you just come down here like a nice little girl?" one of them said. "Nobody's gonna dig up anybody's grandmother."

"Bullshit!"

"Look, I hate to do this, but if you don't come down nice, you're going to come down not nice. Know what I mean?"

She flipped the officer the bird.

A sergeant barked orders and the cops began to move among the protesters. The Nanticokes were well schooled in non-violent resistance. As the officers approached, they let themselves be carried to the waiting squad cars without struggle. But the angry young woman remained defiant. While the agents of the law carried away her comrades, she sat at the controls of the big dozer she had claimed with arms folded across her chest, dark shades masking her eyes, her jaw set. After finishing with her associates, the cops turned back to deal with her in force. Tanaki watched with keen attention. And, as he watched, a phrase began to go through his mind, an insidious ear-worm that he could not turn off: *the nail that sticks up . . . the nail that sticks up . . . the nail that sticks up . . .*

Suddenly, without warning, and to the surprise of himself as much as everyone else, Tanaki broke from the cover of the trees and dashed toward the captured bulldozer. Dust spit from his sneakers. The angry young woman turned in amazement. When Tanaki reached the dozer he leapt without missing a step, planted a foot briefly on the tread, and propelled himself onto the machine's seat. He landed with a thud that left a hollowness in his chest. Instinctively, remotely, he turned the key in the ignition and grabbed for the most prominent looking lever. The cops stumbled back as the grumbling dozer turned wildly on itself, first to one side and then the other, while Tanaki struggled to master the controls.

"What the hell are you doing?" the protester screamed over the din of the dozer's engine.

"I don't know!" Tanaki spit through gritted teeth.

He managed to swing the monster in a widening arc. The cops ran clear. One grabbed a walkie talkie.

"The boy's gone completely crazy," Reynolds said to Buzz. He wiped the sweat from his brow with his handkerchief.

"Stop this thing, you maniac," the woman yelled. "You're going to get us both killed."

Tanaki screwed up his face in consternation. "I'd love to, but I don't know how!"

The dozer careened madly, bumping over mounds of earth

that had been turned up in the excavation. Tanaki experimented with various levers but accomplished nothing more than to cause the scoop to bang up and down willy-nilly, tilting and clanking. Just as a squadron of state troopers roared up, the machine pitched into a shallow trench and slammed to a stop, hurling Tanaki into the dirt, the young protester against the rig's control panel.

The cops ran to the grinding, smoking dozer. Two of them grabbed a shaken and dust-covered Tanaki. A third clambered onto the seat and stopped the machine. The woman, though not injured, was too rattled to put up any but the most ineffectual struggle. She was cuffed and hauled unceremoniously to a squad car.

After booking, the cops released everyone except the angry one and Tanaki, whom they charged with trespassing, resisting arrest, and assault on a peace officer. They were consigned to adjacent holding cells in the old county jailhouse. The woman sat on a bench staring straight ahead, still wearing her dark shades. Tanaki stood in the middle of his cell and tried to figure the whole thing out. "I'm sorry if I made things worse," he said. He looked at her, but she made no move to respond.

"I don't know what on earth got into me." He held his arms away from his body in a quizzical gesture.

She stared at the floor. Tanaki sat down. She turned calmly.

"What I don't get," she said, "is what the hell did you hope to accomplish with that crazy stunt?"

"That, I'm afraid, is something I can't give you an answer to."

"Are you even Indian?"

"No, I'm from Michigan."

As soon as the remark left his lips, he realized that it

was idiotic.

"You're strange," she said.

She seemed to relax a little, leaned back and propped herself on one elbow. Tanaki's thoughts drifted to his own situation, and how he was going to get out of it. He figured he was going to need a lawyer, and he only knew one: Valerie Stanton. But he didn't know if he should call her. He had phoned a couple of times since their Ocean City outing but she had seemed distant and steered the conversation to environmental issues. When he brought up the possibility of getting together again, she complained of a heavy workload and said that she would let him know.

Okay, he thought to himself, maybe the trip to the beach hadn't exactly tripped her trigger. But at the very least, he thought he could say that they were friends. And he was embarrassed at the thought of explaining his situation to a complete stranger. Somehow—he wasn't sure why—he knew that Valerie would cut him a break, help him without making him feel like a loser. When a deputy came by the cell, he asked if he could make a call to Baltimore.

After the deputy returned him to his cell, he spoke to his accomplice. "You might like to know," he said, "that I've got a friend coming down, and she's a lawyer. Hopefully she can get us out of here."

"Oh. And when will your *friend* be getting here?"

Raised eyebrows emerged above the rims of the angry one's shades.

"No, really," Tanaki chuckled, feeling on the defensive, "she's just a friend." *Hell's bells*, he thought, *she doesn't miss a thing!*

He shuffled aimlessly around the cell. Though he could

feel the woman's gaze, he tried to behave casually. It was quiet. They must have been the jail's only prisoners. He stopped in the middle of the cell and turned toward her.

"Were your grandmother's bones really dug up over there?"

"Why do you ask?"

The sharpness in her reply rattled him. "I was just concerned." He ambled to the window at the back of the cell, where he stood for a minute and watched the day's last clouds float by. "You know," he said, making another attempt at connection, "I've been doing some reading about the Shore. And I've got to tell you, I find the history of this area downright fascinating."

"I hope you're not reading that bullshit, the one by Huntley, that they pass out at the public library."

"Is there something wrong with the book by—what was the name, Huntley, did you say?" he fudged.

"Is there something wrong with it! For crying out loud, where have you been? Living in a cave?"

Tanaki tried to suppress the pained expression that painted his face.

"Look," she said, more conciliatory now, "I've seen worse. At least Huntley mentions First Americans, in spite of his obsession with the ignorant conquistadors who savaged my people and raped the land. Above average for a white man, I suppose."

Tanaki needed to change the subject. He didn't have a dog in this fight, yet he felt an unpleasant heat directed his way. "I suppose that was some kind of cemetery down there."

"I don't know if cemetery would be the right word. Full of tombstones and flowers. That's not how things were done in the old days . . ."

She fell silent and fixed her gaze into the darkening cell. Tanaki stood chin in hand, waiting for more elaboration. His discomfort was growing palpable when she finally continued.

"There was this hut—it was up on stilts—called a Chicisoan. You would probably think it's gross."

"Don't worry about me," Tanaki offered readily. "Grossing me out is no easy matter. After all, I've dissected just about every living organism imaginable."

"I guess that's one way to learn about life," she remarked dryly, "by destroying it." She turned slightly toward him.

Tanaki didn't know how to respond. She faced forward again and seemed far away. But after a moment she began to speak anew, as if in a dream: a depth dream of ancestors and carnal earth. "First, using seashells, they would scrape the flesh from the bones. Then they wrapped the bones in the skin. After everything dried out, they would pick the bones clean and bury them with those of the rest of the ancestors."

Tanaki approached the bars between the cells. He grabbed a couple of them, leaned his weight against the cool metal. "So, basically, that was a mass grave over there?"

He let the silence expand until it engulfed him. Then he spoke in self-defense, against the silence, against the bars, against the striking dark beauty of the young woman in the next cell. "What I'm trying to say is," he explained, "it would be hard to determine if the bones in that grave were specifically those of *your* ancestors, in particular."

"What's that supposed to mean?"

She reminded him of a spiny lobster he had once tried to tag. He recalled how fiercely it had wielded its formidable defenses.

"Nothing," he replied. "It's not supposed to mean anything."

He dropped the bars and wandered back into his cell, where he stood with hands in his pockets for a moment, feeling at odds with himself. He sat on the bench that ran across the back wall of the cell, lost in a reverie of ancient bones.

Her voice cut suddenly through the twilight.

"Who *are* you, anyway?"

"David Tanaki." He spoke absently, for she had interrupted his thoughts. He continued in the same tone, thinking aloud. "I wonder why they would give such special treatment to the bones?"

She allowed his question to settle fully into the gloaming. When she spoke, her voice was sparse and emphatic. "That's where the spirit lived."

"Ahhh." Tanaki turned slowly toward her and grew more alert now, his reverie fulfilled by her answer. "And . . . what about you? What do you call yourself?"

"Melanie Kersey. With white people, anyway."

"Do you think I'm white?"

She squinted carefully at him. "To tell the truth, I'm not sure."

"I'm not either," Tanaki replied with a small laugh. "I'm not sure what any of it means. But are you saying that you have another name? An Indian one, perhaps?"

She scuffed her boots across the floor. Stalled. "I've never been that crazy about it," she said after a moment, and her voice grew less confrontational, almost friendly. "It always seemed so prissy," she confided. "But since I've been in the movement, I have been using it more. My grandfather tells me that the morning I was born, there was a quarter moon rising . . ."

She seemed exasperated for a moment and confused, and

then she rose suddenly and strode to her cell's high window. "But what's that got to do with anything? Just call me Melanie, for crying out loud."

Tanaki would have liked to know more, but after a brief glance outside, Melanie returned to her bench and lay down, her face to the wall. Realizing his own fatigue, Tanaki leaned back against the wall, allowing his body to experience the energetic letdown bound to follow the adrenaline rush of the afternoon. He stretched out with arms crossed under his head. His thoughts splintered into a hazy collage of the day's confusion . . .

He was asleep in moments.

Valerie's voice came to him through a fog of half-consciousness. He struggled to focus on her blurred image, which was further complicated by the pattern of bars that stood between them. She wore a powder blue suit and her hair was in a pony tail. She looked real sweet, standing there smiling, saying his name. "David . . . it's time to wake up. Oh, David?"

Tanaki rose woozily and walked slowly over to the bars. "I guess you're going to want to know how I got into this mess." He tried to chuckle, but what emerged sounded like the constricted venting of air out of a balloon.

"I'm afraid I'll have to, if I'm going to get you out of here."

Tanaki walked back to the bench while the deputy who had accompanied Valerie into the cell block opened the heavy steel door. Valerie entered and sat down as the door clanked shut. Tanaki had not finished enumerating the extraordinary events of the day in halting, jagged phrases when the deputy suddenly reappeared. He spoke as he once again opened the door.

"Good news," he said matter-of-factly, "you're free to go."

He didn't look at Tanaki. Instead, his eyes moved from the

lock to the floor; and then to Melanie Kersey, who had roused herself at the sound of jangling keys. She answered his smile with a deliberate grimace.

Tanaki looked at Valerie with widened eyes. It all seemed too sudden. As far as he could tell, she hadn't even begun to work her lawyerly magic yet. Or had she managed some kind of deal before coming to the jail?

She turned to the deputy.

"You're releasing him?" Her voice betrayed the fact that she shared Tanaki's surprise.

"That's right."

"What about the charges?"

"Been dropped."

Tanaki felt almost cheated. It seemed so anticlimactic.

He was actually beginning to protest when Valerie drowned him out.

"Thank you very much, Officer," she said as she rose. "If you'll just give my client a moment to collect his things."

She stepped toward the door and waited there for Tanaki.

Tanaki rose and addressed the deputy. "Wait," he said, "what about her?" He nodded toward the next cell.

"What about her?"

"Isn't she getting out?"

Staring hard at Tanaki, trying to silence him with her eyes, Valerie maintained a pleasant smile for the benefit of the deputy.

"Didn't receive no instructions about the girl."

Tanaki beckoned Valerie to the back of the cell. "Look," he said, "I got her into this mess. I think we ought to try and get her out of it."

"David," she whispered, "let me tell you something. These

people don't take too kindly to outsiders coming down here telling them how to run their affairs. I think you had better just get out of here while getting out's on offer. I'll see what I can do for her. I'll just need a little time."

She looked over at Melanie; Melanie affected a bored, detached air.

Tanaki was at a loss for words; Valerie took him by the arm and directed him through the cell door. He wanted to offer Melanie some kind of assurance, but the situation seemed to call for an immediate exit. The deputy escorted him and Valerie down the hallway. When they reached the lobby, Valerie turned and addressed the officer. "I'm with the University's legal defense project. Be advised that your staff will be held fully accountable for that woman's safety." She calmly turned, and she and Tanaki left the building. Her Miata sat at the curb with the top down.

"I thought you said they don't like people coming down here, telling them—" Tanaki began.

"I just couldn't help it," she said tersely. She pulled her keys from her purse. Tanaki stood for a moment and drew in the deliciously cooling air. Valerie opened his door and pressed it closed after he was ensconced in the low bucket seat. As they coursed over the asphalt rivers of Bristol County, she thought outloud.

"Why would they have dropped the charges? That's really weird. I can't imagine it's simply because you're affiliated with the research center." She reached down and turned off the radio. Cogitation covered her face like a cloud. "Tell me more about that construction site."

Tanaki explained the earth-moving equipment, the upturned earth, the hardhats.

"This just doesn't add up," she said. "That entire area is off-limits to new construction." She pulled at her hair tie and shook out her hair. Her face lightened. "I don't know, maybe they got some kind of exception. It's late. I'll look into it tomorrow, when I'm back at the school."

They cruised past darkened woods interspersed with wayside hamlets of broken board houses desperately in need of paint.

"Why don't we find a room in some little motel?" Tanaki asked. He reached over the console and lay his hand in her lap.

She kept her hands on the wheel. Stared straight over the dash into the tunnel of light cast by the Miata's headlamps. "Hmm, better not," she said, to all appearances completely uninspired by his proposal. "I've got classes in the morning."

He delicately drew back his hand.

An awkward silence ensued. Then, with a little shake of her hair, Valerie gestured vaguely toward Tanaki and spoke again. "David," she said, "I like you in many ways, and we have some important things in common. But I've really been dwelling on our trip to the beach. Don't get me wrong, I can appreciate your caring about those birds. But when I spend that kind of time with a man—like we did that night—I need a little more attention to be paid . . ."

He couldn't manage to respond.

"I'm not trying to make a big deal about it," she said. "I guess I'm struggling with some boundary issues. How about if we just be friends for now?"

"Sure, that's fine," he said, but he knew a brush-off when he heard one. He turned and watched the passing shadows as they sped toward Cambridge.

15
Be the Bird

IT STARTED SOON after the waxwing invasion.

That's when the Bluebird began to use the phrase "Be the bird."

Tanaki had also been affected by the events of that day. His loss of identity, that look in the Bluebird's eyes. The strange rapture of their lovemaking. In fact, he had wandered about for days suffering from a sort of temporary amnesia, oblivious to his day-to-day obligations—uncertain, for that matter, who he even was. He had gone so far as to avoid the Bluebird, in spite of several telephone messages. He felt that he had to be alone. It had all been too powerful. He couldn't digest it, and he was worried.

Finally the Bluebird sent a telegram. "Must see you. Everything strange. And a little scary. Quit hiding from me. Blue—"

They met in Bruges over the weekend. In spite of his apprehension, when he saw her coming across the courtyard in front of the hotel something melted away. All sense of danger was dispelled, any urge to fight for his individuality gone. Nothing remained but the need to hold her, to be with her. They walked the cobbled streets of the town, skirted the canals, and stood on small arching bridges to watch the swans drift along the canals.

The call from Moeller came a couple of months later. At

the sound of his greeting, Tanaki conjured a vivid image of the brilliant German's immaculately groomed Old World polish.

"I don't want to worry you," Moeller began, "but I need to talk to you about Ani."

"Ani?"

"I hope you won't find this . . . *presumptuous* is the word, I believe?"

The question was a rhetorical stall. Moeller's command of English was impeccable.

"I'm sure you needn't worry. Please, go on."

"Thank you, David. I knew I could count on you." Moeller coughed. "As I said, it's about Ani."

"Right."

"Well, it seems that you and she have become—how shall I put it—quite close?"

Another rhetorical stall. Tanaki and the Bluebird, while not brazenly thrusting their affair into the faces of their colleagues, had made no particular attempt to hide it. In fact, Tanaki was convinced that Moeller and Pannenburg had secretly abetted their romance in mysterious ways. Joint projects suddenly materialized, requiring close collaboration, and the Bluebird swore that she hadn't intrigued in arranging them. (Tanaki knew that he hadn't; not that he wouldn't have liked to; he simply hadn't been clever enough to pull it off.) In the occasional paranoid moment, Tanaki even wondered whether their older colleagues—their mentors, in fact—hadn't orchestrated his love affair as part of some private research agenda. Or on a bet. The two of them, after all, loved that sort of thing. He could picture the many occasions, sitting in some café, when they would place large wagers on when the first wheatear would appear, or on who would receive some academic appointment. And they both loved to discuss sex in all its many permutations. As for Moeller, he had a particular penchant for placing human lovemaking in the broader context of mammalian mating, reveled in coming up with witty comparisons between human courting behaviors and those of other animals. It more amused than bothered Tanaki to think that, even prior to their introducing him to the Bluebird, these two graying observers of life may have placed a healthy wager on how long it would take the two youngsters to hop in the sack. He just hoped that he hadn't disappointed them. And he wondered: did they also have money riding on when the relationship would end?

"Go on . . ." he said warily.

"It's just that Ani has been acting a little, shall I say, *unusual* lately." A note of distress clawed its way through Moeller's habitual veneer of calm control.

Still Tanaki remained guarded. "Unusual? In what way?"

"That's just it. It's hard to describe." A nervous hitch in Moeller's voice now.

"Go ahead and tell me what's on your mind, Dietrich. I can sense how concerned you must be."

"Thank you, David. I knew . . . It's the cage. You see, the cage . . ."

"Which cage?"

"*Zugenruhe* . . . it's the *Zugenruhe* . . ."

"The cage you use for Zugenruhe experiments?"

"Yes, that's it. Thank you. I knew I could—"

"Dietrich?"

"Yes?"

"What is it about the Zugenruhe cage!"

"She's in it."

"You mean the Blue—I mean, Ani? She's in the Zugenruhe cage?"

"Yes, exactly. That's exactly it."

"What's she doing? Cleaning it?"

"No, David."

"Dietrich, please, just tell me. What is it that Ani's doing in the Zugenruhe cage?"

"Hold the line a moment."

Tanaki heard the receiver clack into its cradle. Then there was the sound of an extension being picked up.

"David, are you still there?"

"Yes, I'm still with you."

"Good. Listen."

Now Moeller must have taken the phone from his ear, because in response to his questions Tanaki heard nothing but the hollow echo of the researcher's cavernous laboratory, which had been built like an aviary. It was a hollowness he had come to associate with fond afternoon phone calls from the Bluebird. For a moment he heard nothing else, and then he slowly became aware of the rattling of metal. A loud "chirp." And then another. There was something wildly plaintive about the calls; it was no bird that Tanaki recognized. The chirping continued, changing rhythm, varying in volume. Moeller's voice came on the line again.

"That's her!"

"What, that bizarre chirping? That's Ani?"

"Yes, David. Please come quickly. I'm afraid that something has gone terribly wrong."

Tanaki didn't bother to ask Pannenburg's permission to borrow the station's jeep. It wasn't clear what was going on at Moeller's lab, but the quavering quality in the great and cynical scientist's voice had rattled him deeply. His mind raced as he sped toward Cologne, groping for an explanation for those bizarre chirps. He thought back over the last few months . . .

Tanaki had managed to shake off the events associated with the waxwing invasion after the weekend in Bruges. He had classified the experience as an extremely interesting phenomenon, worthy perhaps of further thought when he had more time and leisure, but for the time being filed away in a nice, secure box in his mind. He was working with a group of Swedish biologists with whom he was reprising Perdecci's classic experiment, but with more sophisticated controls. He considered the study paramount to his career, and felt that he couldn't let anything get in the way of its successful completion. He was following the only tried and true method he knew. He planned his work, and he was working his plan.

The Bluebird had reacted differently.

Over the course of the preceding summer she had lost interest in scientific studies in which only weeks before she was passionately involved. She took a wry interest in Tanaki's enthusiasm for the experiments he was organizing with the Swedes. After he described, in great detail, the lengthy preparations that were underway, all the ingenious controls he and his colleagues had devised, she looked at him as one might look at a child, leaned back on the day bed in his room and said, "Why not simply *be* the bird?"

"I can understand—conceptually, that is—what you're getting at," Tanaki said. "But I really don't see how you expect me to put such a vague protocol into practice."

She just smiled at him, a mysterious, Mona Lisa smile.

"Well?" He stood looking at her, his hand held out as if waiting to receive some tangible object.

"Honestly, David," she said with an exaggerated frown, mocking his seriousness, "I'm not sure, either."

When they loved each other, she urged him to find again that place where they had been on the day of the waxwings. Holding him, she would coo softly in his ear, or make fevered fluttering sounds as she ran her fingertips along his back. He tried to ignore it, kissing her passionately, as if by main force he could obliterate an experience that threatened to turn his world into chaos. He felt a pull toward some vortex from which he was certain they would never return.

He was prepared to resist to the death.

Next she began a series of, to say the least, unorthodox experiments. First she attempted to live on the diet of a bird for an entire week. Nothing but worms, seeds, and berries. Later, against Tanaki's strident objections, she had him take her out in Pannenburg's jeep and drop her at remote places with which she was utterly unfamiliar. She would then attempt to find her way back without looking at road signs or consulting a map, while Tanaki, back at the station, worried himself sick. Most of these outings ended with a tired phone call in the middle of the night, telling a relieved Tanaki that she was in such-and-such a town, would he please pick her up. But it must be conceded that on one occasion she arrived triumphantly at the station after two days, smiling and waving as she emerged over a dune.

As autumn approached, and Tanaki became increasingly involved in his experiments with the Swedes, he began to lose patience with the Bluebird. He felt that his reputation, perhaps his entire career, was riding on the new study. The Bluebird's recent fascinations—and her rejection of the methods that she and Tanaki once shared—left him alone in his preoccupations.

One day he exploded.

"Damn it, Bird," he barked angrily from his desk, "I'm getting tired of hearing about this 'be the bird' crap. Maybe it would be better if you just kept it to yourself from here on out."

She was stunned. The era of gentle playmates was tragically over. Seeing her hurt, Tanaki quickly backpedaled. He tried to explain. "Listen Bird," he said, "I'm really jammed up with this study right now. And, to be frank, I feel like you've gone a little outside the pale on this thing. I mean, the stuff you're into lately is kookiness, not science."

"I'm glad you've told me how you feel about it." She cast down her eyes.

He should have held her then. He knew that. But he didn't. Somehow, it wasn't part of the logic of the situation. His study was supposed to start soon—had to start, you couldn't tell birds when to migrate—and he couldn't waste time with the Bluebird's moodiness. He would deal with her later, he told himself, when the study was completed. He picked up his pen and resumed writing in his notebook while she collected her things. She touched him on the shoulder as she walked past, saying goodbye so quietly that he wasn't sure whether he had heard or merely imagined it.

"I'll call you," he said without bothering to look up.

That was the last time they had spoken. He allowed himself to wonder hopefully, as he approached Cologne, if the routine in the Zugenruhe cage wasn't some silly joke: a little gag to break the icy silence that had reigned between them for two weeks. But that didn't square with the genuinely frightened tone of Moeller's voice, or the unearthly quality of the chirping Tanaki had heard over the telephone.

16
Nanticokes

THE FACTS surrounding Tanaki's arrest and detention awakened no small amount of curiosity in Valerie. The day after securing his release, she spent the afternoon working in the university's law library, digging out information on land use on the lower Shore. She found no record of any exceptions to the moratorium on development. From Tanaki's description, the construction project was significant. It sounded like a good four or five acres had been cleared, with several earth-moving machines on the site.

Was some renegade builder operating in flagrant violation of the law?

Why were the charges against Tanaki so suddenly dismissed?

The next morning she made calls to several offices in the state bureaucracy, but no one seemed to know anything about the matter, or in any case wish to discuss it. She called Tanaki to confirm the site's location; he reminded her that Melanie Kersey was still languishing in the county lockup. She let him know she was already working on the matter.

The sun was at its zenith in a pale blue sky as she zummed along the sticky asphalt of a deserted county road. A dragonfly hovered above the windshield for a split second before disappearing in the rush of wind that sculpted the body of the car. She listened to the radio while scanning the roadside for landmarks by which Tanaki had described the construction site: a white clapboard house with a spotted dog on the porch, its large barn in back in need of paint; a broken-down pickup of antique vintage on cinder blocks; a sharp curve in the road; a stretch of pine forest. And then, the site.

She made note of each of the landmarks as she passed them. The frame house. The spotted dog, running alongside the road, yapping at her wheels. The barn in back. The pickup. The stand of loblollies, branches and needles waving in the mild breeze. And then—nothing! She pulled off the road and stared into the clearing that followed the stand of pines. She turned off the radio. Sure, there was a clearing. That much checked out. But there was no sign of construction equipment, nor of any other human endeavor. What's more, the ground didn't appear to have been disturbed, was in fact covered with grass!

She took a hard look at Tanaki's directions, mentally counting off the turns she had taken, enumerating the landmarks, right down to the frame house with the dog, the barn, the pickup, and the pine grove. She was certain she had come to the place he had described. She drove directly to the county records office, hesitating only long enough to note the street address of the clapboard house so that she would have some point of reference for the grassy plot.

Sitting at a battered table, surrounded by dusty files, she located the parcel's plat, determined the plat number, and searched the files for ownership. The parcel had recently changed hands. It was now owned by a corporation listed as

"Seabreeze, Inc." Aside from a popular line of cosmetics, the corporate moniker incited no reverberations. She would have to stop in Annapolis, on the way back to Baltimore, and check the state's incorporation records. From the land records bureau she walked across the town square to a bail bondsman's office. She arrived at the jailhouse in late afternoon and presented some papers to the deputy at the front desk.

"I'll have to clear this," he said.

"I understand," she replied. "Can I go back while you take care of it?"

"Don't see why not."

Melanie Kersey sat on the bench at the back of her cell, slouched against the wall. She didn't bother to straighten up when Valerie approached.

"Look who it is," she said, peering up through her dark shades, "I suppose you're here to straighten out little boyfriend's mess."

"Ms. Kersey, I'm here to help *you*. . ."

Melanie stood up. She removed her shades and slowly approached the bars. "I didn't ask for your help," she clipped out. "Just like I didn't ask for your geeky boyfriend's help. If he hadn't played the hero and almost gotten three county cops killed, I wouldn't be stuck in this filthy hellhole." She turned and sighed. After a moment, she resumed in a philosophical vein, as if reasoning with herself. "I should have known he'd get off, with his high-priced city lawyer. Even though he was the one responsible for everything!"

"Now, Ms. Kersey—" Valerie tried to protest, speaking at Melanie's back.

"And I should have known what I would get," Melanie continued, ignoring Valerie. "The same bullshit we Indians have always gotten—the shaft." Having concluded, she stared out the window, apparently hoping that Valerie would just go away.

Valerie let the silence sink in. She wasn't insensitive to Melanie's remarks. She was well familiar with the history of First Americans on the Eastern Shore, and was aware that, like First Americans all over the continent, they had invariably gotten the short end of the stick in their struggles against technologically and numerically superior Euro-American adversaries. She too turned around, leaned back against the bars, and ran through a brief history of the Nanticoke people in her mind, searching through that shrouded fog for some wedge into the psyche of the young woman unjustly caged behind her . . .

The original inhabitants of the Eastern Shore had at first graciously accommodated the earliest English settlers. They eagerly traded with the colonists and offered them assistance in establishing their rudimentary communities. But relations between the two groups were soon marred by the colonists' sharp trading practices, the relentless encroachment of their settlements on Indian hunting grounds, and cattle that marauded through Nanticoke gardens of beans and maize—and occasionally ended up on Nanticoke dinner menus. Though most of the ensuing altercations were small fare, on several occasions these conflicts erupted into open warfare.

In the early eighteenth century Maryland's governor tried to establish harmony by reserving lands along Chicawan Creek where the Nanticokes could live unmolested by the newcomers. But though the Nanticokes acceded to this reduced status, they continued to be subjected to predations by the avaricious colonists, predations the governor was powerless to prevent from his capital on the opposite side of the Bay. When the harried Nanticokes received an offer to join the Iroquois on the banks of the Susquehanna River, most of them packed up and migrated northward. A few dozen diehards stayed behind, however, reluctant to leave the land where their ancestors' bones rested. But the colonists soon forced these hardy souls entirely off the reserved lands. This remnant settled near the coast on Indian River where, having adopted the ways of the European settlers, they gained their subsistence from farming and fishing. They lived there inconspicuously until shortly before the Civil War, when the vicious dynamics of racism brought an unwelcome scrutiny to their community.

Lewis Sockum was a Nanticoke Indian who lived at Indian River. A profitable general store, and a number of shrewd land purchases, had made Sockum a rare success in his community—and a target for the greed and envy of his white neighbors. In the midst of the racial paranoia that followed John Brown's raid on Harper's Ferry, they accused him of selling gunpowder to his son-in-law, Isaac Harmon. Harmon, the state averred, was a mulatto, and thereby not allowed to own firearms. The copper-toned Sockum countered that Harmon was in fact a Nanticoke Indian like himself.

The state's key witness was a frail old lady named Lydia Clark, reputed to be the sole Nanticoke Indian still conversant in her native tongue. Her testimony—given under threat of eviction by her prominent white landlord—began with an Irish widow named Chancey. Chancy, Lydia Clark related in halting, broken phrases, owned a plantation not far from Indian River in the years following the Revolution. On hearing of a slave ship stranded on the bar, so Clark's story went, Chancey hied herself to the waterfront in hopes of acquiring a field hand. To complete Clark's tale, it turned out that the handsome young man Chancy selected was a prince of one of the most prominent Congo statelets. His many noble attributes were not lost on the lady, and before the season turned she was big with their first child. A dozen more followed—so Lydia testified—and the mixed children of this illicit romance, shunned by the white community, took husbands and wives from among the Indian River Nanticokes. Lydia further testified that not only Isaac Harmon, but Lewis Sockum—as well as the rest of the Nanticoke Indians living around Indian River—were in fact the issue of these marriages. Under the "one-drop-of-blood" theory then enshrined in state law, their princely African ancestor, were her story true, rendered them officially "colored," and subject to all of the persecutions that designation entrained. The court decided to accept Clark's story, while it ignored her vociferous assertions that, as far as she was concerned, both Sockum and Harmon were Nanticoke Indians, like herself. As a consequence, Sockum was fined twenty dollars for selling powder to his son-in-law. What was worse, he was declared "colored" himself, and thereby deprived of the right to bear arms. Unwilling to bow to this novel oppression, he sold out and left the state in disgust.

If there was a bright side to this sad tale, the trial shook the Nanticoke community at Indian River out of its complacency. For the first time, the Nanticokes organized to protect their rights, and Lewis Sockum became the first and greatest hero of the Indian River people. The demonstration that landed Melanie Kersey in jail, in fact, could be traced directly back to the activism inspired by Sockum's ordeal.

But Melanie had no way of knowing, as she stared out the window of her cell, that the impeccably dressed city woman on the other side of the bars knew more about the history of her people than she and most of her kin. Valerie had been teaching a seminar on the development of property rights in the state for six years and owed her job at the University to her dissertation for the LLB: *Trouble in the Garden: Planters and Nanticokes, 1631-1789.*

"Ms. Kersey," Valerie began slowly, carefully, turning into the bars, "I know you have every reason to be upset. The legacy of the kinds of injustices perpetrated on Lewis Sockum and the rest of your ancestors isn't altogether behind us. But if we work together, I think we can make some of today's battles come out a little better."

Melanie turned disjointedly. She looked at Valerie with a mixture of skepticism and amazement in her eyes.

"I'm just beginning to investigate what went on at your burial grounds the other day," Valerie continued, "but from what I've learned so far, it already smells more than a little rotten."

"What did you find out?" Melanie asked desperately.

"They've stopped digging, for one thing. What's more, someone has covered everything up, as if it never happened."

Melanie revolved on herself. "What!" she exclaimed.

"Listen," Valerie said, "I'm going to stay on this thing until I figure out what's going on down there. And I'll be happy to help your group with any legal issues that arise concerning your tribe's interests."

Melanie responded slowly, skeptically. "Yeah, but what will it cost us?"

"Nothing."

Melanie's face still bore mistrust. "Are you serious? I mean, there's got to be some catch . . ."

"Of course I'm serious. We can work it through the University's legal defense project. But I'm going to need your help. So let's get you out of this awful place."

Something like a muted joy invaded Melanie's features. She started to collect her few belongings that lay on the bench. Then her shoulders slumped, and she turned with a dejected air. "Wait a minute," she said, "there's no way I'll be able to swing the bail money."

"Oh," Valerie said as she dug her keys out of her purse, "I guess I didn't mention it. The bail's been taken care of."

Melanie stood dumbstruck for a moment. Then she eagerly said, "I'll pay you back." A film of tears had formed over her eyes.

The deputy was coming down the hallway. Melanie collected her things while he unlocked the door. She ignored him as she left the cell, addressing Valerie convivially.

"I totally blew the whole passive resistance thing." She laughed through her tears.

"I'm sure it's not easy," Valerie said. "But you put yourself on the line for something you believe in. I really admire that."

Melanie put an arm around Valerie's waist and touched her head briefly onto her shoulder as they strolled out of the cell block. "Do me one more favor, will you?"

"What's that?"

"Find your boyfriend something hipper to read than *Albion's Spawn in the Great Shellfish Bay*."

Valerie was about to protest that Tanaki wasn't her boyfriend. But she suddenly thought better of leaving the field open. "He's reading that?" she asked incredulously.

The two broke into girlish laughter, the deputy looking on in dumb wonder as they left the jail.

17
Revolt

AS JULY MELTED imperceptibly into August, Folker's regime became so onerous not only to Tanaki, but to his colleagues on the Center's staff, that a clandestine meeting was organized to discuss the situation. Tanaki was notified by DeForrest who, whistling nonchalantly, casually approached his research cube one afternoon and held a sheet of orange paper through the doorway. Tanaki wheeled his chair over and took the flyer with a puzzled look. He unfolded it and read the large capital letters:

> FOR ALL OF YOU WHO ARE
> SICK AND TIRED
> OF THE INCESSANT
> AND UNNECESSARY
> MEDDLING WHERE HIS %#*@*
> DOES NOT BELONG
> OF OUR SO-CALLED
> "ADMINISTRATOR,"
> MEET FOR DISCUSSION.
> PLACE: THE CANTEEN
> TIME: FOUR THIS AFTERNOON

Tanaki couldn't help but smile at the animus expressed in

the announcement. In his effort to maintain a professional demeanor, he realized, he had failed to own his growing anger at Folker's antics. He nodded affirmatively to DeForrest and then turned to look out on the Bay. Small whitecaps danced on the aquamarine surface. He recalled that Folker, accompanied by Cynthia, was in Annapolis for meetings. He felt an irrepressible thrill at the idea of holding a gripe session in their absence.

When he entered the canteen a couple of minutes before four, many of his colleagues were already there. Several had been out and around the Bay, to judge from the sun on their faces, the splotches of mud on their clothes, and the fatigue in their postures. A few leaned against the vending machines that lined one wall. Others sat at a half-dozen or so tables that occupied the better part of the room.

Tanaki recognized them all, though he didn't know any of them well. They had chatted on the occasion of chance encounters in this room, in the supplies room, or around the docks. He had seen them at staff meetings and even consulted a few about their research. But he hadn't socialized with any of them. He worked late so often, and most of them were married or otherwise occupied. Besides, on his rare evenings off, he usually found himself looking forward to dinner at the Yamaguchis.

At the far end of the room Beth Delantis sat at a table with a fan of paper in front of her. She wrote industriously, looking up from time to time to gauge the turnout. Tanaki had passed a couple of profitable and pleasant hours one afternoon picking her brain on her specialty, planktonic life. She had been at the Center for several years. She spent a lot of time peering through a microscope, when she wasn't out on the Bay collecting specimens. Her face was browned by hours in the sun and salt air.

Shortly DeForrest came through the door. Beth noticed him, made eye contact, and raised her eyebrows in a questioning gesture. With a nod DeForrest indicated that it was time to begin. He turned and closed the door, and Delantis spoke.

"I guess you all know why we're meeting here."

A chorus of "oh yeses" and "mmm-hmms."

"I've taken some time to draw up a short list of our grievances. If it's okay with you, I'll start by reading it. Then I'd like to get your input."

Affirmative nods.

"Here it is," Delantis began. "Number one: Unexplained and unprecedented interference with our research schedules."

More nods.

"Number two: Incessant requests to do public relations work."

Inarticulate grumblings.

"Number three: Failure to communicate policy to staff in a coherent fashion."

"You mean in any fashion!" someone blurted from near the Coke machine.

"Number four: Bogus rationales for previously stated interference."

Raised eyebrows.

"And"—her voice grew quiet here—"Number five: A growing sense of paranoia?"

She looked up, seeking the eyes of her colleagues. They looked at the floor or otherwise averted their faces from her persistent gaze. Perhaps she was striking too close to the heart of the matter.

REVOLT

Tanaki sensed the discomfort in the room, but he didn't share it. To the contrary, he felt strangely energized. Having buckled under to Folker's meddling all spring and summer, trying not to be the damned nail sticking up, he experienced a tonic sense of liberation in Beth's rebelliousness. So when her eyes scanned to his he didn't waiver but returned her gaze, smiling calmly and nodding. Slowly, affirmatively. She didn't avert her eyes either but returned his smile. Then, continuing to look at him, she gently slapped her list of grievances with the back of her hand and said, "So what are we going to do about all of this?"

Tanaki sensed the collective attention of his colleagues bear down upon him, led there by Beth's unabated gaze. He felt a sense of implosion, as if the weight of all those stares were compressing something inside of him, forcing the essence of his being into a tighter and tighter bundle until release was the only natural consequence. Suddenly, all the expectation in the faces of his colleagues became irrelevant. He even ceased to notice Beth's continuing stare. He pushed back his chair and rose to speak.

"I don't know what everyone else is thinking," he heard himself declare, "but I say we've got to make some kind of protest. Folker's meddling has played hell with my research already, and if I don't get down to the lower Bay sometime soon I may as well write off this entire season."

His colleagues made small rustling noises, shuffled their shoes on the floor, toyed with their flyers.

"I mean, I've done research in a lot of settings, but I've never seen anything like this. Either this man is crazy, some kind of control freak, or there's something else—perhaps something less than kosher—going on."

"What exactly do you mean, less than kosher?" Beth asked.

"I'm not sure. But this whole experience with Folker has an aura of unreality about it. You ask for explanations and you get some cock and bull story about the Coast Guard, or the weather service. We're not idiots, after all. We can see that the weather's not bad. I'm starting to feel like we're being gas-lighted or something."

There were looks of recognition throughout the room.

"Do you have any suggestions?"

Tanaki thought for a moment. "Well, for starters, somebody's got to talk to Folker. Confront him with all of this nonsense, and not take any moonshine for an answer."

Beth looked around the room. "Any volunteers?" People shifted in their chairs, coughed. The standing ones moved their weight from one foot to another.

Finally DeForrest spoke up. "Why don't you speak to him, Dave?" he said. "You seem to have a good handle on the situation."

Tanaki looked around the room. His colleagues gazed upon him like the inhabitants of some hopelessly besieged town, he about to be sent through enemy lines for help. Moved by their haplessness, but with a sense that he was over-extending himself, he humbly agreed to present the staff's grievances to Folker. He also agreed to report his findings at another meeting to be arranged as circumstances might permit.

There was no question of seeing Folker immediately, for he would be at the conference in Annapolis for several days. Tanaki was grateful for this fact, because after the meeting broke up and everyone stood chatting over Cokes and chips, he knew that he had done it again, gotten himself involved in something beyond his main agenda: migration research. He mentally ticked off the events like the beads on a rosary: the impassioned speech in Baltimore the day he met Valerie; the episode at the beach with the gulls and the trash; and most recently, his run-in with the law over Melanie Kersey and her protester friends. He felt a vague sense of fear. It was like being at sea with someone else at the helm, someone whose face you never see, whose voice you never hear, but whom you are certain you know intimately.

He had once known what he was about. Sure, there was a big world outside his studies and research. But he had always been certain that it was nothing he wanted to get himself mixed up in. He thought about Melanie. She was still sitting in the county jail, as far as he knew. And what about Bob Haskel: a prisoner in his own home, beleaguered at every step, his lawn covered with geese guano, his wife perennially visiting friends and relatives? Then there was the Bluebird. The mere thought of her came like a stab at his heart. Look what her originality had gotten her. There was a line it seemed you couldn't cross without risking personal difficulty, inconvenience, or in the worst possible case, annihilation. His father wasn't without reason, he reflected. There was a certain comfort in being down there with all the other nails. And now he'd gone and done it again, popped himself right up into hammer range. As the Honda coasted down Talbot Street he forcibly put the meeting with Folker out of his mind. He would cross that bridge when he came to it.

When he entered his apartment he noticed the red light blinking in the twilight. He strode directly to the answering machine and pressed the play button. After a couple seconds of icy static, Valerie's voice came over the speaker, sounding pinched and far away.

"David, Valerie. I've been looking into that construction site. Nothing very definitive yet, but things are looking exceedingly strange. I'll keep you posted. And oh, I took care of your girlfriend down in Bristol. She loves you to death, by the way, the operative word being *death*. . . (laughter). I'll talk to you soon."

Tanaki sat down and looked out the window at the magnolia branches' dark forms moving languidly in the breeze. Valerie's crack about Melanie reverberated in his ears: the operative word being *death*. He thought that he and Melanie had gotten onto a pretty friendly basis before he left the jail. "I guess after being locked up a couple more days—" he thought. Deeply troubled, he felt an urge to apologize for the trouble he had caused her. And then, as he settled back in his overstuffed chair, he wondered why he would feel such concern for someone he had hardly gotten to know. She was attractive, but probably too young for him. And there wasn't much common ground. She seemed the epitome of a local girl, and he was anything but a local boy. All the more reason he couldn't understand why the idea of seeking her out, making things up to her, rose to the foreground of his consciousness until it crowded out every other concern. Even his research. Even the fateful meeting with Folker.

But perhaps that explained it! he thought. The entire thing was a trick his mind was playing, relieving itself of anxieties over real issues in his life by conveniently substituting this tangential concern, and then focusing all its attention there.

It was nine o'clock. He switched on the lamp and picked up a book DeForrest had loaned him: *Albion's Spawn or Caliban's Scourge?: English Colonization in the Chesapeake Deconstructed.*

18
Joe Pasquath

TANAKI WOKE in the morning with one thought on his mind—find Melanie Kersey. Lying in bed, he stared at the ceiling. "If this is a trick my mind is playing on me, it's a damned persistent one," he said out loud. He tried closing his eyes, hoping he would fall into some dream and wake up thinking about getting to work, but it wasn't any good. He couldn't shake the idea of Melanie. He had a feeling that if he could talk to her, explain himself, everything would turn out fine: his research, his difficulties with Folker, even his eel-tracking study. There was nothing logical in that expectation. But it was as real as the sunlight falling on the bedroom floor, as real as the cardinals singing out back.

Of course there were practical difficulties to be considered. He had no idea where he might find Melanie, for instance. He didn't know where she lived, not even remotely. He could ask Valerie, but then again—

In the shower he devised a strategy that wasn't particularly clever but which struck him as such, so unused was he to intrigue. He decided to call Valerie and tell her a white lie, something about having wound up with one of Melanie's belongings. When he returned to his bedroom, wrapped in a towel, he looked at the clock beside the bed. It was seven o'clock. He figured Valerie would still be at home. He searched through the scraps of paper scattered on his nightstand. Only having called Valerie a couple of times, he didn't know her number by heart.

She sounded groggy when she answered. He told her in an unwavering voice that he had found a piece of what looked like Native American jewelry stuck in the laces of the tennis shoes he was wearing the day of his arrest. "I guess it must have fallen while we were on the dozer," he said.

Valerie yawned.

"It looks like an earring" (he was inventing as he went along). "The hook part somehow got caught in the laces of my tennis shoes . . ."

"It's funny you didn't notice it at the time." Another yawn.

"I know. I guess it's the color. It kind of blends in. Anyway, I thought I might be able get her address from you, so I could drop it in the mail."

"It's probably just inexpensive costume jewelry. I don't think you need to worry about it." Valerie's voice was warm, and Tanaki's room suddenly seemed oddly barren.

"I don't know about that," he countered adroitly. "It looks like it could be valuable. After all, I feel like I've given the kid enough grief."

"All right," she said drowsily. "Hold on a minute."

She put down the phone. Tanaki pictured her walking around the room in her nightgown, drowsy and fuzzy, and felt lousy lying to her. She came back on the line.

"David?" She sounded more awake now.

"Yeah, I'm here."

"You're not interested in this girl, are you?"

He tried to sound jocular. "Valerie, come on, I just want to return the poor kid's jewelry."

"Good," she replied, laughing, "because she thinks you're extremely strange."

The address was in Salisbury, one of the larger Eastern Shore towns, about a half hour down the highway toward the beach. Tanaki decided to go there directly after getting dressed and having breakfast. He didn't call first. That would just give Melanie a chance to blow him off. He knew that if he showed up in person she would be more likely to grant him a hearing.

It was going on ten when the Honda pulled up in front of the squat, brick buildings that sat at the end of a road that went nowhere, just after a railroad crossing. There was no one out and about. Everything was quiet except for the sounds of birds in the battered locust trees that stood haphazardly along the dusty street. The sun was bright, but the heat still at a manageable level when he stepped out of the car. He crossed the street, entered the building, and climbed to the second floor. A tousled young woman in a baggy sweatshirt answered the door and looked at him through bleary eyes, straining to make out his features in the dark stairwell.

"Hi, I'm looking for Melanie."

"Who are you?" she asked forthrightly.

"I'm a friend of hers."

"Are you part of the Nanticoke Association?"

He told his second lie of the day

"She's at her grandfather's . . ."

The grandfather lived in a remote area near Chicawan Creek, that tributary of the Nanticoke River around which the Nanticoke Indians' ill-fated reservation was established in colonial days. Tanaki took several blacktop roads past farmsteads and chicken coops before turning onto a dusty, rutted track that ran through pines and hardwoods. As he approached the creek the nature of the forest changed. There was a greater admixture of ash and hackberry, and the pungently sweet odor of damp soil filled the air. An old blue compact was parked against the brush where the rudimentary road ended. He stepped out of the Honda and heard the soft rippling of water. There was a footpath through the woods. A wooden marker in the shape of an arrow, covered with cracked white paint, was affixed to a tree at its head.

The path slowly converged toward the rippling sound as he walked over the moist earth, taking in the profusion of insect and bird calls that filled the woods. After a hundred yards glimpses of a crude dwelling appeared through the trees. He felt uneasy approaching unannounced: an intruder in these quiet precincts, disturbing Melanie's visit to her grandfather. But whatever had propelled him this far—to call Valerie, to take the morning off from his research, to lie shamelessly twice in one day—propelled him onward through the trees.

He needn't have worried about arriving unannounced. As he came around a bend which placed him on a line of sight with the shack he had seen through the forest, a chorus of dog yelps shattered the silence of the woods. Three or four mongrels had mobilized around the end of the path, and they furiously barked at the stranger who leaned against a tree with one hand. Within moments Melanie appeared behind them, peering through the mottled light of the woods. Tanaki stepped into the middle of the path and waved his arm in a broad gesture. He tried to look casual, as if to say, "I was just driving by, thought I'd stop in to say hello . . ."

Melanie strode toward him with yelping dogs preceding her steps. When she was ten or so feet away she asked over the snarling animals, without a trace of friendliness, "What are you doing here?"

He groped for words, indicated the hounds with a searching gesture of one arm. He finally managed to get out, "Could we talk somewhere?"

She turned and walked toward the shack as she spit over one shoulder, "Come on."

The dogs must have picked up a cue from Melanie because they desisted in their persecutions. By the time they all reached the shack, in fact, Tanaki and the hounds had acquainted themselves in the most friendly fashion. When Melanie's grandfather emerged from the low shelter into the clearing which surrounded it, a laughing Tanaki was at the center of a whirl of leaping, yelping mutts.

"Look at that!" the old man exclaimed. He stood by and watched Tanaki cavort with the dogs. "He's not a whit different from these crazy animals of ours!"

Taken aback, Tanaki was certain that the old man was prepared to lay into him. He was about to protest that his intentions toward Melanie were entirely innocent when the old man spoke again.

"That's really beautiful!" the man said, almost to himself. He shook his head and chuckled, and then he turned away and began to lay out the dogs' food.

Tanaki felt Melanie wince at her grandfather's arguably kind remark. The dogs pantingly left Tanaki to attend to their feed.

"This is the guy who got me locked up last week," Melanie said coldly.

Her grandfather looked up from the dogs' dishes. "You don't say?" He gave Tanaki a good looking-over. "Let me shake your hand." The old man stood and proffered his hand to Tanaki. "You done my granddaughter an immeasurable favor."

"I don't know about that," a nonplussed Tanaki replied. He felt another wince from Melanie's direction. The old man continued.

"Sure you did," he said. "I passed a spell in the county lockup myself once upon a time. And I can tell you, until you been caged, you really don't know what it's worth to be free!"

The old man's remark created a sort of void, what is sometimes called angels passing. In that silence Tanaki looked around and noticed that the old man's shack sat only a few yards from Chicawan Creek. It was a low structure of board which, had it ever been painted, showed no lingering signs of the operation. It had the appearance of being built in stages, with no unity of design between subsequent additions. Whatever integrity the homestead possessed was on account of the tatterdemalion appearance of the whole. There were a few chickens pecking in the dirt and a wire cage in the back. A canoe lay in a patch of weeds near the creek.

"By the way," the old man said, "My name is Joe Pasquath."

Turning slowly, Tanaki briefly took Pasquath in. Short, with a thin and wiry frame, his gray hair straggled over his ears and overlapped his collar in the back. His sunken cheeks, bony jaw, and knobby chin were covered with a prickly white stubble. He wore a pair of baggy old jeans and, in spite of the heat, a loose-fitting flannel shirt.

Tanaki introduced himself. Joe invited him in and asked Melanie to make some coffee; she preceded them over the threshold and disappeared into the dimness of the shack. Joe offered Tanaki a seat in the cabin's main room and, evincing a curiosity that Tanaki found surprising, soon had the young biologist carefully detailing his work at the Center. He listened intently, while Melanie stood in an adjoining alcove brewing java, as Tanaki outlined all of his elaborate plans and scientific procedures. After Tanaki enthusiastically described his eel experiment, Joe asked him to wait. He scrambled up, went through a doorway that came off the room at an odd angle, and returned with a cylindrically shaped piece of basketry about three feet long. He held it in front of his chest, with one hand on either end.

"Ever seen one of these?" He stretched the object toward Tanaki so that he might examine it more closely.

Tanaki revolved the cylinder in his lap, scrutinized both ends.

"Looks like some kind of trap." He glanced at Melanie for reasons he couldn't explain. She was pouring coffee from a steel kettle she had just removed from a kerosene burner.

Joe nodded his head and smiled eagerly. "That's right. And you can have it."

Tanaki wasn't sure what he would do with it. After all, he wasn't much of a collector. He began to protest, "No, I really couldn't . . ."

"Go ahead," the old-timer said. "You can catch your eel in it."

Tanaki didn't want to hurt the old man's feelings, tell him that the Center had far more sophisticated devices for trapping eels. He was about to thank him for the gift when Joe continued. "I know you got plenty of fancy devices for capturing animals at the research station. But I'll bet none of em's got the kind of power this thing's got."

Melanie brought over the coffee. "Grandpa," she said as she set the cups on a table, "I doubt this guy's into that kind of stuff. He's what you'd call the scientific type." She shot Tanaki a glance and walked back to the alcove.

Tanaki was about to protest, not out of any real disagreement with Melanie's remark, but because he didn't want to seem disrespectful to the elder Pasquath. But Joe preempted his response.

"Don't worry," Pasquath said. "I know all about scientists. They believe in their own kind of magic. Only it doesn't always work!" The old man slapped his thighs and broke into a spasm of hearty laughter. Then, as if to make certain Tanaki not read any bitterness into his observation, he came over and patted him on the shoulder. Tanaki smiled gamely; he was willing to take a little teasing.

"The real reason I came," he said, "was to apologize for having stuck my nose—obviously unsuccessfully—into Melanie's business the other week."

Melanie was tidying up the kitchen counter. "What's the point?" she asked. "It's over and done with."

"I'm not so sure about that," Tanaki responded earnestly.

Joe shifted his gaze from Melanie to Tanaki as each spoke, observing every nuance of their exchange unabashedly, almost . . . scientifically.

Tanaki continued, but with evident difficulty. "I don't know what's been getting into me lately. I end up doing something impulsively, without thinking ahead . . ."

"What's wrong with that?" Joe interjected.

Melanie laughed. She came back into the room and stood over the men with her hands on her hips. "It would appear to be some kind of control-freak thing, Grampa."

"What's wrong with that?" Joe repeated.

Melanie didn't respond, but her face twisted into a frustrated grimace.

Tanaki had come to conciliate, not to fan the flames of further controversies. "Actually, Melanie has a point," he said. "I am a bit of a control freak, to be honest."

Melanie's expression softened, but only slightly.

"It's part of my work," Tanaki said. He groped in his mind for words to deploy. "Or maybe my work is part of me, I don't know. Control, when it comes right down to it, is largely what science is all about . . . trying to gain some control over this crazy universe we all call home."

Tanaki's remark hung in the air a moment, and then Joe spoke.

"But the more science we get," he said in a musing tone, and to no one in particular, "the more things seem to be going haywire."

Melanie sat down with the men. Joe then turned to Tanaki.

"Don't get me wrong," he went on. "You scientists have some pretty amazing medicine. Jet planes, satellites, all that. Some of you guys are even trying to save the Bay. That's undeniably powerful. But still, everything seems to be heading downhill." Joe fixed his eyes on the floor for a moment, and then he suddenly raised them, as if freshly inspired. "Maybe it's because everybody's sitting around staring at their televisions. They don't notice what's going on! No matter how hard you try and save the Bay, as long as people are staring at that box, you'll never win. They can't feel the Bay through that box. They can't smell the earth." The old man took a deep draught of creekside air through uplifted nostrils.

Tanaki was beginning to feel uncomfortable. But before he could indulge the sensation, Joe stood up and again patted him on the shoulder.

"You're a nice boy," he said. "You'd be good for Morning Moon."

Tanaki was so embarrassed that he hardly registered that Joe had revealed Melanie's Indian name. "Morning Moon," for her part, maintained a steady cool as she said sardonically, "Grampa, I think you're losing it."

Driving back to Cambridge Tanaki tried to focus on the projects that awaited him at the lab. He and Reynolds had tests to run on the radio transmitters, for one thing. And there were those trips to the lower Bay, if only he could find some way around Folker's blasted interference . . .

But his mind kept drifting back to Joe Pasquath, and more specifically, to the moment when he had handed him the wicker eel trap, which now lay on the passenger seat beside him. That image, full-blown and fulgent, kept reappearing at interstices in his thoughts like the through-line of some ephemeral fugue. It pulled at him so hard, in fact, that he finally gave himself over to it, allowed the memory of that transaction to completely occupy his mind. Then, after a moment or two, this first image began to alternate with another, similar image. As in the first one, he was receiving an object from an old man. Only Tanaki was still a teenager, and the old man wasn't Melanie's grandfather.

It was his own.

This second image soon grew to transcendent proportions, absorbing all of Tanaki's attention, except for the small parcel of awareness needed to keep the Honda moving in its appointed lane. The sun was bright, and Tanaki and his grandfather were on a fishing pier. His grandfather was handing him a bucket full of mullet.

Tanaki's thoughts raveled back through time and memory to that distant summer of his fourteenth year. He had gone to California to spend a couple of weeks with his grandparents. He hadn't seen much of them growing up, and his parents feared that if he didn't visit them soon, he might never have the chance; they were getting on in years, and neither was in the best of health.

He could picture his grandfather perfectly. Short and stocky, close-cropped white hair. His mottled skin weathered by years working in the California sun: first on his farm; and then, after the war, doing landscaping work. He took Tanaki fishing several times during that summer's visit. But what emerged from the depths of Tanaki's memory about this particular day was a conversation about the youth of Tanaki's father. Tanaki son had never really thought about the fact that his father had once been young himself. His father had never said much about his youth, and it had never occurred to Tanaki to ask.

The boy Tanaki saw his father, first and foremost, as a rule-maker, the source of all the strictures he tried so hard to abide in his yet callow life. He was the prophet of the nail that sticks up, a guy who had figured out the system and now went steadily about his life as an industrial engineer. There were enigmas, certainly, the odd moment when the guard came down, like the night he had to be rushed to the hospital with an inflamed prostate, when he sat groaning on the bed, drenched in sweat and suffering, wrapped in the wet towels Tanaki's mother repeatedly replaced to bring down the fever.

But these episodes were few and far between, and did little to challenge Tanaki's view of the family patriarch as a guy who had things under control.

The male camaraderie that emerged on fishing trips brought him closer to his father's most elemental, inarticulate being. But it didn't tell him much about Ken Tanaki's private thoughts or experiences. So when his grandfather began to reminisce about the days before his father was his father, but was simply Kenny Tanaki, Tanaki listened with rapt attention. He somehow knew that he was receiving a precious gift, one that would never be offered again.

It started with fish.

"Your Pa always loved fishing trips," the old man said, sending his line reeling gaily out over the water.

"Me, too," Tanaki enthused.

His grandfather sighted down his line, checked how it lay, and then gave it a gentle tug.

"Now that I think about it," the old man ruminated, "being so far away from water probably didn't make that camp any easier for him."

"Camp?" Tanaki's parents had never made any but the most elliptical allusions to their experiences as captives of the United States government during the Second World War.

The old man swiveled his head slyly toward his grandson. "What? Your folks never told you about the internment camp?"

"There was something about it in Social Studies class once," Tanaki said. "But when I brought it up with Mom and Dad, they said it was over and done with, and that I should just forget about it."

The old man gave his line another tug, gently slipped the

reel a little. "I can understand your pa not wanting to talk about it." He smiled ironically as he reeled in his line and recast. "We all hated that camp. But your pa got more, well, more steamed up about it than the rest of us."

"Really?" Tanaki remarked incredulously. His father—with his corporate suits, his briefcase, his steady, workmanlike approach to everything—seemed too collected to have ever been *steamed up* about anything.

"Believe me," the old man went on, "I knew how he felt." He peered into the distant haze. "It wasn't easy for your grandma and me, either, selling our farm for pennies to the dollar. Folks come round and offer next to nothing for what we'd spent our entire lives working for. They knew we only had a week to pack up and get out. They were getting what they wanted all along, anyway. To get rid of us Japs."

Tanaki stiffened. His grandfather freed one hand and squeezed him hard over the top of the shoulder. He laughed through clenched teeth at his erstwhile neighbors' stupid pettiness.

"But what about Dad and that camp?" Tanaki was impatient to hear more about his father's hidden histories.

Tanaki's grandfather brought his line to his mouth, used his teeth to break it so that he could attach another hook. "For starters," he said, "they put us out in Arizona. And let me tell you, boy, that desert sun beat down on you like a broiler. As for your pa, well, he couldn't get over the fact they made us Japanese live in those internment camps. It was more of a shock for the younger ones, I suppose, than for us older folks. We'd gone through the Alien Land Law, the Asian Exclusion Act, and just more plain meanness. I don't know, maybe we still had more of that old *gaman* spirit in us."

"*Gaman?*" Tanaki repeated, his face screwed up in confusion. "What's that?"

The old man tossed his rebaited line into the water, let it float free for a moment. He was thinking, translating from the sounds of his boyhood to the language of his adopted country. "*Gaman?*" he finally said. "It means sticking it out, no matter what. Even with everything working against you." Tugging determinedly on his reel, he grew more animated. "Just stick to the job you've been given, and try to ignore the problems. No matter what the obstacles are, just keep trying!"

"It bugs me when I hear things like 'slant-eyes,'" Tanaki suddenly confided.

"It was even worse in your pa's day," the old man said. "The rotten ones at school would call him Chink right to his face. And when farms went up for sale, people put up signs that said 'Japs Stay Out.' Your grandma and me told Kenny to ignore it, just to concentrate on his studies. He was an American citizen. Not a foreigner, like us. It was a free country, I told him, and if he showed them that he was good as anybody else, they'd have to let him succeed."

They were silent for a moment. Tanaki's grandfather reeled in his line. "I'm not sure I believed it myself," he confessed with a chuckle, "but what else could we say?"

The old man crouched down over the mullet bucket, took one of the creatures out, gutted it, and began to cut bait. As he worked, occasionally throwing pieces of offal over the rail to frantically squawking gulls, he spoke quietly to his grandson, recounting ancient legends . . .

"The trouble started," he began, "at the camp school. Your pa, you see, he wouldn't sing that song with everybody. What's it called, 'Tis of thee?' 'My country,' that's the part Kenny didn't like. He said if it was his country, why was he locked up in some stinking cage?

"Your grandma and me had to go to the school and talk to the principal. We were worried sick. We were sure your dad was ruining his chances. I tried to talk to him, get him to cool his jets. I told him that the nail that sticks up gets hammered down. But he wouldn't listen. He said, real excited, 'You told me to concentrate on my studies, and I would succeed. And now look! The only thing my blessed concentration has gotten me is a concentration camp!' I got so mad I did something I never did before. I hit him right smack across the face. Hard as I could."

Tanaki's grandfather stopped speaking and gazed out over San Francisco Bay. His mouth tightened, like he was trying to swallow but couldn't. There was nothing but the sound of waves roiling below the pier, punctuated by the seabirds' antic cries. He arranged the freshly cut bait pieces on an old rag and gave one to Tanaki. Then he stood up and baited his own hook.

"After that, after I struck him," the old man took up again, and he brought his arm back in a soft arcing motion before swinging it effortlessly forward, "your pa started to stay away from home. Later I found out that he was hanging with some of these camp boys who wanted to fight the system. You know, not cooperate with the authorities . . ."

Tanaki, trying his best to imitate his grandfather's artful cast, slung his line awkwardly out over the railing. The rustling of the waves against the pier, the sun piercing through the deep blue air, fluffy white clouds that banked one upon one another in the northern reaches: they all seemed to yearn for the story to continue, to draw it inexorably from the far reaches of the grandfather's mind . . .

"One day they came round to recruit boys for the war," the old man took up again. He shifted his stance to maneuver his line, squared himself solidly to the rail. "It was this sergeant, as I recall, came by our place. And if you can picture it, no sooner had the guy got out three words than your pa moved right up in his face. I'll always remember how he said it. 'What do you take us for,' your dad said, 'a bunch of idiots? You classify me enemy alien, and then you lock me up like some wild beast. And now you expect me to volunteer for your god-forsaken suicide squad, so I can get my butt shot off for your so-called democracy. I've got to hand it to you, though. That's really going some, for sheer brass!'"

The old man chuckled and spit over the railing, relishing the memory of his son's reckless gutsiness. Tanaki, for his part, was mesmerized by this new image of his father—now sedately ensconced in corporate America—speaking Truth to Power. He urged his grandfather to go on.

"I was so mad," the old man said, "I could hardly see straight. I was dead sure they would arrest him after that. Maybe take it out on the rest of the family, too. But I couldn't talk to your pa. He quit listening to me, after that time I smacked him."

The grandfather stopped speaking, closed his eyes and collected himself for a moment. "You know about your Uncle Frank?"

"I always heard he died in the war."

"Yeah, that's right." A new silence now arose, engulfing both the boy and his grandfather. Then, after a moment, the old man looked down on Tanaki. "I don't guess anybody ever told you the rest of the story?"

"I don't think so," Tanaki replied.

JOE PASQUATH

The grandfather let out a sigh. He reeled in for a moment and then, as he began to speak, just let his line drift. "After your pa dressed that sergeant down," he recounted soberly, "everything got real quiet around our section of the barracks. Me, well, I was still mad as hell. And your pa—when he was at home, which wasn't too often—wasn't talking to anybody. As for your grandma, she would just pace around the cabin, stewing all day. She was worried sick about me and Kenny fighting, for one thing. On top of that, she was scared as hell about what the authorities might do if they found out what your pa was up to with those new pals of his. She tried her best to make peace between us. But I wouldn't give an inch, and neither would your pa."

The old man looked over the bay, and he bit hard into his lower lip. He reeled his line a little, let it out again. He felt his grandson beside him, felt the boy of his blood glancing at him, wanting the story's end, thirsting to receive the sacred family sorrows . . .

"The way Frank was," the old man began again after a moment, "he could never stand to see anybody upset. He was like that. A sweet kid; easy going. And man was he fast. Always number one in track . . .

"Anyway, I guess the tensions around the shack finally got to him. Because one day, without saying a word to anybody, he went over to the recruiter's office and enlisted. He never said it, but I know he figured that if he signed on, they'd let the rest of us be. Well, your grandma was beside herself. And your pa, when he found out, he tried to talk Frankie out of it. He even said that he'd go in his place. But it was too late, Frankie had signed up, and they had him for good."

"What happened then?" Tanaki's voice was filled with awe

and dread.

The old man spoke slowly, precisely. "Your pa was right about those suicide squads. Frank was in the 442nd Division. All Japanese. They put those guys up against the toughest Nazi troops in Italy. And man, they got chewed up real bad."

Tanaki could hear the old man's throat tightening. He saw the thin film of tears on the skin below his eyes. After peering into the water for a moment, his grandfather abruptly raised his face to the sky.

"But they did us proud," he said, choking back tears. "The most decorated damned unit in the whole, filthy war." He loudly cleared his throat and collected himself. There was a pull on his line. He reeled feverishly but lost it. He gathered his line in and began to rebait it.

"When your pa heard about Frank," he went on, clenching his teeth as he forced the hook into a chunk of mullet, "he wanted to kill some Nazis like nobody's business. Marched over to the recruiting office in a big huff. But they already had him marked for a troublemaker, and they wouldn't take him."

Tanaki exhaled loudly. "I never knew a thing about any of this!"

The old man laughed quietly. "Yeah, it's funny some of the things parents don't think their kids ought to know." He glanced toward his grandson. "It's like when your pa was a boy. I didn't make much of the troubles your grandma and I went through when we first came to America. The way they spit on us at the docks. Crowds gathered around with signs that said, 'Japs Go Home.' I didn't want to spoil his view of his native country. But you know, maybe if I'd been more realistic, that camp wouldn't have been such a shock to his system."

Now they fished in silence awhile, until Tanaki's grandfather began, out of the blue, to speak again.

"Not long after Frank died," the old man took up now, digging to the depths of his being, determined to finish this gift of past to his grandson, "something really strange happened. I was out by the border of the camp, looking at the desert through this chain-link fence. Sometimes, you see, I'd go out there where it was quiet, just stand there and let my mind wander. There was something about looking out over all that land. It reminded me, I guess, that there was more world out there, outside the camp.

"Anyway," he went on after a moment, "it was getting near evening. That's the time of day when your eyes can really play tricks on you. Especially in the desert . . ."

Tanaki's grandfather shifted his rod to his left hand, and he brushed the bottom of his nose vigorously with the back of his right index finger as if trying to dislodge something, but there was nothing there. He shifted the rod again and wiped the back of his left hand slowly and solemnly across his mouth. He seemed to choke up a little, but he fixed his eyes resolutely on his line and tugged and pulled, reeled and relaxed, and finally he began to speak again.

"I was just standing by that fence," he said, "looking off into the desert, when I saw something moving toward me. It was real small at first, in the distance, and I couldn't tell what it was. But then, as it got closer, I could see that it was a person, walking. I just stared, because I couldn't figure who would be out there. I mean, there was nothing but desert for miles around. Then, after another minute or two, I could tell that they were wearing military fatigues, so I figured it was part of the camp guard. Well, that's when this guy, whoever it was, started to run. Straight at me, with a big smile on his face. And then I recognized who it was. But it couldn't be! It was Frankie! Running toward me, his arms spread wide, like he was going to give me a big hug or something. Then, as soon as I realized it was him, he up and disappeared on me.

"It was just a mirage," the old man concluded, "but I cried like a damn baby."

Tanaki was half way across the Choptank bridge before he realized that he had passed Cambridge. As he turned at a break in the median, he saw his grandfather standing at that concertina wire–topped fence in the lonely Arizona desert. He thought about Joe Pasquath's remark: "Until you been caged, you don't know what it's worth to be free."

When he got home he found a note from the Yamaguchi sisters taped to his door jamb. It was an invitation to "Sea Festival and Dinner" for the coming weekend. Wondering what "sea festival" might be, he wrote a short response on the same piece of notepaper, light blue with pastel flowers around the border, walked up the creaking stairs to the third floor, and taped it to the sisters' door with the original piece of scotch tape.

19
Sea Festival

SATURDAY MORNING Tanaki walked to Yamaguchi Enterprises. The building was festooned with bunting, and a couple dozen modern fishing boats crowded around the docks with bright pennants flying from their spars and bridges. He walked through the front office and into the large, cavernous processing area behind. Some hundred feet away, Setsuko gave instructions to a crowd of fifty or more men; they shook their heads in acknowledgment or just calmly listened. Tanaki thought of Margaret Brent handling the mutinous soldiers after Ingels' Rebellion . . .

Not wanting to get in the way of company business, he stayed near the door to the front office, quietly observing. One of the company's vessels bobbed gently at an indoor slip; it was decorated with banners and pennants like the ones in the harbor. Nariko emerged from around a corner and greeted him. She seemed in a good mood. There was a sort of glow he had never before noticed.

She took him by the arm and led him to where Setsuko and her employees now milled toward the Ebisu shrine on the opposite wall. Nariko and Tanaki stopped short of the melée of movement that engulfed the god's abode. With Setsuko directing every move, the men split into four groups. Each group laid hold to one of the carrying posts, like those of a palanquin, that extended from each corner of the ornate structure. On Setsuko's three-count they crouched to maneuver the poles onto their shoulders and heaved the god into the air. Ebisu, though sorely bobbled, remained undisturbed, smiling in his maniacally gleeful way throughout the operation.

The deity was maneuvered to the boat in the interior dock, and with much grunting and groaning, much sidestepping and twisting and turning, was placed in a prominent position on the bow, face forward. The Yamaguchi crews secured the shrine with boat lines and dispersed to take up positions on the vessels Tanaki had seen in the harbor, which comprised the entire strength of Yamaguchi Enterprise's Chesapeake fleet.

Setsuko and Nariko escorted Tanaki onto the boat containing Ebisu and Setsuko directed the skipper to get underway. The boat backed out of the hangar and proceeded slowly through Cambridge harbor with the remainder of the Yamaguchi fleet falling in behind. When the flotilla emerged into the Choptank it headed for the Bay. It was a bright August day, with slowly drifting cumuli in the sky and just enough choppiness on the surface to make it interesting. The pennants flapped gaily in a winsome breeze as, for the next several hours, the vessels marked a wide circuit through the estuary at the leisurely pace of a royal procession. The god Ebisu led the way, his head jutting forward, a fishing rod in his right hand, a squirming sea bream clutched under his left arm. When the fleet anchored around noon, the combined crews joined the Yamaguchi sisters and Tanaki on the flagship for a feast, the preparation of which was supervised by the sisters in the ship's galley. It was terribly festive with the breeze ruffling the pennants, the colorful seafood, warm sake, hearty companions, and a karaoke contest in which Tanaki was persuaded to belt out a hammy rendition of *Feelings*.

Before directing her fleet to again get underway, Setsuko climbed to the bridge and addressed her employees. She first reminded them of the purpose of the day's festivities—an expression of gratitude for the bounty of the sea, upon which everyone associated with Yamaguchi Enterprises depended for their livelihoods. Then she removed a roll of FAX paper from the back pocket of her jeans and said: "I also have a message from our father that I'd like to share with you." She unrolled the paper. "I offer my greetings and wish you good cheer on the day of your sea festival," she began. "And I offer my humble gratitude to the *kami* for all they have done for my family and for our company. It has been over thirty years since I founded Yamaguchi Enterprises, with only one boat and the dream to provide my fellow human beings with nourishment from the sea. Japan was still suffering from the effects of the tragic war, but I knew that the *kami* would not fail to provide for our needs if we worked with pure hearts. And now I am amazed at what has been accomplished. Our fleet of ocean-going vessels is one of the world's largest, and when I visit Tsukiji, our great fish market here in Tokyo, it fills my heart to see so many buyers crowded around our auctioneer as he chants out all the seafood we have on offer. I am proud of everyone who makes this possible, and I feel a special affection for our employees at the Chesapeake branch, who work so hard with my two daughters. They tell me that you have taken the words of our credo to heart: 'sharing both good times and bad, we will cooperate, and not forget to encourage one another.'"

Setsuko stuck the paper under her arm and called out, "Let's give ourselves a big hand." She clapped at her employees while they in turn cheered and hooted. Nariko, who had come to her side, took the fax paper from her sister and, when the tumult had abated, turned to the assembled watermen.

"Before we go, there's a little more here. . ." she started shyly. "I'd like to read it to you."

The sailors strained to hear Nariko's small voice over the big and raucous Bay.

"There is a shrine at the Tsukiji fish market," Nariko read gently, caressing each of her adored papa-san's words as though it were his hand, his forehead. "Each day the shrine's priests offer prayers to . . . console the souls of the fish who have . . . offered their lives for our benefit. Unfortunately, many of our fellow human beings, even my own . . . countrymen, are not taking good care . . . of the life of the seas. I am afraid that," she struggled, "if this continues, we will be in for a painful . . . rectification. That is why Yamaguchi Enterprises does not engage in fishing practices that. . . endanger the survival of any species. And you have my promise . . . that we will never change . . . our policy. I will continue to work with our . . . foundation to bring better . . . regulation to the fishing industry."

The Bay seemed to have grown ghastly quiet. Nariko stared at the shiny fax paper. Tears had come to her eyes, whether from the contemplation of man's failure to appreciate Nature's gifts, or at the thought of her sorely missed Chichi-san, it could not be said. In any case, as the sailors watched on, beginning to feel a little sad themselves, Setsuko gently took the fax paper from her sister's hands and, putting an arm around her shoulder, addressed their crews.

"Father closes," she said cheerily: "Today I hope you enjoy the beauty of the sea and feel the manifold blessings of its bounty. Sincerely, Matsuo Yamaguchi."

There was a cheer for the venerable founder, and then the crews dispersed to their various boats and continued their procession through the Bay. It was late afternoon when the colorful flotilla chugged up the Choptank toward Cambridge. The expansive summer light was softening; the god Ebisu seemed just as jubilant to be returning home as he had been to venture forth. After returning the god to his customary place, where he would remain until another year of seasons had passed across the face of the Bay, the employees of Yamaguchi Enterprises went their separate ways. The Yamaguchi sisters and Tanaki walked up Talbot Street. They were weary from a day in the sun, but each felt a fullness that only wished to be expended in some noble and generous action.

Tanaki felt right at home as he sat on a tatami in the room that glowed of sunsets. He could hear the crackle of grilling flesh and smell a mélange of aromas, a mixture of seaweed and brine, fish and sesame oil, and the charring juices that dripped from the cooking fillets. Intermingling with it all was the scent of the perfume that, like so much else, the two women shared.

He reflected on the many evenings he had spent with them during the spring and summer: walking through the neighborhood or down to the river to watch the swans; sitting on the porch; or retiring to the backyard where someone had long ago established an intimate garden with statues and stone benches, a fountain that no longer worked, and a trellis covered with unruly roses whose scarlet petals littered the flagstone walkway. He remembered the *O-bon* festival, watching the *toro* lanterns float into the river, and the sisters in their kimonos.

Surrounded by the aromas of cooking food, he also recalled

a couple of memorable meals. One evening they had served him carp:

"We hope you like it," Setsuko had said. "It was Nariko's idea."

Nariko blushed. Tanaki glanced at her and decided that she looked more vulnerable than ever.

"It's sort of . . . for boys day," she had said into her plate as she clamped a clump of noodles in her chopsticks.

"Boys day?" Tanaki asked.

Setsuko stepped in to explain, as usual. "Of course we realize you're not a boy. But Nariko was concerned that, since you never had a boys day, it might be good for you."

Nariko seemed to shrink into herself. Setsuko continued, "You've never had one, have you?"

He assured them that he had never heard of the rite.

"You've never seen the photographs?" she asked incredulously. "Those colorful paper tubes, like big fish, that everyone hangs on power lines and roofs?"

"When you look up at the blue sky," Nariko added, "it's like the sea, full of carp . . . swimming in the wind." The sisters held their arms overhead. They swayed and swam back and forth, being the fish.

"You know," Nariko said with a tone of great seriousness, "only the carp could fight its way past the rapids."

"Yeah, that's how the legend goes." Setsuko turned to Tanaki. "According to the myth, only the carp had the determination to make it upstream, to be transformed thereby into a dragon." Now the girls metamorphosed into dragons, making ferocious faces and noises. Tanaki scowled and snorted back at them until they all collapsed in laughter.

"I'm afraid it's a little late for boys day," Setsuko said as she reached for her sake cup. "It should be celebrated on the third of March. But I imagine this will do."

"What about girls?" Tanaki had asked. "Didn't you females have a special day of your own?"

"*Dolls* day," Setsuko said wryly. "We got to set up these cheesy dolls in front of the family altar, and then we had to fix dinner for everyone. Some holiday."

"And peach blossoms . . ." Nariko began, "symbols of"—the two women looked at each other, holding back laughter, and then completed the thought in unison—"grace and gentleness!"

When they finished laughing, Setsuko said, "Needless to say, we liked boys day better."

On another occasion clams and abalone had been on the menu:

"Clams," Setsuko had said pertly as she placed several on Tanaki's plate. "The symbol of union."

Tanaki looked at the mollusks, watery and soft in their half-opened shells, and suddenly understood. "Ah—two joined shells."

"Exactly," Setsuko replied as she lowered herself onto her tatami. "That's why we Japanese always serve them at weddings."

Then Nariko had spooned several of the abalone onto his plate, their shells rattling against the china. "These abalone are symbols of—"

" –unrequited love," Setsuko provided matter-of-factly.

"Of course," Tanaki replied. He picked up one of the large snails to examine it closely. "One shell."

"We used to give them as . . . offerings . . . to the *kami*," Nariko added. "The meat was cut in strips, and dried, and attached to the gifts at shrines. Now we use . . . folded strips of paper instead. I guess they're cheaper."

"Interesting," Tanaki proffered, still examining the specimen. "It is the symbol of unrequited love that you offer to the *kami*?"

Now, on this night, the evening of the Sea Festival, eel was on the menu. Fatigued from his day's outing in the sun, Tanaki was reclined on his elbows when Setsuko and Nariko followed one another out of the kitchen. They carried trays packed with steaming dishes. He pulled himself up and commented on the delicious aroma that accompanied the meal into the room.

"Eel, for the ox days!" Setsuko announced ceremoniously. She lowered the first tray onto the table in the middle of the room.

"It helps . . . to stand the heat," Nariko said.

"I hope you don't mind eating it," Setsuko teased coyly. "We know how very fond you are of the poor creatures."

"Let's see." Tanaki picked through the dish with his chopsticks. "This doesn't appear to be one of my personal acquaintances . . ."

Nariko smiled at him and blushed.

"We were going to prepare it *kabayaki* style," Setsuko added. "But we decided an *unadon* would be more informal. I'm afraid Nariko was a little disappointed that she couldn't break out the lacquered boxes."

On the table were three large bowls filled with jagged chunks of eel meat, all half-submersed in a cloudy broth. The sisters had steamed the locally caught fish the evening before and cut them into long fillets. "Steaming removes the oils," Setsuko explained, "makes them nice and tender." While Tanaki listened to them crackle under the grill from the living room, they had basted them with soy sauce and sweet rice wine. Three smaller bowls contained a soup of eel liver, soy, burdock root and cooked egg.

Carefully sampling the pungently delectable eel meat, Tanaki couldn't help muse over a more fortunate specimen: alive and free, it bided its time in some quiet corner of the estuary, already knowing that this would be its last season around the Bay. It could feel its body changing, its eyes bulging, its skin undergoing a brilliant alteration—a still undiscovered creature to whom Tanaki had attached the most extravagant dreams of adventure and glory!

Setsuko interrupted his reveries. "The *unadon* style was invented at the Floating World, you know. That's what the history books say, anyway." She fixed her gaze on a darkening window. "All those sixteenth century Edo merchants, what a crazy bunch they must have been. And such an interesting departure. From Buddhist renunciation, to wine, women, and song!"

"*Ukiyo*," Nariko intoned, evoking the power of the original term.

"Yes," Setsuko added enthusiastically. "A world, not solid and anchored, but *floating*. Always changing. Tragically without permanence." She looked at Nariko with an amused smile. "That was the traditional Buddhist concept, anyway."

"But—" Nariko tried to interject, but to complicate her usual difficulties, her mouth was stuffed with eel, and Setsuko finished her thought. "But," she said, looking toward her sister with a smile on her lips, "the Edo merchants looked at it, oh, I guess, a little differently."

"Sumo, geishas, Kabuki . . ." Nariko managed.

"Right. Those merchants figured, "Hey, if this world is

floating, if it's all going to evaporate like so much dust in the wind, we had better party hearty while we can!"

The sisters laughed together while Nariko filled Tanaki's sake cup.

He lifted the cup to his lips. "You know," he said, "nothing ever stays the same in an ecosystem. In a way, that's what's so fascinating about it. And what about migration? It's all about movement. Everything in nature is always shifting, reorganizing itself. I see how transience can be sad. But it's also exhilarating. In fact, I think I prefer things that way."

Setsuko raised her cup in a toast. "David," she said, "with some luck, we may make a Japanese out of you yet."

Tanaki spiraled his cup up in a twisted way, making his best clown face, and then downed the sake in a single gulp.

20
Seabreeze, Inc.

WHILE TANAKI SPENT his summer deepening his acquaintance with the Bay and the Yamaguchi sisters, Valerie pursued her investigations into the construction site where had occurred the most dramatic gesture of Tanaki's life. After securing Melanie Kersey's release in Bristol County, she had stopped in Annapolis to look into "Seabreeze, Inc." in the state's incorporation records. This led to a paper trail of Byzantine complexity. Seabreeze was owned by a corporation called Tidewater Properties, which was owned by Bay Enterprises, which in turn was owned by . . . and so on. As far as she had been able to make out, there were fourteen separate corporations involved in either a pyramidal or laterally interlocking network of ownership. For days and weeks she sat at worn tables in dingy rooms poring over land transactions and corporate statements. She was determined to unravel a conundrum she had decided could not be allowed to exist in the same universe as herself; in the same universe as the law school, with all the sensible weight of *stare decisus* behind it; in the same universe with the sun-blessed beach; in the same universe with the glorious and glittering Bay.

She phoned Tanaki over Labor Day weekend. "Something very strange is going on out there," she said. "There's a determined, clandestine effort underway to buy up property along the lower Shore. It's all so complicated, I still haven't gotten to the bottom of it."

"Who's buying it?" Tanaki tried to wrap his mind around what all this might mean. Land transactions were not something he had ever spent much time thinking about.

"It's hard to tell," Valerie replied. "There are a bunch of separate corporations involved, but they're all related. They're probably just fronts for the same enterprise. Whoever it is, they've been very thorough about throwing up a smoke screen around their activities."

"I don't get it," he asked. "What are they trying to hide?"

"Normally," she said, "when you find this kind of clandestine land acquisition going on, it's a sign that a developer wants to obtain a large, unbroken tract. They break into separate enterprises, and these smaller firms buy the land one parcel at a time, keeping everything completely hush-hush. That way they don't drive up prices by letting on that a corporation with deep pockets is interested. It's a fairly common practice. But what bothers me about this situation, is why would anyone be interested in that land, since the legislature has placed a moratorium on development down there?"

Tanaki couldn't fit this legal puzzle into any of the categories by which he customarily sorted out his world. "It sounds funny," he said, "but what does it all add up to?"

"I'm not sure," Valerie said. "I've got a friend who works at the State House. I'll see what I can find out."

"Okay."

There was a brief silence, and then Valerie picked up again. "When I'm finally clear of all this research," she said, "maybe we can get together. You know, have a chance to talk about some other stuff."

Tanaki agreed and signed off. He wondered what *other stuff* might be. He was sure he had detected a certain sultry quality in her parting words—something he hadn't heard since their beer-soaked evening in Ocean City. Was she thinking about giving their relationship another go? He began to lose himself in that intriguing thought, but disturbing reflections came crowding into his mind. Wait a minute, he thought. Corporations gobbling up property along the lower shores of the Bay? That was exactly where Folker had been messing with his research!

The thought of Folker reminded him that he hadn't yet confronted the director with the staff's grievances, as he had promised to do at the canteen meeting. Folker had been away, and then Tanaki had been busy on the water. And then, the more he thought about it, the more he had questioned the wisdom of playing the heavy for the staff. Why had none of the others volunteered, after all? They were interested, Tanaki finally figured out, in something he had failed to take into account: self-preservation. What if Folker up and terminated his fellowship?

Anything was possible.

Yet Valerie's news—all the more disturbing for the mystery of it—was working its way ever deeper into his mind. Though he didn't comprehend it all, he sensed that something terribly wrong was happening, and that something had to be done to stop it, whatever *it* was. Ferreting out hard facts seemed the first step. He had a strong hunch that Sea Breeze, Inc.'s secretive land grab and his problems with Folker were not unrelated. In fact, he thought it not unlikely that Folker held the key to the whole boggling riddle.

He spent the rest of his holiday weekend doing household chores, idling, and mentally turning over the idea of confronting Folker with his concerns. But as he stood beside Reynolds in the Center's shop Tuesday morning, silently examining the latest alterations to the tracking gear, he still hadn't decided what he would do.

"Something's bothering you." Reynolds spoke calmly, not shifting his gaze from a transmitter that he turned from one angle to another.

Tanaki didn't reply. He feared that merely to speak would start the proverbial slide down that slippery slope . . .

"You may as well get it out," Reynolds said, "or it's gonna eat you alive. Just like one of your eel buddies gulping down some soft-shell crab."

Instead of responding, Tanaki excused himself and went to the station's canteen. There he sat for half an hour trying to talk himself out of what he was about to do. He reviewed his career in his mind: the long years of college and graduate school, his doctoral research in Europe, the stint in India, huddled freezing and wet at tundra swan breeding grounds in northern Alaska. He thought of his grand design to follow the eel, and all the rest of his treasured research plans. Realizing that he was about to place every bit of that at risk, he agonized until he couldn't stand as much as one more moment on the horns of this particular dilemma.

He burst into Folker's office and began to speak without bothering to greet him.

"Guy, there are a number of us on the staff who would like to know what's going on around here." He was breathing funny and his face was flushed. Like most people who normally avoid confrontations, he was little practiced in the art of conducting them elegantly.

"Dave, what on earth are you talking about? Please, sit down."

Tanaki didn't move. "We'd like to know what's behind all of these restrictions on our research. Go here, don't go there. My plan for the season is seriously compromised. And I'm not alone." Though he knew it wasn't for the best, his voice was rising.

"Dave, please, you're getting yourself overwrought. Come on, sit down."

Tanaki took a seat in the leatherette chair that faced Folker's desk, inwardly vowing not to leave without an answer. "Listen Guy," he said, "there's something strange going on"—he heard himself echoing Valerie's words—"I know it, and I'm sure you do, too."

He noted a crack in Folker's composure, an awkward hesitation before responding. "Dave, there are things that it's not important for you to know. Administrative matters, boring stuff. That's why I'm here. To take care of that kind of business, so you guys can have your hands free to do the science. That's what you want, isn't it?"

"I want to go down to the lower Bay and finish my work in those salt grass meadows."

Folker swiveled around to face a window that looked out on the Bay. He seemed at a loss for words.

"Who's buying up all that land down there?" Tanaki shot at him.

Folker's chair spun back around as if driven by an unseen hand. His voice was now tremulous. "Dave," he said, "I don't know how to tell you this, but you're treading on sensitive ground here. Very sensitive. And if I were you, I'd try to go along and get along. There are bigger players than you—bigger than me, too—in this game."

Tanaki looked at him in stunned silence.

"Listen," Folker went on, "I don't know about you, but I've got a mortgage, and a wife, and kids. I care about my job. This isn't my research center, and it isn't yours. We're hired to do a job. I follow orders from the folks who sign my paycheck. I'd advise you to do the same."

The tremor in Folker's voice was gone. His face had grown red, his attitude hardened. Tanaki sensed that he wouldn't get any further with him.

"So that's it," he said as he rose to go. "You're taking orders from the folks who sign your paycheck?"

"I'd advise you to do the same," Folker repeated.

Tanaki walked out. He didn't bother to close the door behind him.

21
Chirp!

WHEN TANAKI ARRIVED at Moeller's lab the light was already fading around the soaring spires of Cologne's Gothic cathedral. He hurriedly parked the station's jeep in the graveled space in front and jogged toward the door of the nineteenth century mansion of brick and stone that Moeller had converted into one of the premier centers of avian research in the world. A breeze laden with moisture blew out of the sky to the northeast with a force that told Tanaki the season would soon be changing. The wind struck his face, and with it a fugitive thought crossed his mind: hordes of Swedish starlings—the subjects of his much anticipated study—would soon be heading this way.

He banged the ornate knocker and stepped back, shifting restlessly on the flagging before the entrance. He was preparing to knock again when the door glided open to reveal a weary-seeming Moeller. The older scientist, normally impeccably groomed, needed a shave. The knot of his tie was loosened. His collar was unbuttoned and his jacket rumpled, as if he had slept in his clothes. A few strands of thinning hair fell across his forehead.

The foyer was dark and the hushed establishment possessed a funereal air. Tanaki silently followed Moeller along the hallway leading to the research labs. "She will eat nothing but bird seed." Moeller sounded as horrified as if he had said, "She has become a vampire!" As they advanced toward the laboratory, Tanaki heard the same erratic chirping he had heard over the telephone. Looking neither at Tanaki nor at a large cage that stood nearby, Moeller opened the laboratory door and stepped aside—as if, by doing so, he could step out of the disturbing predicament in which he found himself.

Evening was falling fast, the hour when Zugenruhe—migratory fidgets—reaches its peak. Tanaki watched in sudden horror as the Bluebird hopped wildly about the Zugenruhe cage, the dimensions of which allowed her only limited latitude for movement. She repeatedly threw herself against the sides of the enclosure as her strident chirpings grew in pitch and intensity. Tanaki rushed to the side of the cage.

"All right, Bluebird," he shouted over the chirps, "we get it. The joke's over."

She appeared to take no notice of him.

"Bluebird, come on. You're making me a little nervous now. Besides, Dietrich's not used to these kinds of gags. Give it up!"

She stopped hopping long enough to peer into Tanaki's eyes with the same wildness of the day of the waxwing invasion, that pool of inarticulate infinity. Then she emitted an especially loud chirp. She wore a yellow knit dress and she had done something awful to her hair. It had been cut almost entirely off. What remained stood straight out in little tufts. She possessed the awkward appearance of an unfledged nestling.

Tanaki's concern rapidly mutated into a pervading fear. He looked at Moeller, who was slumped against the wall, still unable to look in the direction of the cage. The famous scientist had been right. This was no joke: something was frightfully wrong with the Bluebird. Tanaki felt a need to do something, anything, to bring back the old Ana—the Bluebird he knew, even with her kookiness and moodiness. But she seemed so unreachable, so alien. What's more, Tanaki's will was beset by horrible misgivings. Perhaps, he suddenly thought, he was complicit in all of this. Wasn't it he who had rushed to pick her up on the day of the waxwing invasion? Hadn't he driven her to remote locations so that she could try to navigate her way back? Hadn't they compared one another to beluga whales and blackpole warblers?

Hadn't he called her "Bluebird?"

Unable to face his reflections alone, Tanaki floated, as if in a dream, to where Moeller crouched against the wall. He asked him how long Bluebird's aberrant behavior had been going on.

"About a week or so," Moeller replied weakly.

"Why didn't you call me sooner!"

"I didn't want to trouble you. I hoped it might—go away."

Tanaki felt more unhappy at that moment then he had ever remembered feeling, afflicted by a pain so intense he thought he might actually cease to exist were it not eradicated. He stormed over to the Zugenruhe cage and shook it frantically.

"Bluebird!" he shouted, "Bluebird!" She appeared not to notice him.

He leaned against the metal of the cage, exhausted with emotion. Finally he quietly pleaded. "Ana. . ." He paused and said it again, "Ana. . ."

Whether it was because the restless time of twilight was passing (the windows of the lab were now mere rectangles of violet darkness); or had to do with the subdued tone of Tanaki's voice (or the evocation of her real name); the Bluebird calmed down. Coming to stand in front of Tanaki, she gazed at him steadily through the wire of the cage. He would have expected her now to speak in the most normal fashion, except for the crazy hair and that look in her eyes—that look in her eyes!

She stood, her arms hung loosely at her sides, and said, "Chirp!"

Tanaki didn't have the power to respond. He looked at her sadly.

"Chirp!"

22
Bay World

THE MORNING AFTER confronting Folker, Tanaki handed Cynthia a request for one of the station's boats. His destination was marked as "Elk Neck and other sites in the upper estuary." He had no particular plan in mind. He had assumed that facing the director, after his agonizing internal struggle, would yield the answers he was looking for. Instead he was left with a greater sense of mystification. Something now told him that the answers, if they were to be had, were out there: out among the wide, blue waters of the Chesapeake.

While he waited for a reply he looked up Mark DeForrest, whom he found in one of the larger labs straining something through a stream of Bay water raucously gushing through a fat steel intake pipe.

"What's up, Mark?"

"Hey!" DeForrest replied as he looked up with surprise. "Just collecting data for one of my studies. What can I do you for?"

"I talked to Folker yesterday."

"Really?" DeForrest said. He laid the strainer on a nearby counter and began carefully to pick through it's contents. "What about?" he asked abstractedly.

"You know," Tanaki said, a little incredulous at DeForrest's seeming cluelessness, "the meeting we all had."

"Oh," DeForrest replied. He turned from his work, took Tanaki by the elbow, and walked a few yards from the counter. "I didn't think you were going to follow through on that." There was a remote quality to his voice, as if his interest were purely academic.

Tanaki didn't know what had gotten into DeForrest. He had been as keen as anyone to get to the bottom of Folker's antics. Now he seemed blithely unconcerned about the entire problem. "Perhaps I should report to Beth. Do you know where she is?"

"You didn't hear?" DeForrest turned suddenly to face Tanaki. "She's not around anymore."

"Not around anymore?"

"It seems that Folker needed someone to represent the Center on this international exchange." DeForrest raised his eyebrows. "Looks like she'll be in Madagascar throughout the winter."

"Madagascar? That seems awfully sudden."

"Seemed that way to me, too. She barely had time to pack her things."

"Do you think this had something to do with the meeting?"

"One would have to assume . . ."

"But how would Folker have found out?"

"There's always one fink in every operation."

Tanaki contemplated the streaming water, which still gushed golden green from the intake pipe. "Damn," he said. "Imagine how she must have felt about leaving her research mid-season!"

"I don't guess she liked it. But she didn't have much choice, did she?" DeForrest made as if to return to his work.

"Listen Mark," Tanaki said, "I didn't learn much from Folker. He told me that he takes orders from the people who sign his checks. He says he's got a mortgage, and kids, and all that bunk."

"Well, I guess I can relate to that. I've got 'em myself." DeForrest walked back over to the basin and Tanaki followed. "But Mark," he said, "where do we go from here?" He strained his voice over the rushing water.

DeForrest turned and faced him. "I'm not sure, partner. Beth was the one spearheading this thing. It looks like she'll be out of commission for a while. As for myself, I'm pretty jammed up with this study." He gestured toward the basin, the counter. "Maybe we ought to let it drop for the time being. What say we talk again in a few weeks?"

After shoving off from the station's dock, Tanaki asked Reynolds to make directly for the opposite shore. When they were well past the channel, beyond the point at which a possibly observing Folker could distinguish the cruiser from other boats—day sailors and cabin cruisers, the odd waterman—cutting along the skin of the Bay, he asked him to rudder hard and make for the lower estuary.

"Okay, Dave," was Reynold's only response, though a broad smile betrayed his pleasure in the unexpected decision.

As the cruiser made for south the traffic thinned out and the breeze picked up. There was an astringent bite to the air that heightened Tanaki's senses and cleared his mind. The more oxygenated water of the lower Bay was an extravagant blue; a bright September sun danced on the surface. By mid-day the gently waving spartina that fringes the eelgrass meadows below Smith Island came into view along the shore. Tanaki asked Reynolds to take the cruiser into the shoals. They dropped anchor and winched the dinghy into the water.

About fifty yards into the grass bed, Reynolds' oar struck against some obstacle. The dinghy was brought alongside a concrete footing, it's bland whiteness wavering a few feet below the surface. Reynolds struck it again with the oar to make sure it was real. The footing's edges were sharp: the concrete seemed newly poured. Struck dumb with disbelief, the two men paddled on through the bed, Tanaki's original research plans completely forgotten. They encountered similar footings at regular intervals, elements of some kind of infrastructure.

But for what?

They hurried back to the cruiser and spent the remainder of the day working down the shoreline. Like western explorers striking out across watery prairies, they paddled the dinghy into one broad eelgrass bed after another; in each instance they encountered the same strange evidence of construction activity lurking beneath a surface that reflected the afternoon sun like a burnished shield. Both of them were perplexed, and uneasy. The network of footings was clearly the work of an organization with considerable resources at its disposal. And it seemed that every effort had been made to cover any tracks left by the construction. Other than the broken, branching matrix of angular concrete, the shallows now seemed undisturbed. A sun-baked breeze soughed lazily over the grass beds as it had for eons, its whisper punctuated only by the sudden plunge of a common tern piercing the surface in pursuit of its prey. It took an immense effort of imagination for Tanaki to envision the commotion of heavy equipment, barges, and cranes that must have been required to put these foundations in place. Perhaps the underpinnings had something to do with Folker's prohibitions on working the lower Bay. But why all the secrecy? And what were these drowned structures for? On the trip back to the Center, he and Reynolds speculated about what they had seen.

Reynolds felt certain the military was behind it.

"Let me tell you," he said, "I've seen how these boys operate. People be used for experiments—like guinea pigs!—and they never even *knew* it. Dope 'em up on LSD, and then watch 'em go out of their minds. Just for grins! Now, that ain't cool. And, hey, dropping A-bombs on whole islands in the Pacific. And did they ask folks' permission? No, sir. Acted like it was their *due*. Let me tell you something else. It might be a lot safer for us if we never saw what we just saw. You know what I mean?"

Rattled by Reynolds' speculations, Tanaki waited until he got home to phone Valerie. He hadn't dared call from the station. "I've got to talk to you," he said when she answered. "It's about the Bay."

"I'm glad you called. I've got some news for you, too." There was a long moment of silence.

"I'd rather not discuss it on the phone."

"Me neither."

"This may sound strange," Tanaki said, "but I'm feeling paranoid over here. Can we meet on your side of the Bay?"

He sensed her thinking. "It may not be much better over here," she said, "but all right. I'll have Russell meet us."

"Russell? Who's Russell?"

"He's that friend of mine in government. Remember, I mentioned him before."

Valerie sensed wariness in Tanaki's silence. "Don't worry.

He's trustworthy. I know him well."

"How well?" he wanted to ask, but he knew that would sound foolish.

The pancake house, right off the highway between Annapolis and Washington, was built like a Dutch windmill. Gaily painted blue and white, its big wooden blades sat rigidly defiant of wind and breeze; when Tanaki entered beneath them he felt an irresistible nostalgia for his years in the Netherlands. He found Valerie at a sunny table with a robustly built man sporting sleekly styled hair and the square-jawed good looks of a Clark Kent. Out the window the windmill's blades partially obscured the frenzied, shorebound traffic hurtling along the highway. He sat down and said, "This seems fairly secluded."

Superman took a careful look around. "It's not bad," he said. "But still, you never know who might be listening." After a brief silence, Valerie spoke with an air of forced conviviality. "David, this is my friend Russell."

"Pleased to meet you." Russell rose to give Tanaki an iron-gripped handshake across the table. When he sat down, he smiled questioningly at Valerie. No one seemed to know how to start, or to want to. Finally Valerie began, *sotto voce*. "David, you won't believe what I'm about to tell you."

She looked at Russell—whether for verification or support, it wasn't clear.

"Something's definitely wrong in Denmark," he remarked.

"I've got a shocker for you, too," Tanaki replied.

Valerie slipped a manila folder out of the briefcase that sat beside her chair and laid it on the table. It contained a stack of paper three inches thick. "This," she said, gesturing to the folder, "is what I've had to go through to figure out who really owned that piece of land where they arrested you."

"Amazing, isn't it?" Russell spoke with the amused resignation of a seasoned political infighter.

"Well," Tanaki asked, "who *does* own it?"

Valerie spoke in a forced whisper. "The same slimeballs who now own just about the entire lower portion of the Eastern Shore, that's who."

Tanaki hastened to describe the odd structures he and Reynolds had discovered in the eelgrass beds. Valerie shot an alarmed glance at Russell. "Bastards!" she exclaimed under her breath.

"Not too surprising, unfortunately."

A waitress brought their food. Russell looked approvingly over the dishes as she laid them around the table. "Looks like the fat's in the fire, now," he said. He sipped from his orange juice, put cream in his coffee and stirred it.

"Wait a minute," Tanaki interjected. "I'm in the dark here. How about giving me some background?"

"Russell works for a government entity that must remain nameless," Valerie said.

"Look," Russell said, "land use isn't my area. But because of where I'm situated I, well, I hear things."

"Hear things? Like what?" Tanaki asked.

Russell spoke casually as he buttered his toast. "Like there's a corporation called Global Enterprises that bankrolls the campaigns of some key players in the government." He settled in then and addressed himself to his bacon and eggs.

"David," Valerie said, "how does the concept 'Bay World' strike you?"

"Bay what? What are you talking about?"

"What I'm talking about is a fun-filled family theme park twice the size of Disney World, with pavilions about the early settlers, the Indians, the oyster wars, simulated trawling, tonging for oysters in fakey creeks, swan rides, fish rides, a massive roller coaster that veers out over the Bay. Oh, I could go on and on . . ."

"Val," Russell put in between mouthfuls, "don't forget the luxury condos, discount super mall, the offshore casino—that special blend of the surreal, the ostentatious, and the tacky."

"Where?" Tanaki asked.

"David. . ." Valerie began.

"Where?!" he repeated.

"Isn't it obvious?" Russell supplied. "Those footings you found . . . they've made their move."

"But Valerie"—Tanaki groped—"Valerie said that there's legislation on the books . . ."

"Sure there is," Russell said. "Unfortunately, that's really never stopped anybody." He took up his napkin and wiped his mouth in broad strokes. "The fact is, a powerful member of the legislature, who represents one of the state's conservative backwaters, has assured his buddies at Global that he can work some kind of fix. They were advised to go ahead with the preparatory phases of their scheme, that somehow everything would be smoothed out in the end."

"Smoothed out!" Tanaki asked in astonishment.

"Sure," Russell said. "You've got to remember, for some of these wing nuts, nature is just an obstacle to be obliterated in the name of commerce and industry."

"But how could they have put those footings in place without anyone noticing?" Tanaki stammered.

"Where did you say these structures are located?"

"A few miles below Smith Island."

"Aha!" Russell cast a wry look toward Valerie. "Not too

creative, but sometimes the most brilliant tactics are the most obvious. I figured something was up," he went on, once again taking Tanaki into his purview, "when one of Global's subsidiaries got a contract to dredge the channel down there. Now it all makes perfect sense. In the wee hours, they could just shift their equipment into the shallows . . ."

Tanaki felt a helpless rage. "But they'll destroy entire ecosystems! This can't be allowed to happen!"

Russell turned to Valerie. And when he spoke, a quiet alarm had invaded his voice. "Remember," he said, "if anyone finds out where you've learned this, it would mean career death for yours truly."

"Don't worry." She placed her hand reassuringly on his.

The three sat silently for a moment. Tanaki couldn't help but fix his eyes on Valerie's hand lying so comfortably across Russell's. After a moment, Valerie raised her eyes to Tanaki.

"There's one other thing I think you should know," she said.

"What's that?"

"The Center's director . . ."

"Folker?"

"Yes," she said, "Guy Folker."

"What about him?"

"We've uncovered some distinctly unsettling information."

"What's that?" *How much worse can this get?* he thought.

"His last employment, before coming to the Center . . ."

"Yes?"

"Was with an outfit called Offshore Enterprises."

"Offshore Enterprises? Who the heck is that?"

Valerie squeezed Russell's hand in a funny way and looked soulfully into his eyes. She sought confirmation, reassurance—fortitude, perhaps. "Offshore Enterprises is a wholly owned subsidiary of Global Enterprises," she said. "In other words, it looks like Guy Folker is some kind of plant."

Tanaki placed his head in his hands. He felt utterly crushed. It's true that he himself had come to suspect that there was something deeply wrong with Folker, had even sensed an odd unease on his first day at the Folker's house. But a very important part of him had always wanted to believe that there was some benign explanation (plain old incompetence, for example, as disturbing as that would be) behind Folker's mysterious and exasperating behavior. His world of science was like a chapel to him, a chapel of truth and integrity. It would require a major revision of his most fundamental assumptions about life to accept that the outside world—a secular world, if you will, of business, and money, and greedy speculators—had forced its way into this hallowed sanctum.

Noting Tanaki's mood, and eager to move beyond the sense of gloom that now clouded their luncheon, Valerie took a practical, can-do tone. "What about an anonymous call to the press?" she mused to Russell.

"We could try that," he replied, "but they'll just concoct some story about needing to stabilize the shoreline, or some such other horse crap. That will buy Global Enterprises enough time to solidify their support in the legislature. They'll ballyhoo all the tax revenue, all the jobs the theme park will generate. Also the campaign contributions Global is prepared to spread around like the most pungent fertilizer. What's more important, it will give them time to roll out their advertising campaign. Because you see, they're counting on the public to back them up. When it comes right down to it, they figure that the citizenry is more interested in roller coaster rides, shopping, and one-armed bandits than spawning grounds for fish."

"The sad thing is," Valerie said resignedly, "they may be right."

"I can't believe this!" Tanaki exclaimed. He rocked his head in exasperation.

"I've got to hand it to them," Russell said. "All the preparations were made in absolute secrecy. Environmental groups haven't had a chance to mobilize. And once everything is in place, resistance will be futile."

"But those footings," Tanaki whispered pleadingly, "they're there for anyone to see."

Valerie placed her free hand on Tanaki's, completing a circuit between the two men. "David," she said, "This may be bigger than we are."

Tanaki wanted to weep. Pulling his hand away, he got up and left the restaurant, nearly colliding with the surreal windmill blades on his way to his Honda. He soared eastward over the bridge, utterly disoriented. His mind was crowded with concepts he had never expected to grapple with: Bay World, Global Enterprises, campaign contributions, political fixes. And what was going on with Valerie and Russell? Maybe she was just following her blessed instincts! Perhaps he should learn to do the same, he thought. But his erotic yearnings seemed trivial compared to the hideous news he had just heard. How could some developer ravage a beautifully delicate ecosystem, just to create a crude, plasticized version of reality? Who would speak for the powerless creatures of the marshes; the bottom feeders; the young of the many species that depend on the cover of the grasses as they grow to maturity? How will the shoppers, the roller coaster riders, the gambling junkies feel when there are no more crabs and rockfish, a stinking brown sludge pond where once was the glittering jewel of the Bay?

He returned to the Center, but only because there was no place else to go. His patience for work was nil. He tried to look up DeForrest again but learned that he was on the water and was not expected to return until evening. He could think of no one else to unburden himself to; Reynolds was up the Potomac with a survey team. Wanting to be alone, and especially to avoid Folker, he went to the lab where he and DeForrest had spoken the day before. It was deserted. He knocked about the drab space, uneasy with himself, turning jets on and off, splashing water into the basins. He went to the windows and looked out on the Bay. The sky was clouding over, the Bay's turbid waters gray-green.

He sat on the lip of one of the holding pens and considered whether to wait for DeForrest to return. In his restlessness, he asked himself what he hoped to accomplish by sharing Global's designs on the estuary with his senior colleague. DeForrest hadn't seemed terribly interested in his meeting with Folker, an encounter which had filled Tanaki with dread in its anticipation, frustration in its consummation. And the references to the older man's kids and mortgage, and to the work that he meant to complete before the season turned, wasn't all this his way of letting Tanaki know he couldn't afford to risk the treatment doled out to Beth Delantis—if not worse?

It was all too clear that Folker was willing to play hardball.

Tanaki went again to the windows. A thick overcast had settled in and the water was getting choppier. He figured DeForrest would have to return soon. But he was finding it increasingly difficult to find a reason to wait. As he pondered the events of the last couple of months, it seemed that Global Enterprise's planned assault on the estuary had become an intensely personal matter. After all, it was he who had blundered into the construction site at the Nanticoke burial ground, he who confronted Folker, he who turned up those footings down in the salt grass meadows. For reasons he could not begin to fathom, fate seemed to have placed the entire problem of Bay World squarely in his lap.

This thought occasioned a frisson of nameless terror.

Tanaki left the Center and walked aimlessly, jaggedly, through Bristol, past the guest houses and nautical gift shops of the main drag, trying to escape a problem he did not have the stomach to confront. He plunged into quiet side streets past clotheslines in backyards, where children too young for school rode ludicrously small tricycles in wobbly circles in the middle of the deserted blocks. There seemed no place for him. He couldn't bear to go back to the lab, and there was nothing at home but the silence of his apartment. The Yamaguchis would certainly be at work. He felt vulnerable, yet strangely aggressive at the same time.

He found himself driving eastward on the main highway toward Salisbury. When he pulled up in front of the squat buildings across from the railroad tracks, he noted the dry leaves of the locusts rustling in the gathering wind. He climbed the stairs devoid of thought. He knocked and then leaned against the door jamb, letting his shoulder support his weight.

Morning Moon sounded far away through the door. "Who is it?"

"David Tanaki."

"WHO?"

"TANAKI."

She opened the door and, sensing his despair, gazed at him with pity in her eyes. He extended his arms like a supplicant. She moved to his embrace.

Tanaki sat on the edge of the bed, immersed in an aura of richly colored rugs and tapestries, baptized in the earthy warmth of Morning Moon's skin and the forest-scent of her hair. While he laced up his sneakers he explained, in as measured terms as he could muster, what he had learned at the meeting with Russell and Valerie. Morning Moon moved hastily about the room; she was preparing to leave for her waitressing job at an Ocean City restaurant. After looking in the mirror to attach a pair of beaded earrings, she came to the bed and sat beside him. She allowed her weight to rest against him.

"This Bay World business sounds pretty serious."

"Serious? It would be a total disaster. Somebody's got to do something to stop it!"

Melanie wrinkled her brow a little. "That somebody wouldn't happen to be you, I don't suppose?"

Tanaki reeled back as he answered her. "I don't know if that would make a lot of sense," he said. "I mean, there are people who are trained to do this sort of thing. They've got the experience, the skills . . ."

"You mean, like your *friend*, Valerie?"

"Well, yes, like her," Tanaki replied, so preoccupied with his dilemma that he utterly missed Melanie's insinuations. "And others, too. Politicians. Protesters. Advocacy groups. Me, I'm a scientist. My job is to get the data, try to make sense out of it. It's up to other people to create policy, enforce the rules . . ."

"Other people? Oh, like the good folks over in Annapolis? The ones who are maneuvering, at this very minute, to sell the

Chesapeake down the river, so to speak?"

Tanaki was at a loss. Melanie pulled a small leather pouch from her jeans pocket. "I've never heard so much bullshit in my life," she added flatly. "And, to be frank, I know you're definitely crazy. But, for some weird reason, I feel like you've got the makings of a warrior. There's something I want to give you, but you've got to promise you'll keep it on your person every minute until this thing is over."

"What is it?"

She opened the pouch and removed a shiny black stone covered with indecipherable markings. There was a small hole near one edge. She held it in the open palm of her hand. "It's a power stone. It'll keep you safe." Tanaki's face betrayed his skepticism. "You don't have to believe it, dummy," she said. "Just wear it."

She took a thin leather thong from her nightstand and threaded it carefully through the hole in the stone. Then she raised her arms and placed the thong around Tanaki's neck. "Promise!" she said.

Tanaki didn't know about the stone, but he felt overwhelmed by the confidence Morning Moon seemed to place in him (however qualified it may have been). "Okay, I promise," he said, and he bowed his head for reasons he couldn't understand.

They emerged from Melanie's building into the late afternoon. It had stormed while Tanaki was inside and though the earth was wet with rain, the now placid sky was broken only by floating bands of inconsequential cirri. On the way back to Cambridge he stopped at the refuge where he sat looking over the marshes for an hour or more. When he arrived home, his apartment seemed lonely. He was free of the sense of manic agitation he had experienced earlier, but without any focus for the undirected energies he now felt budding within. He looked into the backyard and noticed Nariko sitting in the garden by the defunct fountain. He descended the creaking staircase and walked around the old Victorian. After greeting his friend he sat beside her on the bench she occupied.

"What's up?" Nariko asked gaily.

Tanaki responded in solemn tones. "Things are a complete and awful mess. That's what's up."

"Oh." She squinted at him with eyes that felt his pain. "Do you want to talk about it?"

He scuffed his shoes in the earth before the bench. "It's all so screwy, I hardly know where to begin."

"Just start . . . anywhere." Her kind gaze was filled with infinite patience.

Tanaki picked up a fallen twig and began to break it into ever smaller bits. "It's something involving my work. Even bigger than that, really. As big as the whole, wide, wonderful Chesapeake."

"Wow," Nariko half-whispered, and her eyes widened. "Not something good, eh?"

"No," Tanaki said sternly. "In fact, it's something too bad to even believe. If you can imagine it, some mega conglomerate is trying to take over the Bay. And this guy who's in the know, Russell, says there's no way that we can stop it."

"Take over the Bay? Con—glomerate?" She shook her head slowly but emphatically. "I can't believe . . ."

"What's worse, my boss at the Center," Tanaki went on, "it looks like he's mixed up with these bastards and their stupid scheme. Damn!" he exclaimed and cast bits of twig aimlessly at the ground. "I feel so frustrated!"

"What?" Nariko exclaimed in turn. "Big bossman mixed up?"

Tanaki explained the situation in detail. Nariko listened with keen interest. And then she asked, quite simply, "Why not fight the bastards?"

"Fight . . ." Tanaki said incredulously. "But how?"

She responded with a placid smile and upturned hands.

"Look, Nari," Tanaki tried to explain, "Russell is probably right. This thing may be too big to stop. Besides, I have no idea what to do. And if I do something stupid, and it all backfires, it could literally demolish my career."

Nariko waited silently for a discreet interval. Then she asked, quietly and humbly, "What's more important? Your career, or . . . the magnificent *kami* of the Bay?"

Tanaki was at a loss for words. They sat in silence for a moment.

"Remember Ato-san, and his philosophy of pure action?" Nariko ventured helpfully. "Maybe you're having what-might-happen thoughts, and you're blocked."

"I'm blocked, that's for sure." There was the bitter taste of impotent exasperation in Tanaki's voice. He gazed among the trees that stood in the yards of Mrs. Stafford's and the neighboring houses. "Aargh! The cards just seem so stacked against us!"

Nariko picked up a petal that had fallen onto the bench from the broken rose arbor. She pinched it between thumb and forefinger, turned it over as it caught the day's last sunlight from different angles. She proffered it briefly toward Tanaki, but then released it to the breeze that played gaily through the yard.

23

The Eel II

RISING AFTER a night of broken sleep and strange dreams, Tanaki moved uncertainly to the bathroom. He peered into the mirror and tried to recognize the man who stared back at him. The result was inconclusive. He put toothpaste on his brush and vigorously cleansed his teeth, as if he could so easily scrub the whole matter of Bay World out of his life.

He stood in the middle of the living room, as he had done the day he rented the apartment, and tried to feel some directional instinct. Nothing emerged. He rang Morning Moon's number, thinking she might be able to help, but there was no answer.

He sat on an orange crate and gazed at the magnolias. Sunlight fell on the floor. Life was going on, but he felt at a loss, every impulse turned inward and finding a dead end. Sitting still became unbearable and, driven by his discomfort, he went back to the bedroom. Applying himself to dressing with an exaggerated vigor, he discovered that with a little effort he could force the manifold horrors of Bay World out of his mind. For reasons of self-preservation he decided to spend the day concentrating on something he understood better, and from which he could expect to derive a comforting sense of purpose. Yes, he would devote his day to preparations for the

THE EEL II

eel study!

After overcoming Tanaki's reservations, Reynolds had assembled one of the most sophisticated telemetry systems ever used in animal tracking experiments. He had fielded a number of attachment devices on live subjects, whom he harried around the Center's holding tanks to put the equipment under maximum stress. After then testing the gear throughout the Bay, he and Tanaki agreed that the odds were at least even that they would be able to follow a spawning eel as it valiantly made its way through deep ocean toward the Sargasso Sea . . .

Tanaki signed out a boat, and he and Reynolds headed across the Bay and south to the wide mouth of the Patuxent River. They carried a couple dozen wire eel traps of the most modern design, along with Joe Pasquath's antiquated wicker version. Tanaki had little confidence in the Nanticoke relic, but as Reynolds had taken a shine to it, he agreed to bring it along. "Now, that's what I call an eel trap," Reynolds had said when Tanaki walked into the Center's maintenance shop after returning from Chicawan Creek.

They motored upstream for a couple of miles and began to drop traps, attaching plenty of line and small marking buoys before throwing each one overboard. Reynolds insisted on placing Joe Pasquath's personally; at his insistence, the boat was anchored near the mouth of a shallow creek. He waded up the shady watercourse and in ten minutes returned empty-handed, with a big smile on his face.

"That one's gonna hit. I just know it." He was still smiling as he climbed into the boat. "I just *know* it." He rubbed his hands with the gusto of a much younger man.

Being out on the water had been good for Tanaki, but by the time he and Reynolds returned to the Center he once again found himself feeling rudderless. The stratagem of concentrating on the eel study had worked temporarily, but there was nothing further to do until it was time, one week out, to check the traps. He didn't mention the matter of Bay World to Reynolds, uncertain how far he should widen the circle of *cognoscenti* until he had decided how to respond to the situation. Returning home feeling tense, he was grateful to find an invitation to dinner at the Yamaguchis posted on his door. He figured Nariko's solicitude was behind it, but that didn't especially embarrass him, so accustomed had he become to the pervading goodwill the sisters lavished in his direction.

24

Blowfish

AT SEVEN SHARP Tanaki walked up to the Yamaguchis' place. Setsuko let him in. Though he was certain that she had been thoroughly briefed on his discussion with Nariko in the garden, she didn't mention it. Nariko was in the kitchen, as usual. But contrary to custom, Setsuko didn't excuse herself to help her sister finish preparing dinner. Instead she remained in the living room with Tanaki, topping off his sake while they discussed the changing autumn weather, the seasonal migration patterns of Yamaguchi Enterprise's quarry, and the upcoming local elections. He guessed that a decision had been reached not to leave him alone. While he appreciated the sisters' concern for his troubles, he began to feel that he had worried them unduly.

"So," he asked, "why aren't you helping Nari with dinner tonight?"

"I'm not exactly, well, qualified to prepare this dish," Setsuko said, elegantly tipping a stoneware sake decanter over Tanaki's cup.

"Really?" Tanaki said. "I didn't know there were qualifications for cooking dinner!"

"For *fugu* there are."

Here was one Japanese word that Tanaki did understand,

since it applied to a fish, and a notorious one at that. He repressed the sudden sense of alarm he felt as he replied, his rising voice suggesting nothing more than casual curiosity, "We're having blowfish?"

"I hope you don't mind," Setsuko said. "I know they say that a man who's his own sushi chef has a fool for a customer, but Nari has her first-class license from the Ministry of Health and Welfare. And she learned right at the top, a two-month course at Tsukiji, Tokyo's famous fish-market." She turned toward the kitchen and raised her voice. "Right, little sister?"

Nariko stuck her head around the corner and smiled cheerfully at Tanaki.

"Don't worry, David-san," Setsuko continued. "You're not going to end up like Bando."

"Bando?" he asked.

"He was little sister's and my favorite Kabuki actor."

"Was?"

"Sadly, yes. You see, he got a little cocky one night after a particularly successful Tokyo performance, and he talked this sushi chef into serving him a fugu liver. That's where the poison is most concentrated, you know."

"Yes, that's correct," Tanaki said.

Nariko rounded the kitchen wall. She carried a lacquered tray full of porcelain dishes in her outstretched arms.

"His last performance consisted of writhing and drooling on the floor of a sushi house," Setsuko went on. "No wonder they don't let the imperial family eat the stuff. Right, little sister?"

Nariko set the tray on the low table that sat in the midst of the tatamis and stood very erect, a schoolgirl about to recite her lessons. "The poison is found in the liver and ovaries," she began. "One thousand times more potent than cyanide, it attacks the motor-nervous system. Within twenty minutes it overwhelms the respiratory system. There is no known antidote."

"Very good, little sister!" Setsuko said. "I see you still remember your sushi training. What's it been, like, five years now?"

Tanaki noticed that Nariko hadn't hesitated once during her recitation. He was also struck by Setsuko's references to her as "little sister." He couldn't remember her ever addressing Nariko that way in the past. He recalled their account of girls day, with dolls and peach blossoms, symbols of "grace and gentleness." Their carefree laughter echoed in his mind. But things were different tonight; their words and movements felt studied, formalistic, some kind of *shtick*. He might have guessed that they were clowning around to distract him from his worries—except for Setsuko's tantalizing references to the dangers inherent in eating blowfish, followed by assurances that "little sister" would make sure that he would survive the ordeal. It was like the good-cop, bad-cop routine from all those old movies he used to watch on TV. But if he were under investigation, of what crime was he suspected? Had Nariko, through some uncanny feminine intuition, sensed that he had come from the embrace of another woman when they spoke in the garden the evening before?

The Yamaguchis were arranging dishes on the table. As they knelt beside it, Setsuko resumed the conversation.

"In fact," she said, "Nariko completed the final exam well before the rest of the class. How long did it take you, little sister? I can't quite remember the exact figure."

Nariko held up four fingers.

"That's right," Setsuko continued. "Four minutes." She looked at Tanaki. "Amazing, isn't it? Most of the class took the full fifteen minutes to separate the good parts from the bad. But Nari has always liked to work fast. And she's never gotten too sloppy. Not yet, anyway!" She threw back her head with a hearty laugh and took a solid slug of sake.

Tanaki belted down a large gulp of the warm brew himself and examined the dish that lay before him. On a small plate, a couple of carrot garnishes surrounded a few toasted blowfish fins. Setsuko placed an empty bowl in the middle of the table.

"We usually start with the fins," she explained. "It's best to pour sake over them." She held a fin delicately over the empty bowl, poured from her cup, and then bit into the morsel with extreme delectation. Nariko followed suit.

Tanaki took a tentative nibble. "I don't get it," he said. "What's the attraction in eating something that could kill you? Isn't it like Russian roulette, only played with fish, instead of a loaded revolver?"

"Some connoisseurs say they just like the flavor" Setsuko explained, "though of course there are scads of tasty fish out there. It's also supposed to be an aphrodisiac. I guess the sex fiend types go for it for that reason."

"Sex fiends!" Tanaki thought. Maybe they did know about him and Morning Moon. He took a long, slow draught of sake and began to feel incredibly lucid—or to lose lucidity altogether, he wasn't sure which. Outlandish thoughts began to infest his mind: it occurred to him that his friends the Yamaguchis could be preparing to murder him! There was always that undercurrent of attraction between them. Maybe they considered him "theirs." After all, he reasoned, they were from a very different culture. Who knew what kinds of ideas might be caroming around in those crazy Japanese minds, although they'd always seemed normal enough? The fugu provided a perfect set-up, he thought. They would just say that it had all been a horrible accident!

"Not finishing your fins?" Setsuko asked solicitously. She and Nariko gathered up the plates. "Oh well, that's the least interesting part, anyway." She whisked Tanaki's dish away and followed Nariko into the kitchen. They returned moments later with more trays.

"Now for the sashimi," Nariko announced proudly.

She and Setsuko arrayed the dishes on the table and sat on their haunches. Before each of the diners was a plate with strips of fugu fillet arranged in the shape of an animal. Setsuko's was a crane; Nariko's a sea turtle; Tanaki's, of course, an eel. Small bowls contained the traditional sauce of soy, daikon, chopped scallions, bitter orange, and red pepper.

"We're supposed to eat this?" Tanaki asked.

Setsuko laughed. "What else would we do with it? Play frisbee?" She pincered a piece in her chopsticks and gazed at it longingly. "I realize it's usually eaten in the colder months."

"Less poison," Nariko interjected as she chewed.

"But we didn't feel we could wait that long," Setsuko resumed. "Who knows where in this wide world you'll be after your fellowship at the Center ends?"

Tanaki stared at the eel design and wondered what to do. Further additions of warm sake to his body chemistry had intensified the feeling of lucidity—or its antithesis—to the point where it would soon no longer matter.

"You know," Nariko said, "it could be . . . the Floating World."

Tanaki stared at her, as puzzled as ever.

"You asked why people eat fugu. Well, the Floating World."

Tanaki remained stubbornly bewildered.

Setsuko glanced at her sister. "Perhaps Nariko means to say," she explained, "that the floating, shifting nature of all of this, this reality, if you like, becomes crystal clear when we are faced with the"—she gestured now with her eyes toward the sashimi clasped in her raised chopsticks— "the abyss, shall we say? Ato-san, when he was alive, always liked to remind us that life gives us no choice but to act, even in the face of utter uncertainty." She smiled benignly at the morsel of fugu, still dangling there from her chopsticks. "But he also said that we should be sure to enjoy life's delights while doing so!" Now she chewed into the fugu with a look of supreme delectation. After swallowing, she said, "I hope that's what you meant, little sister."

Nariko, nodding and chewing, mumbled her assent.

Tanaki looked at Setsuko. She smiled at him, and he could have sworn that he detected a wink. He clasped a sizable portion of the eel design with his chopsticks and, not bothering with the sauce, stuffed it decisively into his maw.

25
Disposition of Forces

TANAKI AWOKE with an emperor-sized sake hangover. He made a big pot of coffee and sat in the breakfast nook watching sparrows play in the magnolias. As his mental fog dissipated, he couldn't help but laugh about the events of the evening before. Those Yamaguchi sisters were always full of surprises! In the cold morning light, he realized how absurd had been his paranoia-, stress- and sake-induced suspicions. In fact, he felt a perfect calm, the kind encountered in the eye of a hurricane, and a new resolve. It was fueled by a gut knowledge that he couldn't stand still; nor could he go back to the time before he knew about Bay World, the footings in the eelgrass beds, or the desecration of the Nanticoke burial ground. He now faced something he could not go over, under, or around.

As his father used to remind him, he would just have to go through it.

After his third cup he rang Valerie to get Russell's number. He had had a chance to think about the two of them and had decided that it was none of his business how she satisfied *her* instincts. He couldn't help admire everything she was doing to protect the Bay and hoped that they could remain friends. Considering what he had shared with Melanie, things seemed to have worked out for the best. He apologized for his hasty departure from the pancake house.

"You were certainly freaked out," she said. "I hope you're keeping your head on straight."

"Don't worry about me. I'm as right as rain." He spoke confidently, concealing his remaining doubts from himself as much as from her.

"I guess Russell won't mind your contacting him. But remember, he's a little skittish about all of this. You know, his whole career could blow up if . . ."

Tanaki reached Russell at the statehouse. "Sorry about the way I ran out on you guys the other day," he opened. "This whole Bay World thing really threw me for a loop."

"Don't worry about that," Russell said. "It was perfectly understandable. Just remember"—his voice grew hushed here— "our conversation was strictly off the record."

"I completely understand," Tanaki said. "But if you don't mind, I was hoping I could ask you a few more questions, get a little more detail."

There was a brief silence on the other end of the line. When Russell's voice again broke the dead air, it was a near-whisper. "I can't talk here," he said hurriedly. "I'll give you my home number. Call me this evening."

Tanaki spent the rest of the day working on his notes, making calculations for his eel study. He called Morning Moon again, but again there was no answer.

That evening he called Russell at home. Driving, hard-rock music blared in the background. "Sorry if I sound winded," Russell said. "I've just been pumping some iron."

If his muscles get any bigger, Tanaki thought, he's going to have a hard time buying shirts.

"I want to tell you," Russell started, "I feel like I should have done something on this business sooner." He paused at intervals to catch his breath in shallow gulps. "I've been so wrapped up in certain other issues that are particularly dear to my heart. This thing just didn't get on my radar screen like I wish it had. I heard tidbits here and there, but until Valerie called, I didn't put it all together."

"I understand. But do you have any details on when this thing is supposed to happen? I mean, when do they plan to go forward with the whole enchilada?"

"As to the whole enchilada, as you put it, I couldn't say. But it seems they plan to start putting some of the initial apparatus in place before winter sets in."

"Are you sure?"

"There are some regulatory hurdles they need to clear, but their backers in the legislature seem to think they're in the bag. They've probably managed to place pliable plants in the pertinent agencies, just like they did with your pal Folker."

"Some of the apparatus, sometime before winter. Is that all you know?"

"That, and look for them to come by sea. Oh, and the under cover of darkness."

"By sea, under—?"

"I know it sounds ridiculous, but that's what I've heard."

"No more details?"

"I'm afraid that's all I know. I'll reach out if I hear anything else. I'd better not stay on much longer. Who knows who might be listening. Good luck."

Tanaki heard the click of the connection terminated. Russell seemed like a nice enough guy. He felt sort of happy for Valerie. He only wished he had gotten more details. But as he sat in his stuffed chair pondering Russell's remarks, he realized that he would have to go on whatever he had to go on. He was certain about one thing at least: he wasn't going to let anyone spoil the rich and storied Chesapeake without a fight. He sipped a cup of tea, went to bed, and fell into a sleep more profound than he had experienced for weeks. He dreamt that he was an eel, swimming freely and strong in open ocean. He passed fish of various kinds, large and small, but they all bore the faces of people he knew. The Bluebird was there, Reynolds, Valerie, Pannenburg, Morning Moon, the Yamaguchis, his parents—even his grandfather. He heard a strange, ethereal music. Though he was deep under water, sunlight permeated his surroundings, and he could breathe freely. He woke up feeling vital and clear. After breakfast, he called Helen Conway and asked if he could drive over to Easton and talk with her.

"I've been meaning to get in touch with you, too," she said as they waited for lunch in the sun-spangled courtyard of the genteel hotel where he had addressed her club in the spring. She looked down and fussed with her napkin for a moment. "I was hoping," she said shyly, "I might convince you to lead our fall migration tour."

"I'd be more than happy to," he said with a smile. Then he leaned in and spoke quietly, confidentially. "But listen," he said, "I also have another adventure in mind, one that's slightly more . . . urgent, you might say."

"Oh, really? My gals and I are always ready for an adventure. Tell me about it!"

Tanaki described what he knew of Global's plans, and told Helen that he needed a cadre of allies to act as lookouts along the shores of the Bay as winter drew near.

Helen's eyes flared brightly at the thought of Tanaki's

news. "I'm sure I speak for my entire club when I say that we would relish the opportunity to confront these, these, barbarians! Just give me a day or two to contact the other gals, and then let us know what you need."

The next day Tanaki went into the Center. He requested a boat and cruised over the Bay with Reynolds to check the eel traps. Amid the privacy of the churning waters, he filled him in on Bay World.

"So it wasn't the military after all," Reynolds said. "I'll be damned."

"No, but I have a feeling that these guys could be just as scary."

"Listen," Reynolds said, "forget about that. The main thing is, don't *worry*. Take it from me, I've seen some struggles in my time. When you know what you're doing is right, just do what you have to do, and don't let the heebie-jeebies get to you. Now let's see about them eels."

Reynolds piloted the boat up the Patuxent toward the traps. As one wire device after another came up either empty, or with a specimen that displayed none of the physiological changes that would indicate an imminent spawning migration, he evinced not concern, but satisfaction. "I knew we wouldn't get anything with these traps," he said as they pulled the last of them out of the river, dripping with pungent green water and strands of soggy vegetation. "Just let me check that Indian gizmo. Now, that's an eel trap!" And sure enough, a half an hour later, as he tripped toward the boat through the shallows of Sheldon creek holding the wicker contraption over his head with both hands, he hollered out, "We got one! This baby will run, I can see it!"

And Tanaki agreed. The eel's eyes bulged out of its head,

and its new ocean skin gleamed iridescent through the interstices of the basketry. He was pleased. It was a large, healthy female. He judged it to be twelve years old. In the cruiser's portable lab, Reynolds held the wriggling, writhing creature on an examination table while Tanaki measured and examined it from every conceivable angle. Finally Reynolds tenderly fitted the transmitter at the base of a pectoral fin and released the eel back to its home.

Tanaki spent that evening with the Yamaguchis.

"I feel funny asking for your help," he said after he had updated them on what he knew of Global's plans. "I imagine it could involve considerable risk for you."

"The only risk is . . . what-might-happen," Nariko said.

"Besides," Setsuko added, "the Bay has given us so much. How could we see it come to harm, while we stand by and do nothing?"

A few days later Tanaki and Reynolds looked up Buzz Richardson at one of his usual haunts. "I'd like to help in any way I can," Buzz said forthrightly upon learning of the impending assault on the estuary that had nourished him and his family throughout the years.

As autumn ripened, yellow and orange, Tanaki drove to Muddy Creek. He found Bob Haskel in much the same plight as before, only worse. His house was still surrounded by the flock of snow geese the Canadian government had prevented him from leading north the year before; but now there were scores of additional geese, and even swans, early migrants who had gotten wind of the tender-hearted scientist's largesse and decided to crash the party.

He stood on the front lawn surrounded by his squawking wards. The idling engine of his plane added to the din. "I've got to do something. Soon!" he yelled. "I'm hoping I can hold out until the final phase of my research is completed."

"You mean—"

"Yeah, I've gotten this group pretty good at following my craft. Now it's time to see if they can transmit that knowledge to the massive numbers of their co-specifics who will descend on the estuary next month."

"But, Bob," Tanaki protested, "according to your research plan, you've got several intermediate steps before you're ready to lead entire flocks, haven't you?"

"That was my plan, good buddy." Haskel slapped a hand onto Tanaki's shoulder. "But remember what the great John Lennon once said: 'Life is what happens to you while you're making plans.' I'm of a mind to just go for it. Know what I mean?"

Tanaki, remembering that Haskel's wife was still "visiting friends," resisted the urge to remind his colleague about the sanctity of experimental design, the inviolability of research protocols. Taking him by the elbow, he guided him away from the noise of the plane and filled him in on Global Enterprise's whole rotten scheme.

"This means war!" Haskel replied tersely when Tanaki finished his account. Without further comment, he strapped on his goggles and strode toward the waiting Cessna.

Tanaki had decided not to include Valerie in his evolving strategy to make sure that Bay World never see the light of day. He was no expert on such matters, but he was pretty certain that the kinds of things he had planned wouldn't pass legal muster. On Halloween evening, as he sat in his dining nook watching Caspers, Supermans, and a varied assortment of princesses and tramps cavort gleefully along Talbot Street, she called.

"I'm worried about you," she opened.

Cold comfort: the solicitude of a woman who has taken a pass on you. "Worried about me? I'm fine," he declared calmly.

"You say that, but still I'm worried."

"Don't be. Believe me, everything is A-okay."

"A-okay? As freaked out as you were a couple of weeks ago? And now, just like that, everything's suddenly A-okay? I can't believe you just forgot this whole Bay World business. I know that I haven't."

"I didn't figure you had. Only, with your position at the law school, there wouldn't be any point in getting mixed up in—"

"Getting mixed up in . . . what?"

He was speechless.

"David, getting mixed up in what?"

"You know," he fudged. "Making waves, creating a ruckus."

"Nonsense. I only just yesterday filed suit on behalf of Melanie's group."

"But you remember what Russell said. By the time this all works its way through the courts, Bay World will be a done deal. Isn't that right?"

"Russell's a smart guy, and very connected, but he doesn't know everything. You never know what might come up. Meanwhile, we've got to fight this thing with whatever tools we have at our disposal."

"I can't argue with that."

Silence.

"Why do you sound so guarded. Like you're hiding something?"

"I've just got a lot on my plate. Several of my research protocols are at critical junctures at the moment."

DISPOSITION OF FORCES

"David—" She was afraid she was losing him.
"What?"
"Promise me you won't do anything crazy."

Indeed, Tanaki hadn't neglected his research, but regularly evaded Folker's guidelines to continue his investigations in the salt grass beds of the lower estuary. He felt a keen repulsion every time the skiff glided past one of Global's concrete footings, but he did his best to document the invasive structures' impact on the creatures who now lived in their shadows.

He continued to try to reach Morning Moon, but she did not return his calls. He had no time to ponder the reason.

The day after Halloween, he discovered in the mail a manila envelope the corner of which was covered with pale purple foreign postage stamps. His heart sank and rose with a sad elation when he recognized the unmistakable hand—the letters artfully rendered in green felt pen—and the Italian return address.

Over the years since the Bluebird's crack-up, Tanaki had stayed informed of her situation through Moeller. After the episode with the Zugenruhe cage she was committed to a psychiatric hospital, where she refused to utter a human sound to anyone, including Tanaki. Though he spent many weeks at her side—at the expense of the joint Swedish starling study that meant so much to him—when his European grant ran out he made the excruciating decision to move on with his life and accepted a new offer in India. Fortunately, Moeller didn't abandon his protégé. On his regular visits, he kept her abreast of ongoing research, though his companion never responded with anything beyond a strident chirp, if her feelings ran averse, or a soft cooing if she agreed. Over the ensuing months, even these sounds diminished, until Moeller delivered lengthy monologues, utterly unperturbed, while the Bluebird stared out the window in silence. After a year of this absurdist drama, the Bluebird finally handed Moeller a scrap of paper upon which she had scrawled a brief note: a request to meet Perdecci. Though he wasn't sure what his former mentor would make of this peculiar fledgling, Moeller was greatly heartened that she had at last resorted to a recognizable form of human communication. He convinced the Bluebird's parents to arrange a transfer to a hospital near the old Italian's home in Milan and entreated Perdecci to intercede.

The great researcher was bound to oblige one of his favorite students, but he came away so charmed by the Bluebird's fey sadness that he made a regular habit of visiting. After a few months she began to write elaborate notes full of questions about his theories; before a year was out Perdecci found himself engaged in lengthy discussions on animal cognition and consciousness, astounded by what he called, in a letter to Moeller, the Bluebird's "uncanny knack for getting into the very souls of our research's animal subjects."

Tanaki stopped writing after a couple of years. Tired of wounded anticipation and unrequited gestures, he suspected that he had become more of a bother than a comfort. He knew she may have felt abandoned, and resentful of his leaving Europe, but from his point of view he had had no choice. At least Moeller kept him informed of his old friend's life. She finally left the hospital to take a position at Perdecci's university. She hadn't as yet made any efforts toward original research, but Tanaki couldn't believe that her pioneering spirit would remain forever caged.

It was with trembling hands, still standing at the little row of rusty mailboxes that hung to one side of Mrs. Stafford's dark foyer, with its antiquated heirlooms, that he opened the padded envelope. He felt a keen disappointment when he found, not a letter in the Bluebird's hand, but an issue of the British journal *Migration Soundings*. He walked up the stairs to his apartment, sank into his chair, and opened the journal to the table of contents. An arrow in the same green ink of the parcel's address had been drawn to the last article in the issue, "Navigation by Magnetic Sensitivity in *homo sapiens sapiens*."

He hurriedly turned the pages to the back of the journal. The article described an experiment carried out by none other than his onetime Swedish collaborators. They had fitted out a dozen men and women with headgear resembling rugby helmets—there was one grainy black and white photograph—but which contained powerful magnets. This faux rugby team was loaded into a windowless van and transported to a destination with which they were unfamiliar; their route, which involved innumerable twists and turns, covered over two hundred miles of Swedish countryside. At their journey's terminus, the participants were asked to point in the direction from which their travels had originated. A control group was subjected to the same experience but *sans* the magnetized headgear. The purpose of the study, according to the abstract, was "to determine if a statistically significant number of the control group's participants could correctly state the direction from which their journey had originated in the absence of visual cues and, if such an ability did exist, whether the wearing of magnetized headgear impaired that ability, suggesting some role in *homo sapiens sapiens* for navigation through sensitivity to the earth's magnetic force lines." Tanaki eagerly read through the article to its end, where the authors summed up the results of their study with the following words: "Our results showed a statistically significant ability to orient to the point of origination among the control subjects, while no such correlation existed among those wearing magnetized headgear." After the printed text, like a single drop of rain on a desert flower, there were three short words penned in the green felt pen. "Be the bird," it said. It was signed "Ana."

This brief communication, the first Tanaki had had from the Bluebird since her last, fateful chirp, seemed to beg a response of some kind. But he was now at the center of a swirl of events which demanded his complete attention. He had decided to confront Global Enterprises' planned assault on the Bay with every resource at his disposal. At the first sign of the conglomerate's advance guard, he was prepared to set in motion a line of defense that, while lacking in sophistication, possessed the advantages of both surprise and directness.

There was only one unresolved issue. The pursuit of the eel, which he and Reynolds had spent so much time and effort planning, could begin at any moment. Once that eel decided to head for open ocean, a convocation of the president, the pope, and the United Nations could not change its mind. If Global moved first, he could deal with them and then follow the eel. If the eel were to make its move, however, a choice would have to be made. It was one that Tanaki still did not know how he would settle as November's dark evenings came to the Shore.

26
Battle at Sea

IT WAS nearly midnight. Tanaki and Reynolds leaned against a counter in the Center's maintenance shop, quietly chatting about nothing in particular. Other than the two of them, the station was deserted.

They were becoming accustomed to this vigil. They had spent every night for the last two weeks here, watching the glowing red and green LEDs on a small black box, alternating naps on temporary cots, waiting for the unique combination of signals that would indicate that their eel was swimming down the Patuxent and into the Bay. Overnight bags were packed. The Center's ocean-going cruiser stood at the ready with a tankful of gas.

But the two men were also alert to the possibility of another signal: the shrill chirping of a pager on Tanaki's belt that would indicate that Global Enterprises had begun to move through the estuary. Along the lower shores of the Bay, ladies of the Chesapeake Avian Support League peered through lenses of field glasses through which they normally searched treetops for flecked vireos and Baltimore orioles, scanning the dark waters of the Virginia capes for any sign of Global's impending assault.

"Davy!" Reynolds boomed suddenly.

"What?"

"Our eel. She's movin' out!"

"Are you sure?"

"No doubt about it."

Tanaki looked at the tracking receiver. A row of green lights swept through a pattern of repeated elongations. "Looks like it's decision time," he mouthed uncertainly staring, mesmerized, at the display. Reynolds was bending to take hold of his overnight bag when Tanaki's pager began to peal aggressively, audibly mirroring the receiver's flashing lights.

"Jesus, Reynolds, that's Helen. They must have spotted Global's outfit. It's all happening at once!" Tanaki's voice betrayed his agitation. "What are we going to do?"

The older man dropped his bag. He approached Tanaki and took him by the shoulders. "Just relax," he said. "Everything's gonna work out fine. I'm going to get the boat ready, and you've got some calls to make. All right?" Reynolds hustled out the door of the shop, bulging at his sides with canvas bags and radio equipment.

It was dark on the water. The moon was in its first quarter and it had rained the day before, classic conditions for eel migration onset. A misty steam rose from the surface of the Bay. The station's cruiser churned through the dark mass, heading toward the estuary's mouth. Tanaki piloted the craft with the engine at full throttle; Reynolds sat near him on the bridge, his receivers arrayed in an orderly row. When they passed the mouth of the Patuxent, the eel still had not moved from the river into the Bay.

"She's hanging back in there," Reynolds said with surprise. "She came down out of that creek all right, and came right down the river channel. But when she got near the Bay, she circled back and made a pass upstream. She's done it two or three times now."

Tanaki eased up on the throttle. Odd, he thought. Was the eel experiencing misgivings, fearing the dark and strange journey that lay ahead? Or was it just indulging a moment of nostalgia over what for many years had been home: savoring one last time that unique bouquet of scents, that particular signature of water pressure and currents, all those identifying characteristics by which marine animals experience their environments? He thrust the throttle forward. "Let's keep going," he said. "I'm certain she'll get on her way eventually. As long as you've got a signal, I'm all right."

For half an hour they cruised steadily, suspended under the blanket of the night, each lost in his own thoughts. Suddenly the ship's radio crackled. "Yamaguchi One to Tanaki, Yamaguchi One to Tanaki. Come in, Tanaki."

It was Setsuko's voice. Tanaki smiled with satisfaction. She and Nariko had positioned their fishing fleet along the shores of the Bay, paying crews overtime to maintain the nightwatch. Immediately after receiving Tanaki's call from the station, the two sisters had rushed to their slap-speed cigarette boat and skimmed over the surface of the Bay to join the fleet. Setsuko's disembodied voice sounded relaxed and upbeat.

"I've got 'little sister' with me, and we're ready for action!"

Tanaki heard Nariko's laughter in the background.

As the station's cruiser proceeded on its course, the Yamaguchi fleet fell in behind, forming an unlikely battle group.

"Lordy," Reynolds whispered solemnly, "it's like the Pacific theatre all over again."

Tanaki looked at him anxiously. "You gonna be all right?"

"Don't you worry about me," Reynolds responded, tweaking dials on his receivers. "I got this sucker completely under control."

For another hour, Tanaki and Reynolds, followed by the Yamaguchi crews, surged over the Bay seeking their quarry. The forces of Global Enterprises first appeared like a field of stars twinkling in the mist, the distant running lights of their powered barges all that could be seen. Then, as Tanaki backed off the throttle to stand marveling at the spectacle, Reynolds tapped his thigh and said excitedly, "Look at this!"

He gestured toward both shores. Joining Tanaki's fleet now was an odd assortment of old Chesapeake craft; the crab boats were there and oyster boats, and even a few galloping skipjacks, their sloop-rigged sails rockily swaying back and forth. It appeared to Tanaki that there must have been more than fifty vessels. Again the radio crackled.

"Buzz to Reynolds, Buzz to Reynolds, come in Reynolds."

"Hot dog," Reynolds said to Tanaki, "it's Buzz!"

By the time the watermen's boats fell into position, Tanaki's motley fleet was within a football field's distance of the approaching flotilla of barges; hazy outlines of hulking structures could now be distinguished through the mist. Tanaki's group, running without lights, had remained undetected by the pilots of the Global forces. He asked Reynolds to raise Setsuko.

"Reynolds to Yamaguchi One, Reynolds to Yamaguchi One."

"Yes boss?" Setsuko responded cheerfully.

Reynolds handed the microphone to Tanaki. Tanaki gazed over the water toward the Global flotilla and spoke into the device. "I think it's time to see what we're dealing with, don't you?"

"I absolutely agree," Setsuko responded, and after the jolting clank of high-voltage transformers, a blinding blaze flooded the Bay with a garish klieg-light glare. The Yamaguchi crews had turned their night fishing floods toward the approaching barges, and the powerful lamps nakedly unmasked an unbelievable scene.

Floating toward Tanaki's rag-tag fleet were at least twenty powered barges. Each carried a gigantic replica of some wild animal native to the Bay, or a historic figure associated with the tidewater area. There was a tundra swan, several stories high; a sprawling blue crab the size of the research station; even a huge oyster whose shell could open and close, allowing visitors to go inside for a tour of the animal's insides. There were equally sizable replicas of John Smith and Pocahontas, Lord Calvert, and Harriot Tubman; these gargantuan figures swayed and staggered across the surface of the Bay, drunkenly dipping and lurching with the motion of the water; forlorn ghosts returning to the scenes of their long-quieted struggles.

The jig was up; the pilots of the barges now realized that they weren't alone. They began a series of feints and dodges, or perhaps the engines had merely been put in reverse. Tanaki was determined not to let them off the hook easily. He directed the Yamaguchi boats to begin an encircling maneuver. The barges were slow and unwieldy, no match for Yamaguchi's sleek, modern fishing vessels. The enemy flotilla was soon surrounded.

"David-san!" Setsuko's voice broke from the radio. "Request permission to reel in the catch."

Tanaki's voice was filled with relish as he leaned back in the captain's chair and pronounced, "Permission granted."

The fishing boats spooled out immense runs of netting, enmeshing the teetering, fantastical forms in an unbroken web of knotted nylon. Some of the engines began to sputter. Meanwhile the watermen moved in. They approached the barges' propellers and tossed crab pots and oyster tongs into the works.

"Dave," Reynolds said, his eyes intent on the tracking receiver. "She's coming!"

"Where is she?"

"Probably not more than a tenth of a mile up-bay. She'll be passing underneath any minute now."

Tanaki looked out at the struggle on the water; the Yamaguchi fleet and the watermen steadily tightened their nylon noose around Global's barges.

Reynolds swiveled on his seat to face Tanaki. "What do you wanna do?" he asked calmly.

"I'm not sure," Tanaki replied. He tried to come to a decision logically, but one phrase kept coming to the surface of his thoughts: "Be the eel!"

Yes, the eel. It had already gravitated to the Bay's deep central channel, as if eager and ready for the far greater depths of the Atlantic. She felt vigorous and strong; though she hadn't yet gotten used to her bulging eyes, her expanded air bladder. In the darkness of the water she sensed that she was swimming past strange creatures, smelled scents she had never encountered in the protected tributary where she had spent her life. But she did not stop to investigate. She was through with any sense of curiosity, as she was with both nostalgia and trepidation. She was now nothing more than a swimming machine, with a destination and a job to do. If she was aware of the drama being played out on the surface as she approached the scene of battle, it was an awareness of a certain amount of meaningless noise, signifying nothing.

Be the eel. Tanaki allowed himself to indulge the small, silly voice, and pictured her, vigorously sidewinding under the keel of the boat, oblivious to his dilemmas. Suddenly his decision was made. The eel would continue her migration just as her ancestors had done for millions of years, regardless of what Tanaki decided to do tonight. That was her destiny. And Tanaki knew that his destiny was here in the thick of the struggle he had precipitated. After all, wasn't the struggle about the eel itself, along with trash on the beach, political interference at the station, Reynolds' double victory, campaign contributions, venal lobbyists, Indian graves, and all the rest? Having made his decision, Tanaki found himself smiling at the thought that, for now at least, the spawning journey of *anguilla rostrata* would remain a tantalizing mystery.

Tanaki had just begun to convey his resolve to Reynolds when his eyes were drawn, by his colleague's fixed gaze, toward the sky. With wonder he perceived the first faint and finally deafening sounds of flapping and fluttering, squawking and honking, and saw the stray aerial bodies that grew into an endless cloud of geese and swans and ducks. While a transfixed Reynolds chanted, in an emphatic whisper, "Go geese, come on geese!" a buzzing aircraft dipped into the circle of the Yamaguchi spotlights, almost indistinguishable from the riotous swarm of wheeling, shuttling birds that surrounded it. The flocks, which Tanaki estimated in the thousands, swooped down on the pilot houses of the barges, sowing rank confusion among Global's forces.

Tanaki grasped Reynolds by the arm. "Damn, Bob!" he hooted, "you did it!"

Meanwhile parties of watermen came abreast of the barges and began to climb aboard the beleaguered giants. In tacit allusion to a more famous act of subversion, they were nearly naked except for warpaint. And Tanaki couldn't believe his eyes when he saw cutting through the choppy waves, heading directly toward the lead barge, a canoe, with Joe Pasquath paddling and Morning Moon in fringed and medallioned buckskin. A single feather in her hair, she stood proudly in the bow like some exotic Valkyrie. Her hurled spear glanced off the pilot cabin and fell into the Bay, ineffective wood against the thick steel.

It's hard to say what happened next, everything was such a confusion of light and sound. The charges that the disguised watermen affixed to the barges worked better than expected, and after they had retreated to their boats and backed away the entire scene erupted in a flamboyant and noisy conflagration. Barges sank while watermen and the boats of the Yamaguchi fleet rushed in to rescue the pilots. Haskel's fowl slowly dispersed, leaving a rain of feathers drifting through the searing blaze.

Reynolds looked sidewise at Tanaki. "You know," he said, "if we hustle, we still might catch that eel."

A twinge of the old lust for glory took hold of Tanaki; he was reconsidering his decision when blaring sirens shattered the air. The pealing lights of three supercharged police boats quickly closed on the battle scene. Within minutes brusque officers escorted Tanaki and Reynolds off the station's cruiser.

Several miles to the south, deep in the Bay's channel, the eel chugged unperturbed through chill water toward open ocean, the transmitter attached to its pectoral fin sending a signal that no one would ever receive.

27
Home?

WHEN VALERIE appeared at Tanaki's cell her demeanor was coolly professional. "We've got to stop meeting like this," she said flatly.

Tanaki managed a wan smile and stood up as a deputy let her into the cell. He was prepared to give her a hug, but she walked past him.

Reynolds and as many of the watermen as could be arrested by the half-dozen marine police that responded to Global's S.O.S. had been booked and released. The Yamaguchi sisters, generous supporters of the police association, were allowed to walk pending further investigation into their role in the incident. Only Tanaki was being held against a sizable bail, given his prior involvement with the criminal justice system of the county. Morning Moon and Joe had disappeared in the confusion of the moment

Valerie pulled an envelope from her purse. "Before I forget," she said, "I saw Melanie the other day. She asked me to give this to you."

Tanaki was reluctant to reach out his hand.

"You don't have to be squeamish about it," she said. "It makes perfect sense."

He took the envelope.

"I know we had a hard time making a connection," she said. "I'd still like to think that we made one."

"I guess various things got in the way."

"Yeah, various things. Like Russell, for example."

"Russell?" she asked.

"Yeah," Tanaki said. "Aren't you and him—?"

"Me and Russell?"

"You seemed pretty darned cozy at the restaurant."

"David, Russell's a dear friend. But he's gay."

"Russell—gay?" Tanaki stood in stunned silence.

Valerie too was taken aback, and it was a moment before she could even respond. "My God," she said, "you have so much to learn about women!" She took a turn around the cell and shook her head in disbelief. When she came again to face Tanaki, a wicked smile adorned her face. "I ought to leave you in here this time."

"May not be a bad idea," he said, the reality of yet another miscalculation seeping in. "I'm actually starting to feel at home here. And it does keep me out of trouble."

"As if that would be possible." Her expression softened. "In any case, it looks like you're going to have to return to the cold, cruel world. They've agreed to most of our conditions."

"Most of them?"

"All charges will be dropped against everyone. Including you."

"What about this new development on the lower Shore?"

"They're not making any commitments," she said, and then she added, preempting the protest she saw lodged in Tanaki's features, "But look at this." She removed a large envelope from her briefcase and extracted several photographs. "These arrived at my office yesterday. I never heard of this guy. Bob, uh, Haskel or something. Here's the note he wrote."

She held a sheet of notepad paper toward Tanaki. He read the jagged black chickenscratch: "These photos now in the hands of every major press organ in the region."

Tanaki examined the images, aerial shots of the battle on the Bay, lit by the Yamaguchis' floodlights and blazing barges, dense with waterfowl, boats, and sinking gargantuans. He shuttled the photos through his hands. "Bob," he enthused to himself, "you're amazing!"

"These should buy the time we need to fight this thing through more official channels," Valerie said.

Tanaki wasn't certain, but he sensed that he should trust her on this one. "So they're letting me off," he said. "I suppose they expect something in return."

"Two things. First, we don't talk to the press." Valerie turned away as she elaborated, avoiding Tanaki's eyes. "I readily agreed to that, since, although they don't know it yet, this Bob fellow has beautifully taken care of publicity for us. The thing to do now is to get you sprung before these things hit the front pages. When the powers that be see them, they're not likely to be terribly accommodating about—"

He interrupted her rambling. "Okay, that all makes sense. And, second?"

"Second—" She seemed to be having a hard time continuing.

"What is it?"

A tear had formed in Valerie's eyes. "Damned allergies." She reached into her purse.

Tanaki spoke over her sniffling. "Valerie, what is the second condition?"

Valerie turned on herself, faced Tanaki. "They want you

out of the state. Forever!" She began to cry.

He put his arms around her, held her snugly.

"I know it's been difficult," she began jaggedly. "But I was hoping that we might be able to—" Unable to complete her thought, she broke down in luxuriant sobs.

Tanaki looked out the window over her shoulder. A light rain had begun to fall. That's going some for sheer brass! he said to himself.

Though it was sunny, a brisk autumn wind swept down the Bay from the north. The skin on Tanaki's face tightened as he looked over the railing. Ignoring the signs, he had stopped the car at the bridge's highest point—*where steel cables swing like hawsers left behind by a doomed race of Titanic sailors*—to look down on gliding gulls, forming one plane of reality, and then below, toy boats that moved soundlessly across the surface of the Bay. He had spent his last days on the Shore closing out his lab, taking care of personal matters, and saying goodbyes.

He reached into his pocket, removed the note Valerie had given him from Morning Moon, and unfolded it. "Sorry I was so hard to reach," he read, quietly mouthing the words. "I didn't want you to get distracted from what you had to do. I knew you had the warrior spirit in you. Besides, I can't get mixed up with a man right now. I've got to find my sacred path, and that's something I have to do on my own. Keep the stone. Good luck. Maybe we'll meet down the road somewhere."

He contemplated the note for a moment. "Good luck to you, too," he whispered and, holding the waffling piece of paper out over the railing, he released it to the wind. A smile spread across his face as he turned his attention back to the vista of sky and estuary that lay before him. Though he was

HOME?

being run out of town, he couldn't manage to feel persecuted. At his last delicious dinner with the Yamaguchis, Nariko had said, "Now you know what we mean by pure action!"

"I just hope all this pure action hasn't created any problems for your business," he had replied.

"The authorities are trying to make life difficult for us," Setsuko put in. "But we won't let them push us around. We talked to father, and he's behind us one hundred percent." She stopped to refill Tanaki's sake cup. Then she settled back on her tatami and, looking toward the household shrine, continued. "After all this settles, and we feel that the Bay is well and truly safe, we'll probably go back to Japan." She looked affectionately at Nariko. "Nari is pining for home. And I feel like I've gotten my Chesapeake phase out of my system."

Tanaki felt that he, too, was ready to go home. Only he wasn't sure that he knew where home was. As he looked over the Bay toward its northern shoals, he pondered that question and decided that, at the very least, his stint on the Shore had brought him closer. In his buoyant mood he was even willing to allow that reaching home—one day—might just be inevitable. Maybe it wasn't a place at all.

He thought about bridges. Had he sought them, or fled them? Images of people he had met on the Shore drifted through his mind. They had all gotten him over one bridge or another. The Yamaguchis, Reynolds, Bob Haskel, Morning Moon and Joe Pasquath, of course Valerie.

Even Folker.

Mrs. Scofield. He suddenly remembered the beauty of her spirit, her egg salad sandwiches, and how kind she had always been when he slept over at Tom's house. It was a shame about her gephyrophobia. But the important thing is, that in spite of her fears, she crossed the bridge. And with that thought Tanaki felt freer than a bird. He didn't know where he was going, but he would figure something out. He owed his parents a visit. Or maybe he would go straight to the nearest airport and book a flight to Italy, share his adventures with an old friend.

Out the corner of his eye he saw the strobing red and blue lights scale the eastern approaches to the bridge. He walked calmly around to the driver's side of the Honda and started the engine. He felt like an important dignitary as four state police cruisers, sirens screaming, escorted him to the Bay's western shore. They peeled off only as he reached the toll gate that stood like a *torii*, not before the Bay now, but before the rest of the world.

The book is a revised edition of a novel first published
by the Portal Press in 2006.

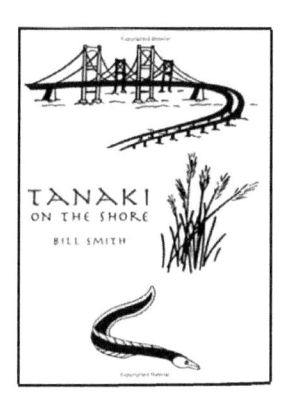

In the summer and fall of that year W. E. Smith read *Tanaki on the Shore* in its entirety at ten different points around the Chesapeake, from Baltmore's Inner Harbor to the Virginia Capes.

W. E. Smith, a native of the Chesapeake region, was educated in Maryland's public schools and universities.

CPSIA information can be obtained
at www.ICGtesting.com
Printed in the USA
FSHW012124010719
59631FS